MW01602264

E.J. OBERMEYER

The Glory McGuire series is fiction. The series will take you into and through the life and adventures of Glory McGuire. The first book, Garden of Death, spans the first four years of Glory's journey in life starting at the age of sixteen.

There is mystery and murder. There is love, hate, deceitfulness, intimidation, and vengeance. You will never know the next unsuspecting victim or the next architect of crime.

The second book Garden of Iniquity spans the ongoing four years in the life of Glory McGuire.

Do not miss the continuing sequel

GARDEN OF INIQUITY

By E. J. Obermeyer, due out in 2012

ISBN: 1466244925
ISBN-13: 9781466244924
LCCN: 2011914983
Createspace, North Charleston, SC
Manufactured in the United States

*This book is dedicated to my
mother, my mentor.
A true and beautiful rose in
every sense of the word.*

*And to Chuck
Teresa, Tobin, and Ryan*

GARDEN OF DEATH

A Novel of Mystery

E. J. OBERMEYER

CHAPTER I

WITH MURDER ON HIS MIND

Whether she was awake or asleep, the blood persisted in reappearing in her mind and in her senses; the vibrant red color and the brutal smell that burned her nostrils. She pictured it over and over, as if it were happening again right then and right there. The visions of coming home to the horror of it continued to circle through her mind. She again felt the chill in the air and remembered the condition of the house, then how the fear soaked within her being, like a sponge, once again, she was breathless.

The sight of her mother was committed to memory as she lay in a pool of thick, red blood, oozing out slowly from under her head, continuing to run out over the great lengths of the mahogany hardwood floor slats. She felt the blood on her own hands. It was sticky. It was thick. It smelled rancid. She tried to wipe it off on her pants.

Her mother was not moving, not breathing…..
She was dead.

Her father, unbeknownst to her at the time, was upstairs, lying dead in his own blood as it soaked the newly laid russet bedroom carpet.

She recalled the exact moment she realized that some madman had somehow managed to turn her world upside down. She was, once again, sick to her stomach.

And today, on June 8, 2003, Garrett Sanders was wishing Glory McGuire good luck and good-bye. He was witness to her boarding the 8:45 a.m. Silver Star Train, after first checking in her luggage. The train was headed northwest; far, far away from Orlando. Its destination, Spalding, South Dakota.

The Silver Star Line makes for a fast journey and this particular one had several more stops than usual, affecting travel time. It would be three days instead of the usual scheduled two.

Sanders' said, as his final words, "I'll be in touch when the time is right." He turned and walked away.

As she boarded the train, embarking on her journey and grateful for the isolation, she was saddened that there was no one to wave good-bye to.

This three-day journey allowed her the solitude she desperately craved, if only for a short time. Having spent her days with people at the shelter, with the police, and with the attorney, she was more than ready for seclusion. She prayed no one would notice her face, knowing it revealed the devastation she wore like a veil. She wanted no invasion of her privacy, no conversation; she had no desire to talk about what had happened.

And just what had happened? She still wasn't certain.

Unbeknownst to her, in February of that year, the evil creature had begun concocting his scheme. Three months prior to that sweet young girl boarding the train, destined for South Dakota, he had put his plan into action.

The day before his departure, May 12th, he was finalizing last minute details. He met with another charlatan, another strange bird, so to speak.

"Okay" this is it," he said. "We're ready. I'll be back soon." With that came a quick and not too affectionate hug.

"Yeah, okay."

"Remember what I told you. Be patient; don't blow it."

"Yeah, yeah, I know. Do you really have to do this?"

Waving his index finger as a forceful indication that he meant business. "You know I do, it's the only way. Mum's the word."

Conviction echoed. "I won't talk. I told you already, and I won't."

"Just see that you don't. You're in this as deep as me, don't forget that. I go down, you go down. We aren't going to let anything stand in our way now are we?"

"I know, yeah, I know."

"I don't need any crazy screw-ups; anything or anyone gets in my way they're dead."

That was his final word. He was on his way.

Early that same day he snuck into the nearby small town bearing an unswerving course for the thrift store. He purchased a non to attractive, ill-fitting blue suit. The straighter he stood the better it fit; he would have to remember that. He found a light blue and white striped shirt, a nice pair of black tie up shoes, and a worn pair of black framed clear lens glasses, as well.

His last purchase, and the most important, was a briefcase. It was an odd looking case, but all that was available at the time.

Reaching home, he donned the clothes, slicked back his thick dark hair tightly to his head, and looked in the mirror. Instantly his psyche was filled with great satisfaction. His reflection assured him that he now transformed into another personage, that being his objective all along.

At the end of that day, May 12, 2003, his subconscious voice was chanting, "*Oh God, this is almost too easy*".

He placed a call, lowered his voice and rasped out his excuse. "Guess I have the 24 hour flu. I won't be in tomorrow." That was all it took for him to escape for the one day he required to complete the task.

In the early morning hours of May 13th, after a restless night in a cheap motel, he called for a taxi to transport him to his 4:45 flight. Optimism saturated his very soul; he was confident and poised. The taxi driver wouldn't remember him, he was sure of that. In a gruff, muffled tone he ordered. "Take me to the airport, Southwest." He kept his head low, very low, and said no more.

Arriving in the airport lobby, he dashed straight up to the Southwest Airline counter procuring a one-way ticket to Orlando. The briefcase was swinging back and forth as he strolled down the length of the almost deserted terminal. If he had been whistling he would have been the perfect image of a traveling salesman, except for the low jingle of the briefcase chain as he walked along.

This, his first flight, gave him the jitters. Suddenly he realized the adventure, though he was sure it would be successful, was beginning to put his nerves in a bundle, but his determination to complete his task was capacious.

Heading to security his mind did a double take as he retraced his process in the placement of each item in the briefcase and those concealed in his sock.

"Put everything in the bin and walk through," the unfriendly uniformed officer touted. He did as requested. Pockets empty and shoes in the container, he walked through and held his breath. Before he was through the scanner he began to chew his lower lip. As nonchalantly as possible, he walked to the checkpoint exit where he was observed but not searched.

He'd made it, unscathed, unsearched. He picked up the briefcase and ran straight through the alley-way leading to the plane.

If they had opened the briefcase they would have seen only blank pieces of paper, nothing more. The counter X-ray had shown the papers in the briefcase and it certainly didn't matter to the security crew if he had actual documents or not.

The items in his sock, well, those were now safe, to his surprise. His careful concealment of them had taken painstaking creativity. The items were under his sock, next to his ankle, wrapped in a solid metal envelope he had constructed a few days earlier. The envelope was then painted with a plastic insulation material making them less detectable.

His ankle hurt badly; the pressure from the metal case bore into his ankle bone, causing the skin to blister. It allowed little give as he walked.

The plane, a 737, resembled the ones he'd seen on TV or at the movies. Amazed at the sheer mass of the plane, he was like a boy in a candy shop, looking at every inch of the interior as he was shown to his seat. He now felt a sense of power and relief.

He sat midway down the aisle next to an attractive, well-dressed woman in her early forties. Luckily she ignored him, spending the flight either reading or dozing off. "G*ood*," he thought, "*the less contact with others the better.*" He had no desire for communication. He needed to travel unnoticed.

The aisle seat suited him. He had no longing to look out the tiny window just to be reminded he was thousands of miles above the earth settling in for a three-hour flight. He lowered his head and spread a magazine in front of him. He hadn't read a word, but flipped the pages only glancing at them briefly.

Instead he reexamined the agenda inscribed in his mind. He had memorized the information he needed to complete the task; he wanted nothing on paper. He wanted nothing that would lead back to him. He analyzed the details over more than once, knowing there could be no mistakes, since he was not a rocket scientist, his review only ensured each task would be accomplished perfectly. His mind created an illusion that his plan was absolutely brilliant.

When offered drinks and peanuts by a beautiful young blond stewardess with a well rounded derriere, he thought, "*I could get used to this kind of treatment.*"

Time passed quickly.

Finally he braced himself for the descent and landing; his hands gripping the arm rests tightly. This would be the only time on this expedition he was formidably afraid.

Much to his astonishment, it was a smoother landing than anticipated. Contemplating the weight of the plane hitting the ground he thought the result would be a much larger jolt than was experienced..

Departing the plane, carrying only the small black briefcase, he looked like any normal frequent flyer. The briefcase resembled others being carried, except for the silver chain dangling from the top handle to the clip at the side.

He summoned a taxi outside the airport lobby. "To the corner of 9th Avenue and Sycamore South."

The location happened to be just past the McGuires' house. The taxi traveled at an uncomfortable speed, darting in and out of traffic lanes like a snake weaving back and forth through rocky terrain. *"Welcome to the big city,"* he thought. He'd never seen traffic, let alone a six-lane highway.

Now was his opportunity, while in the taxi, to remove the metal casing from his sock and place it in the briefcase. His ankle felt immediate relief. He relished the liberation on his rubbed-raw ankle, and prayed it wouldn't handicap his final approach to his destination.

Once dropped at the corner of 9th and Sycamore, he removed the briefcase from the seat, paid the driver and stood upright, straightened his suit, and looked as professional and confident as anyone could. His target was just one block away, 914 Sycamore South, Orlando, Florida. He lavished in the fact that everything had been a breeze thus far.

As he walked he gained appreciation for the climate in Orlando, the foliage and the beautiful spacious homes, along with the delusion of imagining himself living in a place very similar to this; once he was rich, inspired him and gave him pleasure.

It was a glorious day, the sun shone with a morning glow. Its warmth filled him as he kept a steady and self-assured pace along the tree-lined street. The late morning sun was just below the palm branches as to lightly linger and baste the trees and yard shrubs in a golden hue.

Scanning his surrounding, his breath steady, he was relieved that there was little activity in the neighborhood. It was the time of day when most people had left for work and yet late enough that the majority of school kids had already left for class.

He had a confirmed certainty in his mission. He smirked with the knowledge that his appearance bade him the ability to walk the neighborhood freely. Absolutely sure no would give him a second glance and positive no one would be capable of describing him to authorities, other than to state they may have seen a businessman with a briefcase, he felt safe as he walked on.

Now at 914 Sycamore South, from his vantage point from the sidewalk, he grasped the enormity of this all too elegant house. It was a ranch style done in beige and white with a partial gray rock front. *"A celebrity house,."* he thought. His timing in arriving had been precise, he had counted on that.

The place had a perfectly groomed yard, fresh paint, a new roof, and clean, sparkling windows. Flowers adorned every corner of the yard, from yellow, to purple and orange. The colors were brilliant, the blooms generous as they were forced out through the jade, olive, and emerald foliage. He thought, *"Someday, someday this could be mine."*

He strolled casually up to the front door. The floral scents attacked his senses the closer he got to the door. He rang the doorbell.

A pretty, petite woman answered the door. She said hello with a welcoming smile. She was attractive, in her mid forties, sandy colored hair, in a light lavender velveteen sweat suit and matching headband. *"Kind of cheeky."* He thought. He had seen that type of outfit in a catalog once wondering, *"Who in their right mind would actually wear a goofy outfit like that?"* *Now he knew* She apparently had readied herself to go out for a morning run. He nodded politely, struggling to keep a professional guise.

"What can I do for you?"

"Is this the residence of Janice and David McGuire?"

"Yes, it is."

He introduced himself stating the actual town he was from, sparking Janice's curiosity. It was a town Janice was very familiar with.

He was confident enough to tell her the truth, except for his real name. After all, she would never be able to tell anyone he had been there. "I brought information about someone you know there, and it will be of great interest to you and your husband."

Her first thought was to ask if everyone was all right. He assured her they were. He continued talking. "I need to share this family information with him. Is he still in?" Excitedly she began to think she might hear news from someone she thought had been lost from years of absence.

By this time it was almost nine. "David hasn't left for work yet, come in and have a cup of coffee while I get him."

He knew full well David was still home; he'd done his homework beforehand. Using a cell phone he'd call the McGuires' house phone in the early morning hours, for the last few months, once or twice a week, always at a different time and on a different day of the week. He would hang up when one of them answered. He established their routine, who was home and who wasn't. The cell phone had since been crushed and thrown in the local river.

His precise planning, precise timing again had paid off. *"Now* within hours *I'll be on my way."* He thought arrogantly.

He followed closely behind her, first passing the living room then down the hallway, a short distance, to the kitchen. He surveyed each room thoroughly, observing the elegant staging of each detail in the rooms and sensing the layout of the house.

The living room and hallway had fresh cut flowers, obviously from her yard; the aroma, much like the fragrance of the yard, followed him as he continued to the next room. In each room family pictures were strategically placed throughout on furniture and walls. The photos were mainly of David and Janice and a beautiful young girl. *"That's Glory,"* he thought. But then he already knew her name.

"Your home is beautiful. I've never seen anything like it." She thanked him, her head raised a little in self assurance as she said it.

They entered an overly bright yellow and blue kitchen, where she offered him coffee. Using one of those fancy coffeemakers, the kind that holds the little pods, she prepared them each a cup.

He noticed the dining room table with snow white lilies the size of small baseball bats, packed into a large, ornate crystal vase.

As she slipped in another pod he stood on the other side of the counter setting his briefcase on the dining room table. His back was to her.

Opening the briefcase, it made a click as the latch freed itself. She glanced over. He caught a glimpse of her looking and quickly retrieved a piece of blank paper, waving it for her to see, then set it on the table in anticipation of her thinking it to be documents he had brought with him. That was exactly what she thought.

What he in fact was after was his nine inch onyx handled hunting knife and a pair of white latex gloves. He'd had the knife for years. It had once belonged to his father but he never was much of a hunter and had no use for it, until now. He had transferred the knife and gloves from the metal case in his shoe to the briefcase while in the taxi.

He smiled at her. She returned the gesture as she turned from the doorway toward the stairs. "David, come down, we have a visitor, one I think you'll want to meet." David assured her he'd be right down.

His hands quietly inched their way into the latex gloves before she returned to the counter.

As she waited to hear the news he brought, butterflies began to flutter in her stomach. She returned to the counter, reaching for the freshly poured coffee, as he crept up behind her.

Gently reaching forward, he seized the cup from her hand setting it calmly on the counter. Her focus instantly switched to his actions. A look of surprise enveloped her face. Within a millisecond, he curved his arm around her body, rapidly wrenching her shoulder back at an angle causing her full body to rotate until she was facing away from him. Before she had time to speak he quickly and methodically slid the onyx handled knife precisely from one ear diagonally across her throat to the other ear.

After careful research, he had contemplated several techniques to use choosing that knife as the most effective. It would be the safest, quietest, and quickest. There would be no noise; no gun blast, no screaming, and no sounds of a struggle or disturbance at the residence. He simply slit her throat, and there was silence.

She was still upright as he pulled her over to the opposite side of the counter, away from the view of the doorway to the hall. He lightened his grip on her and saw her eyes widen in horror. They seemed to half close in slow motion. He tenderly laid her down. She lay perfectly still.

He watched her as she attempted to inhale but an almost silent gasp came from deep inside her. The air had nowhere to go. Blood gushed generously from her mouth and wounded neck instead, her eyes still fixed on him. She was unable to make an audible sound paralyzed from fright or shock, or both.

Just then David hollered, "Almost done. Just give me another minute or two." When he heard David, he spun around, looking directly at the doorway.

David had not started down the stairs yet. His gaze turned back to Janice. Her eyes were completely closed; she was dead.

He resolved not to wait for David to come down to the kitchen. He commenced his ascension of the stairs as quietly as possible. More family pictures hung on the stairway walls, family, the young girl, a dog. He paused at the picture of Glory and grinned. "*Pretty girl. Pretty, pretty girl.*"

Reaching the top of the stairs he heard David moving around and humming. The sound was reverberating from the last bedroom at the end of the hall.

When he walked in David was standing, fastening the last button on his shirt collar. David turned as he appeared in the doorway. At once David's face took on a look of bewilderment and confusion.

Before David had an opportunity to speak or knew what fate was headed his way, the stampeding stranger headed for him. David felt a full force blow to his midsection, doubling him over, as if he were taking an unsolicited bow. David clutched his middle with both arms and groaned, yet stayed on his feet. Just as his body folded, the assailant leaned over from David's side, grabbing David's neck with one arm, and yanking him to an upright position. In a split second, David's throat encountered the same blow from the blue as Janice's; the wound gaped from ear to ear.

He began to lay David down on the floor next to the side of the bed when an involuntary spasm swept over David's body. It lasted only a moment. David's body discharged one violent shake, a twitch, and then there was complete stillness.

He kept his grasp on David a moment longer, then released him onto the carpeted floor. As he stood there, looking down at David, he felt no emotion, no remorse - just pure satisfaction, and a smirk curled his lips.

His plan was designed to give the effect that a burglary had occurred so he still had work to do. He scanned the master bedroom. To make a burglary scenario more effective, he first swiped his gloved hand across the dresser top, watching in silence as everything fell to the floor. He then rummaged through the bedroom closet and drawers.

He riffled through the bathroom drawers and again slid his hand hastily across the counter top, toppling body lotions, a toothbrush, a perfume bottle, and other toiletries. Each fell atop the other in a pile at the end of the counter.

Then a strange sensation overtook him. His face contorted. Pure evil imbedded itself from his forehead to his chin. It was as if he became possessed. He wickedly dipped his gloved fingers in the blood pouring from David's neck then he proceeded to run the glove across the top of the bathroom counter, the bedspread, and the dressers. He smiled, an evil smile.

He descended the stairs, electing to continue his idiosyncratic behavior. With the remains of David's blood thickening on his gloved hand, he swiped the kitchen counter top.

His next objective was to wipe down any items he may have touched before placing the gloves on while at the dining room table earlier. He used a damp paper towel to wipe the dining room table and the kitchen cupboard doors and handles, and then ambled into the living room while still wearing the latex gloves.

There he moved a few furniture pieces around, brushing pictures and candles off the fireplace mantle, he continued his staging drama for his burglary scenario. He scattered papers from the desk drawers onto the floor.

Standing back and crossing his arms, he surveyed the room. He nodded and said, "Looks like a burglary to me all right."

Back to the kitchen where he placed his gloved hands under the running water at the sink rubbing to get what blood off he could. Then he dried his gloved hands on his pants. He washed up his coffee cup, dried it and put it in the cupboard.

He removed his gloves, placing them and the knife back into the briefcase where the metal casing still lay. Closing the briefcase, he headed to the front door. He stood inside the door a moment, taking time to retrace his steps. Had he wiped everything down? Did he leave anything of his? *"No, all accounted for."*

A smile once again filled the lower half of his ever-so-cocky face, his gratification apparent. Narcissism continued as he considered the task he had so perfectly accomplished.

With the edge of his jacket hem, he opened the front door. There before him, in the doorway, stood a small calico kitten. He shooed the kitten out to the front yard but left the door ajar just enough so the cat could get back in. He wasn't all bad, after all.

Pausing briefly before exiting the entrance completely, he swiftly glanced from this yard to the adjacent yards. No one was outside.

He accelerated his step to get off the McGuires' property at quickly as possible. Once again on the sidewalk, he began walking a steady pace.

Aware that there were only seven blocks to the business district he felt powerful as he strutted along. As he considered that he soon he would be out of this residential area his fearlessness filled his ego like a tumor. Not wanting to break his stride he controlled each step by counting them from time to time. "One and a two and a- stay calm, draw no attention to yourself - three and a four." Then thought, "*It worked. My plan worked.*"

Conscious of the beads of sweat trickling off his brow he quickly wiped off his forehead with the back of his hand after each block.

Arriving at 15th and Elm, just south of a outlet mall and shopping center, he paused. He crossed the street, scanning the area in pursuit of a location to dispose of the briefcase, knife, gloves, and metal casing. He had no intention of taking them back on the plane with him. He knew better than to press his luck a second time.

He located a dumpster at the rear entrance of a men's clothing store. He discarded the metal envelope containing the knife and gloves into one side and the briefcase into the other of the dirty dark green dumpster. Mindfully he wiped each one before depositing them into the dumpster's big open mouth. He leisurely walked back to the intersection and hailed a cab.

Traveling back to the airport in another "can't wait to get there" speeding cab, his thoughts turned to his own genius. It's not an effortless task to pull off what he did, he knew that. Knowing his future was getting brighter by the minute, he relaxed in the back of the taxi with his arms crossed. Laying his head back, he closed his eyes. Overcome with a feeling of exhilaration never experienced before, he was enveloped in total elation.

Once inside the airport lobby he headed straight to the men's room to wash up. His face and hands had become gritty and sweaty during his walk and the constant wiping with the back of his hand.

He removed his suit jacket and tie throwing both into the trash can.

Exiting the restroom, he went to the American Airlines counter, not wanting to use Southwest twice. He booked a one-way flight home. As he sat, again in the aisle seat, and no longer sweating, he felt a great sense of relief.

His window passenger was a teenager who had a set of earphones glued to his head and a CD player strapped to his waist. He was certain the kid would not be a bother, probably couldn't tear himself away from the tunes, which were so loud they echoed through the first two rows.

As he requested a pillow from another gorgeous stewardess, his mind raced. "*Simple in, simple out, simply done and flawless.*" He liked that; he liked that a lot. Then in an almost sinister muted vocalization, he whispered, "Home again, home again, jiggity-jig." And he fell into a deep, restful sleep.

When he awoke, his confidence was at an extreme high. He realized he would never be a suspect, never a target for investigators. In his opinion, he was smoother and cleverer than most, even more so than the police. Unfortunately, ever being able to lay claim to his proficiency was impossible, fame would elude him.

After months of planning, scanning documents, calculating time tables, phoning to find out the McGuires' morning routines, he had promised himself to commit the perfect crime. Indeed he felt he had accomplished just that.

Everything was in motion. Now he would wait Now there was just the waiting.

CHAPTER 2

I BID THEE FAREWELL

Glory agonized for three weeks, then reality set in. Her parents were indeed dead. Exhaustion overtook her. She relaxed in the soft, leather recliner in the observation car of the Silver Star Line and felt at peace as she watched the scenery flash by the window, leading her to an unfamiliar and unwelcomed destination.

The sleeper car became her sanctuary as she slept a great deal during the journey. Her appetite diminished with her tears. The horrifying ordeal of finding her mother and learning of her father had taken its toll.

She wished time travel were possible. If it were she would instantly go back and restore the past; put things back to the way they were before the horrific events that crushed her world.

Apprehension filled her; she was destined to the unknown. Just as she had faced an unknown past – that she would face the day her parents would be dead - one day living a normal life as a carefree sixteen-year-old with a family and the next day alone, abandoned, everything taken away – and now facing whatever lies ahead. Her life had been stolen by a madman, a maniac, a murderer, but she didn't know why. Life as she knew it no longer existed.

She remembered the events too often: seeing her mother and the pool of blood then hearing about her father in a similar condition. She remembered every word the police, Detective Marshall, and Garrett Sanders had told her.

She didn't like to remember any of it, but it was embedded in her memory for time and eternity. She had no control of her thoughts now. Everything was still too fresh, as if it were yesterday.

That day started out like any other. She left the house for school at 7:15. She usually spent her mornings watching early football practice and getting her day's schoolwork in order. The rest of her day was as usual, the studying, handing in assignment, taking notes.

When classes were dismissed for the day, Glory waited for her mother. The students who drove to school had left already, probably to go out for the usual burger and shake at the local Burger King.

She assumed something came up and her mother was unable to contact her to let her know she would be late. She waited. Surprisingly, her father did not come either. She imagined her mother had told no one she was running late.

Glory thought it best to start walking home if she wanted to be there in time to get her homework done before supper. The school, just off the main road a few blocks, was not that far from her home.

She could walk a block and grab a taxi, but she disliked the smells inside a taxi. To her, sitting in a taxi was comparable to sitting next to someone who hadn't bathed in a week. She gladly began walking home.

It was an exceptionally beautiful afternoon, and she soaked in the sun as she walked. With the passing of each car, she expected one would stop and she'd see her mother's smiling face appear on the driver's side - showing signs of rushing all afternoon to make appointments. Then she'd burst out with an exhausted apology, "Oh darling, I got caught in traffic." Or "My appointment ran a little late. Hop in." But no car stopped, ever.

When Glory finally arrived at the corner of 9th and Sycamore South, the hair on her arms rose. Strange, there was no apparent reason for this. She became suddenly chilly. There was no wind, no coolness in the air, yet she grew cold. She scanned the street but saw nothing out of the ordinary. She kept walking.

There was her house. Now she would be safe. She began a rapid walk to the front door, anxious to get in. She noticed the door was ajar and thought her mother had let the kitty out and forgot to shut it; that happened sometimes.

Glory had been born in Orlando and raised in this house. She was familiar with everything inside and outside of it. David and Janice had bought it right after they married and worked years trying to make it a place of pride and distinction.

It was definitely one of the better homes on the block, even though it was an older one. It was a spacious ranch style with gray rock adorning the front. She thought it to be more a sixties look but still stylish enough for today's "home beautiful" world. Her mother constantly redecorated room by room, keeping up with the latest trends in design. When she finally completed the final touches on the last room, she went back and started over in the first room. So every few years, the interior was completely updated.

The gardener was an obvious expert at his craft, an artist of his trade, keeping the grounds pristine. Glory was proud of her home, and she had always felt safe and loved there. It was a happy place.

Opening the door wider with a gentle shove, she first noticed the furniture in the living room out of place. She wondered if someone had been cleaning, moving tabletop items perhaps to dust, and then failed to put them back in place.

Then she saw papers, trinkets and pictures scattered haphazardly on the floor. She knew that as meticulous as her mother was about her home, she would be appalled at this disorder. The chill hit her again.

Just as the phone rang Glory called out, "Mom, are you here?" She wasn't confident entering the house any further was a good idea, but the phone continued its persistent ring. Her hope was that it was her mother calling with a forgivable excuse for being late. She reluctantly and cautiously walked to the phone on the hall table and picked it up. "Hello?"

"Glory, this is Carol from the office. Is your dad there?"

Nearing the living room doorway, scanning the room once again, she had the phone pressed tightly to her ear. "I don't know. Something is not right here."

Not another word was said as she turned in circles trying to take in everything she saw. The furniture and the items on the floor - why would the house be in this bizarre condition, one her mother would never tolerate?

At first Carol didn't catch Glory's drift. "Your dad didn't come in today. I've called several times. I need to ask him a few questions. What do you mean, something's not right?"

Trying to comprehend what it all meant and the eerie feeling drenching her body, Glory was at a loss. "Carol, the place is a mess, and I don't know where mom is and - ………..

With the phone pressed tightly to her ear, Glory had walked from the living room to the kitchen door, stopping before crossing the threshold.

The kitchen was neat, except for what appeared to be a messy red smudge on the countertop. She contemplated turning on her heels and bolting out of the house but couldn't stop herself.

She crossed the threshold and neared the counter, taking one unhurried step at a time. As she started rounding the counter, leading to the dining room, she first saw her mother's legs on the floor. Her mind stopped working. Fear gripped her; terror filled her inner core.

Somehow she found the strength to walk around the full length of the counter but stopped cold when she saw, lying flat on the dining room floor, her mother. She froze. The hair on her arms rose again. Screams began to vibrate inside her a full two seconds before a sound was evident. Then the screams came, from deep within her throat, emerging in panicked jolts.

Carol heard what she thought was a TV horror program. The screams were deafening then changed to uncontrolled sobbing at the other end of the line. Fright filled her.

Still clutching the phone, she raised her voice, shrieking, "Glory, Glory, are you there? Answer me! Are you there? Glory, for God's sake, what's happened?" There was no answer.

The screaming ceased almost as quickly as it had started. Carol waited. She could distinguish only a quiet whimpering sound.

Carol hollered at the top of her lungs, hoping for a response. "Glory, answer me! What's going on there?"

Knowing something was amiss Carol immediately threw her phone down on her desk, ran full speed into David's office, and dialed 911. "Something has happened at the McGuire house, 914 Sycamore South. Glory's there; she's the daughter. She was on the phone and screaming. I can hear her crying, but she won't or can't answer me. Send someone now. Hurry, please hurry."

Of course Glory couldn't respond. There she sat, on the floor, next to her mother, absorbed in shock. She had dropped the phone in her lap and couldn't move.

Within seven minutes, three police cars were front and center at 914 Sycamore South with red lights flashing and sirens howling. The sounds shattered the otherwise quiet neighborhood.

The officers quickly exited their vehicles. First Officer Richards ordered one officer to the left side of the residence, the other to the right side. His instructions to them were to circle the residence, keep their radios on, and let him know if they saw or heard anything or anyone.

Richards was a ten-year veteran with the Orlando Police Department. His major duty was patrolling. He had been dispatched to major crime scenes before but did not find that to be his interest. It was too much work for him. He was six foot and at least seventy-five pounds overweight. He liked patrol. It was easy. He never put much stock into learning anything beyond standard patrol.

Richards approached the front door, which was still wide open. Standing fixed at the entrance, he looked across into the living room.

He called out, "Mr. McGuire, are you here?" No answer. "Mrs. McGuire, can you hear me?" Still no answer.

He unlatched then drew his service weapon and cautiously entered the doorway. He perused the entry, the hallway, and the living room, evaluating as much detail as he could. He took note of the furniture, the odd arrangement of the pieces, and the objects scattered on the floor.

Besides the furniture and papers, knick-knacks lay on the floor, none broken. Pictures lay there too, none torn and no glass shattered.

He continued down the hallway after hearing a barely audible whimpering. "Glory?" He announced his presence once more. "Glory, it's Officer Richards. Are you all right?" Still nothing.

With a steady gait, he headed toward the sound, his hand securely clutching his weapon. With his finger firmly surrounding the trigger, he inhaled deeply, fully prepared for an intruder.

He prayed the girl was safe and wasn't under the control of whoever had entered the premises without an invitation.

The whimpering increased as he neared the kitchen door. He entered and as his eyes surveyed the room, he immediately observed what appeared to be an arbitrary smear of something red on the breakfast counter.

Calculating the direction of the faint sound, he rounded the counter, first seeing a woman's legs then a young girl he assumed to be Glory, sitting on her knees on the floor next to the woman. He presumed it to be the girl's mother.

It was reasonably apparent, even from where he stood, that the woman's throat had been cut. The pool of blood on the floor had streamed from her neck and trailed under the dining room table. He was well aware the wound was fatal.

From past investigations, he knew this meant that when she went down she was not immediately dead. Blood continues to pump from a slit throat until a person bleeds to death; he knew that. It was enough to take her down but not enough to kill her instantly. He surmised it to be a cruel and painful death.

Promptly retrieving his radio unit from his belt, he summoned backup, requesting paramedics before even approaching Glory. He gently touched her shoulder. She wrenched away from his touch.

"I'm Officer Richards. I am here to help you." She nodded but said nothing. He reached down and picked up the phone Glory had in her lap. "Is someone there?"

Carol had raced back into her reception area after calling 911; she was still on the line. She continued to speak into her phone anxiously awaiting Glory's response. She heard her crying, but Glory did not respond. Carol had what felt like ice water running through her veins from the fright she was feeling inside. She wouldn't put the phone down until someone, anyone, spoke to her. She heard a man's voice in the room but couldn't distinguish what was being said. She didn't know if it was someone other than the police, until she heard him speak: "Is anyone there?"

"I'm here. I'm Carol from Mr. McGuire's office. What's going on?"

She received little satisfaction from Officer Richards. "There has been an incident here. I'm unable to give you any further information, and we do have to keep this line free. Someone will talk with you later." And with that he hit "End Talk".

Carol sat in her chair in anxiety and disbelief; at a loss as to what to do next. She went into the bathroom and splashed some cool water on her face. She made coffee, thinking it would give her a boost, while she had time to think. She informed the bank manager of what had happened, and they waited together, hoping to find out more.

Within minutes of Richards' backup call, the back up officers and paramedics arrived. The officers currently on the scene had been busy securing the residence, keeping bystanders back while trying to focus on the surroundings of the house. Richards ordered the new officers to the front of the house with instructions to procure the yellow caution tape and cordon off the perimeter of the residence. He wanted no gawkers entering the area.

He ordered another officer to the rear of the house to do the same, and to remain there until future notice. Then he placed one officer at the base of the stairway, declaring no once was to enter the stairway until the detective unit was present. He reminded the officer, "Keep a sharp eye."

As soon as the paramedics reached the front door, they were directed into the kitchen. He instructed the female paramedic to take Glory to the living room while the paramedics saw to her mother; even though he knew it would be fruitless. Glory did resist, until the paramedic put her arm over Glory's shoulders and let her know they were there for her and would see to her mother saying, "You have nothing to worry about honey. We'll take care of your mother and let you see her before she is taken from your home."

They went into the living room, both being careful not to touch anything in the room, and sat on the couch. Glory put her head in her hands and wept. "Oh my God, who did this to my mother? What happened? Oh my God. Oh, my God."

She looked at the paramedic for answers. Fear had ingrained itself in her wide blue eyes. "Oh my God, where's my Dad. Where's my dad?" Horror echoed in her voice. "He never went to work today. Where's my Dad? Oh, please God, no." Again bursting into tears, she stood and began to walk, transfixed, toward the hall where the stairway led to the second floor.

The paramedic quickly grabbed Glory's arm and guided her gently back to the couch. She told Glory she would be right back then proceeded to the base of the stairway before entering the hall. As quietly as possible, she informed Richards about Mr. McGuire. "See if you can find Mr. McGuire, he never got to the office today." She then returned to the living room, took Glory's hands in her and said confidently at Glory, "Don't worry, we'll find your dad."

Little did she know just where that would be.

CHAPTER 3

GLENN MARSHALL

Officer Richards phoned the Detective Division of the Orlando Sheriff's Department since the case involved a death, apparently a murder, classified as a felony.

Relieved to have reached Detective Glenn Marshall on his first try, Richards hastily told him of the death of Mrs. McGuire. "Appears to be a murder; her throat was slashed." Richards implored him to proceed to the locale as quickly as possible.

Glenn Marshall was the head detective in the division and if he was so inclined he could delegate a case to one of his men. He choose to go to the scene which would land him as the lead in this case.

Glenn Marshall was twenty-six, tall, thin, dark-haired, handsome, and well-built from being an avid participant at the police gym. His lifestyle included a belief in physical fitness no matter what profession one is in. Women would actually stop in the street to look at him, guessing him to be a movie star. His looks were beyond "good."

He dated very little, even in college, because his career took a great deal of his time and energy. He felt he was young and would have plenty of time for a romance later in his life.

Marshall met most rules of manliness, excelling at everything, excluding romance and sports. He had been dubbed a "genius" at a very young age because he excelled at everything he undertook - except sports. He was a brain, not a jock.

His enthusiasm for education earned him high honors and early graduation from North Orlando High School. At sixteen, he enthusiastically enrolled in junior college, pursing a degree in Criminal Justice, something he'd planned since watching *Hawaii Five-0* as a kid. Though it was a two-year course, he accomplished it, in one year, with top honors.

Continuing up the academic ladder and after being accepted by Duke University, he embarked in business courses. He proceeded on to law school, which he aced in less time than his fellow students.

He wasn't a party animal; kept his nose to the grindstone. He had no intention of lingering until he reached the ripe old age of forty to reach his goals, and he knew he didn't have a desire to toil until he reached seventy; his strategy was to retire at fifty.

Cramming day and night, taking more courses than required, he completed his university studies early, as predicted, actually in half the time. Before Marshall turned twenty-two, he was well on his way to success.

As each opportunity presented itself, he grabbed it up like a drowning man grabs a life raft, enrolling in each law enforcement training class afforded him. His ultimate goal was to be a detective for the Orlando Sheriff's Department and; to become proficient in all fields. He always challenged himself to be better - to be the best - at everything he did.

Landing his first position right out of the university, he, like everyone else, started at the bottom and had to take the menial tasks along with any skilled assignments he could get to work his way up. Failure was not an option, and early leaps were his aim.

At the Orlando Police Department, Marshall completed the law enforcement academy in fourteen weeks, the standard course time. He served as a street cop for one year before applying for a sergeant's position. The examination was a cinch for him to complete, he passed without any difficulty. There were two other applicants, but his scores left them out in the cold.

He performed skillfully as sergeant for the police department for two years then applied at the sheriff's office for a position as a rookie deputy. He again passed and readily was accepted.

By the age of twenty-five Marshall succeeded in passing the detective's exam at the sheriff's office, becoming a youngest detective in the history of that office. Within months he was appointed lead detective supervising fourteen other officers.

A few of Marshall's college buddies gave him a hard time over the years because of his obvious brilliance; his test scores and high ratings at the shooting range, he always outshined them. In his pursuit of perfection and promotions, he earned the nickname "Smarty Pants." The name followed him like a sick puppy in each position he held; evidently his colleagues saw to. He took it in stride.

Though he was rather pleased that they recognized his abilities, he did not relish in their enjoyment they when the opportunity arose to use his nickname. "Phone call on three for Smarty Pants." Then he'd wait for the laughter to subside. Some days he'd have to count to ten. *"One of these days,"* he thought, *"I'll pay them back."*

He was not easily angered nor egotistical. He had compassion for his fellow man as well as the victims of crimes he worked on. He tried not to wear his emotions on his sleeve but when the circumstances were right he had no choice. He was a serious man and a proud detective.

Marshall's parents were well educated as was his younger sister, Lela, two years his junior. She wanted to follow in her brother's footsteps; and though she did not graduate early, she did manage to graduate with high honors. She chose to go the local community college, then to the state college. Once her initial courses were complete she was promptly accepted to Yale to pursue her dream of a career as an attorney.

Lela's struggles were different from most or from any Marshall had faced. As a petite brunette she could have been mistaken for a pageant winner. Her features were like that of Cleopatra – she was stunning. Her high cheek bones and violet eyes made people passing her do a double take. She looked far from the standard as a lawyer would be described.

This made it difficult for people, students and professors alike to take her seriously. They thought she could charm her way through most anything but could she convince a judge or a jury of the innocence or guilt of someone, was she strong enough for that – beauty made no difference in a court of law – would she be taken seriously?

She consulted her brother various times during her college years to gather his expertise to guide her through a case. They worked exceptionally well together.

He managed to keep her pumped up and on track. Once in a while, he advised her in lessons in toughness to prevent others from walking all over her, as a female in a man's world. She graduated at the top of her class just as Marshall had been promoted to lead detective in Orlando.

She was quickly scooped up and signed a contract with Baily & Ernstein, one of the largest and most prestigious law firms in central Orlando. It was not long before her power and strength was evident. In court she was a force to be reckoned with. She bowed down to no one. Her arguments took on a new voice, she was now being taken seriously – a bear cat who few wanted to be up against in a court of law.

Now at twenty-six, having a few minor cases - petty local robberies, auto thefts, and assault and abuse -under his belt, Marshall knew the McGuire case would be his first major case with this department and would test him to the fullest.

Even before he reached the scene, determination to exert all his expertise had set in. He vowed that under his watch, no case go unsolved. He would see the perpetrators nabbed and punished. His reputation was at stake as well as his pride.

CHAPTER 4

BACK TO THE SCENE

Marshall wasted not a minute racing to the scene; his unmarked car screeching to a halt after first leaving two short strips of black rubber.

His careful walk toward the residence granted him the opportunity to focus for anything out of the ordinary. He recognized that, inside or outside of a crime scene, one can never assume he will find all the evidence; anyone can miss the obvious.

He knew a little evidence would be found; it usually happened that way. But he remained on high alert anyway.

A cluster of chatty bystanders mulled around the sidewalk of the residence as he made his trek towards the already opened front door. While driving to the scene, he had contacted the forensics lab to come to the scene.

Marshall was acquainted with everyone in the area, including the McGuires. He had been introduced to David at a community function a few years before and had seen him recently at the

Annual Police Awards Ceremony, sponsored every year to honor both officers killed in the line of duty and officers deserving special honors. David was not only the president of the largest bank in Orlando but a member of at least eight community organizations and committees working diligently to see the plans of the community accomplished. His work inside and outside the bank kept him in the public eye, and he was well respected by all who knew him.

Janice worked with high school students, tutoring on occasion, and, was on the hospital board. Marshall had met her only once, and it was brief so he didn't know much about her, except that she was now dead.

Marshall entered the residence. Glancing to the right he observed a young girl, her body shaking with each sob released, sitting next to a female paramedic. She momentarily glanced up when he entered the front hallway.

He quickly made note of her eyes, which were almost swollen shut yet so blue he could see them across the room. She quickly put her head back in her hands and continued weeping. The paramedic put a reassuring arm around Glory, who laid her head on the paramedic's shoulder. Marshall's compassion sprung up full force – he knew he could question the girl later.

He located the first officer on the scene. Richards explained his and the backup officers' actions when they arrived at the home.

After Richards showed Marshall Janice's body on the dining room floor and the paramedics stated there was nothing that could be done for her, Marshall noticed the red smears on the counter. Bending his head low, to get a better look, he deduced it was blood, most likely from Janice's gaping wound. There were no visible fingerprints, which he thought strange. Usually a trained officer could determine where there may be prints, like on glass or a refrigerator surface when it came to a burglary, but not this time.

Continuing his note taking, he turned to Richards. "Get forensics in here as soon as possible and get plenty of pictures, Richards, plenty. And for God's sake, have your officers get the rest of that crime tape up. It has to go entirely around the house not just in front and back. We don't need any sight-seers tramping through this now." Richards complied and said that he had called the coroner's office for transportation of Mrs. McGuire's body.

Richards nervously said, "I searched the downstairs and it appears things had been moved about, apparently brushed off tabletops too. I noticed no real damage has taken place. The TV and other things of value - crystal, electrical equipment, paintings and other collectibles - do not seem to be missing. At first glance it appears this may have been an interrupted burglary. I was just heading upstairs but would prefer you take my back."

Marshall was a little more than perturbed that the upper floor had not already been secured. "No one's been upstairs yet?"

"No, I have an officer securing the stairway entrance and also one outside. I've not heard any noise up there and chose to wait for you to search further."

"Big mistake on your part, Richards." Marshall's anger was apparent but would not change the fact that there has been a lack of progress by Officer Richards.

Marshall and Richards began to ascend the stairs, slowly. They took every precaution afforded them, because there was still a remote chance they would encounter the intruder. Richards had not released his grip on his service weapon since entering the residence.

Both took steady steps, taking note of the pictures of the all-American family on the stairway wall. A quick glance to each other fortified their similar thoughts. *How can this happen in a neighborhood like this, to a family like this?*

At the top of the stairs, with Marshall leading the way, they came upon the first door. Opening it, Marshall assumed it must be the girl's room, because the walls were a pastel yellow, the bedspread multi-colored flowers and the curtains a pale pink. There was no disturbance in the room or in the closet; the clothes appeared to be just as they had been hung. Everything was neatly arranged on the dresser and in the drawers. The window at the head of the bed was shut, and the latch was in the locked position. They shut the door.

The next room was the bathroom. Nothing appeared to be out of place there either. Towels were on the towel racks; perfume bottles, hairspray and a hair brush all lay neatly in place.

The small window was open and there was a screen on it. It had not been tampered with. They closed the door.

The next door was obviously a guest bedroom. At first glance, it appeared nothing there had been disturbed. It was neat and tidy with; nothing in the closet, empty drawers, and a made bed. They closed that door.

The final room, the master bedroom, was at the far end of the hallway. It was a mess, like the living room. A chair sat in the middle of the room, night-stands were pulled away from the wall, and the dresser drawers were open. Items on the dressers had been shoved off and lay on the floor. There were a few hangers with clothes on them scattered about.

To the left side of the bed was David, lying on his back. A paramedic was summoned and instructed to evaluate the body's condition. He appeared at the top of the stairs immediately and went directly to where the body lay. Aware that Marshall was standing nearby, waiting for a determination, but sure he already knew the verdict, the paramedic shook his head. "It's over."

"How long has it been "over"?" Marshall asked. He wondered. *"If he had been discovered sooner, might he still be alive?"* The paramedic assured him he had lain there a long time; perhaps six to eight hours; the blood had gelled in the center of the pools and became dark and thickened on the edges. "Maybe a day as far as I can tell."

Marshall drew near to where David's body was lying, observing that his throat too had been slashed, just as Marshall had seen on Janice downstairs, a pool of blood around his head. And there did not appear to have been a struggle.

The attached master bathroom was in disarray like the bedroom. Items had apparently been shoved off the countertop and lay on the floor almost in one place. It was like a hand had swept across the counter top, toppling everything to the tiled floor and then the hand had stopped. Nothing had been thrown about; items appeared to lie where they fell. Towels had been removed from the towel racks and laid on the floor near the bathtub.

Marshall approached David's body again. The pool of blood around his head soaked into the carpet; appearing halo like. Apparently he had not died immediately either, though it would have taken only seconds for the life to be sucked out of him. It was obvious that when David's throat was cut, he hadn't even had time to fight back.

Detective Marshall made note of the smears of dried blood on the bed-spread, the dressers, and the bathroom counter. Why the trails of blood were left in these three rooms - the master bedroom, master bathroom, and kitchen - was not determined yet, and it confused Marshall. If the smears were intentionally placed there, as if it was for appearance's sake, it was a bizarre act that made no sense. A little blood spray could be accounted for. When a throat is cut the severed area will spray blood, but it was minimal as if to indicate the victim's head was not pulled back but positioned forward to decrease the spray. Marshall had noticed the position of both bodies; their arms were at their sides, their legs straight out - they had not been dropped but purposefully laid down.

Marshall logged everything he saw and heard, noting that the drawers had been yanked out in all three rooms as well as some of the contents. Some items in the drawers were still in a sensible order; only a few papers were on the floor, sparking his curiosity even more. "What could they have been looking for?"

The coroner and forensics' team were arriving just as Marshall and Richards went back down the stairs. Richards stopped long enough to instruct the coroner where the bodies lay and to give direction to the forensic teams. "Marshall says no dilly-dallying. He wants answers, and he wants them yesterday."

Marshall wasted no time in seeing to the girl's welfare. "Richards, get on the horn. I want a female officer here pronto. I want her to accompany Glory from now on. We don't know who did this, and until we do, I want her under our protection." Marshall started for the living room to question Glory. Richards came in shortly thereafter.

Marshall chose an oversized, floral arm-chair across from the couch where Glory was sitting. He told the paramedic that a law enforcement officer would arrive shortly to relieve her so the she could get on with her duties assisting the other paramedics.

Then he introduced himself to Glory.

Understandably shaken the young girl looked at Marshall. "Did you find my dad?"

Marshall knew to go easy with his response as well as with any questions he asked of the girl. "Yes, Glory, we did. I'm sorry but he is upstairs and he as well was a victim."

"You mean he's dead?"

"Yes, Glory, I'm sorry to tell you that, but we will find out who did this."

Glory took the news in silence, looking as if the life had just been drained out of her. Her face took on an ashen color as she laid her head back on the paramedic's shoulder and closed her eyes.

"I hate to ask you any questions, Glory," Marshall said, "but we need to try to find out who did this as soon as possible. The longer we wait, the harder it will be. Do you think you can answer a few questions for me?"

Glory opened her eyes and stared at Marshall. He was taken aback by her pure smooth porcelain skin as he breathed in her unsettling beauty and stared at her deep-set blue eyes, noting that if they weren't swollen, they'd be enormous. He took a mental note of how truly exquisite she was.

"Yes," she quietly whispered.

His first question was to ask her if she had seen anyone or heard anything in the house when she came home and if she had any idea if there were any problems with anyone inside or outside the family. It was a lot to answer but Marshall had only a small window; he needed answers *now*.

In only a faint voice, she said, "No, I didn't see anybody. I didn't hear anything, except the phone ringing. It was my dad's secretary wanting to talk to my dad. I don't think there were any problems in my family."

"Does it look like a burglary to you?"

Glory looked confused. "What does a burglary look like?"

Instantly Marshall felt like an idiot. She wasn't anything but a child, for heaven's sake. His first instinct was to walk out of the room from embarrassment, but he immediately composed himself. "I'm sorry; does it look like anything has been taken?"

Emotionally drained, she was powerless but still willing to answer. She looked around the room. "I don't know. I haven't looked everywhere. Who would do this? Who did it?"

Detective Marshall put his hand on her arm for comfort. "We'll find them, Glory. Don't worry." He knew he would have to talk to her later; this just wasn't the time. As he sat across from her, he said nothing further, just stared.

A female officer arrived to take charge of Glory, and the paramedic left the room to continue her own work. Marshall asked the female officer to take Glory to the Corner Shelter on Davenport Street and have someone stay with her at all times. He also wanted to be notified if the girl remembered anything pertinent.

He turned to Glory and said, "I'm going to send you to a shelter for your own safety. This is Officer

Laura, and she will stay with you until relatives can be notified. You will not be left alone, and I'll talk with you later at the shelter."

He asked Laura to go upstairs to Glory's room to pack a few things she may need, telling her to contact the school, informing them Glory would not be attending for a while.

Glory went upstairs with the officer, shaking all the way, knowing they found her father somewhere up there. She was afraid she might see his body; she wasn't sure she could bear it. The officer walked in front of her, and when they got to her bedroom doorway, she turned around so Glory could not see past her as they entered Glory's room.

Glory wanted to curl up on the bed and pretend nothing had changed. *"Maybe this was a dream and if I got on the bed and closed my eyes when I opened them Mom and Dad would be home"* She closed her eyes.

Laura located a small suitcase and makeup case in the closet. Glory sat on the bed with her arms on her lap, unable to move, eyes closed.

Laura pulled some appropriate clothing out of the closet and the drawers and a couple of pairs of shoes and some personal items off the dresser, and put them into the suitcase. She then retrieved a toothbrush, shampoo, makeup and a hairbrush from the bathroom.

When she returned to the room, Glory's eyes were open. She saw the officer and realized, to her dismay, it wasn't a dream.

They both went back downstairs.

The coroner had finished conducting a preliminary examination on Janice's body. He saw the desperation on the young girl's face, and it was difficult for him to hold his own composure. He wished he could give her words of comfort, but he had none.

As Glory reached the front door, she turned to Marshall. "Please, can I see my mom?" Marshall said she could, but only for a moment. By that time, a coroner's sheet covered Janice from head to toe.

Glory approached the stretcher on which her mother lay. One paramedic folded back the cloth no further than Janice's chin; Glory bent down and kissed her mother on the forehead, backed up, and stared again at Marshall. "Thank you. Please help me." She began to weep. Laura put her arms around her shoulders again and gently led her out of the house.

Marshall had heard a deep sense of need in the girl's voice. But, he thought., O*ther than finding the killer, what can I do?*

Glory was taken to the Corner Shelter in central Orlando, where she would stay until preparations for her care were lined up.

Soon the bodies, completely covered by the corner's customary black body bag, were readied for the ambulance for delivery to the morgue. The coroner's office, located there, would conduct the autopsy.

It was obvious to the bystanders that there had not been an accident at this home; it was something more sinister. When the bodies began to come out of the house gasps were heard throughout the crowd.

They began bombarding the officers and paramedics with questions. The officers assigned outside took control by reversing the conversation; asking them questions instead. Had they noticed anything unusual in the neighborhood - strange people or strange cars? Did the McGuires seem to have any problems? The answers to all their inquiries were a catagorical *no*. All had agreed that both Mr. and Mrs. McGuire were great and there were no problems that they were aware of and also, they had a wonderful daughter.

Some inquired as to the girl's whereabouts. Some were vultures just waiting for every juicy detail they could gather. The bystanders information was of no help.

Even more frightening to them all was the idea there may be a killer on the loose. Some went straight home to check their door locks. Others waited to hear more news. Some were from adjacent neighborhoods and were just curious, not having known any of the McGuire's.

Marshall exited the living room and spoke to the to the coroner in the hallway. "Time of deaths for both was in the early morning hours, possible between eight and ten. "I'll know more after the autopsy, but I can tell you this: the cause of death was homicide. The details will be on the official report."

The bodies had been photographed and bagged for transport to the morgue after the coroner's initial review; accompanied by photos of the bodies' condition, placement and surrounding areas.

The coroner left shortly after talking to Marshall while three forensic specialists began further work at the body sites, searching for fibers, blood, or other evidence.

Marshall retraced his steps back to the living room, where two members of the forensic team were still hard at work. Black fingerprint dust covered much of the furniture and fire-place mantel. Plastic bags sat on the coffee table with bits of various fibers encased in each. Leafing through papers discarded on the floor, Marshall found a business card near the desk. It read, "Garrett Sanders, Attorney at Law." He dialed the number.

"G. Sanders Law Office, may I help you?"

"This is Glenn Marshall, Detective, Orlando Sheriff's Department. Is Garrett Sanders the attorney for David and Janice McGuire on Sycamore Street?"

"Why yes, he is."

"This is an emergency. I need to speak with Mr. Sanders immediately."

The secretary, Jill, informed Marshall that Mr. Sanders was out of the office, but she would contact him immediately. Marshall left his cell number for Sanders to return his call.

Garrett Sanders received Jill's call within minutes. She passed on the information from Marshall about an emergency at the McGuire's.

Sanders arrived at the McGuire residence twenty minutes later, having chosen to drive directly there rather than to make the call from his office. David was his friend; if there was an emergency, he should be with him.

When Sanders arrived, he saw that a large group of bystanders circled the residence and police cars were lined in the front of the house, alarms rang out through his body.

An ambulance was leaving the residence, but no red lights were flashing. Dread overtook him, and he began to sweat.

He parked his car, got out, and headed for the house. An officer tried to stop his approach, but Sanders explained he was the attorney for the McGuire's and that a Detective Marshall had summoned him. The officer nodded in understanding and let him pass.

Even though the door was open, he knocked before entering the house, fearing the worst. Detective Marshall met him at the door, introduced himself, and then proceeded to explain what had happened, to the best of his knowledge.

He gave Sanders a tour of the lower level first, then the upper level of the residence. Sanders grimaced when he saw the bold dark-red stains, seeing where the bodies had been located and his stomach doubled up into knots.

As they came to the downstairs entryway, Marshall questioned Sanders. "Is there anything you can tell me that might shed some light on what happened here? Were there any problems in the McGuire house or with his business?"

Sanders was tearful at this point, still in shock from the tour and the explanation of what may have happened. Being a tough old bird, he held the tears back as best he could. "We've been friends for years. "Though I was his attorney, there had not been much to do legally for him over the past years. But we did socialize." Then, "I thought you indicated this was a burglary."

Detective Marshall asked him again, changing his wording, "Do you know of any problems David was having with anyone personally or financially. And yes, at this time we consider this a burglary."

"No, David and Janice were good honest people. I can't think of anyone who would wish either of them harm." He was visibly distraught. "What about Glory?"

Marshall explained to him that, unfortunately, Glory had been the one who found her mother. "I had her taken to the Corner Shelter and a female officer who will be with her at all times. I mean to question her later, but right now she is still in shock."

Sanders reluctantly offered some new information. "David and I were close since junior high. He has a brother; his name is Lucen. The guy was kind of a loner, a nonconformist, never hung out with us much. He's now living in South Dakota, but the families have not talked in many years."

"Why is that?" Marshall asked.

"They had a disagreement just out of college, or maybe it was high school. I can't remember exactly when it was. They weren't close. Lucen moved away. I don't know why they never kept in contact after that, I just know they didn't. David never talked about Lucen."

"Can you reach the brother and let him know what happened here?"

Sanders assured Marshall he would contact Lucen later that day, adding that he didn't think there were any other living relatives.

"Sanders, Glory is a minor and the only child of the McGuire's. Contacting someone to care for her is a priority, and time is of the essence. I'll leave it up to you to take responsibility for the release of the bodies from the coroner too. I hate to put all this on you, but when you talk to Lucen, find out about funeral arrangements. Evidently he may not wish to handle it and, if there are no other relatives, that sort of leaves you, doesn't it? Can you do it?"

"Yes, I'll do what I can."

"Did you prepare the wills for the McGuire's?"

"Yes."

"I need to know what was in them, and I need to know if there was a life insurance policy and who the beneficiary is."

For a moment, Sanders thought Marshall to be a callous man, just a hard-nosed detective. Then he realized it was information Marshall needed to pursue the investigation. He assured Marshall he would review the contents of the wills and check on the life insurance policy. A big load was just placed on his shoulders, and he really wasn't looking forward to carrying it. He hadn't expected such chaos today.

"As far as I remember, David and Janice wrote a will but it was a long time ago. I don't recall the contents. I have no idea what provisions, if any, were set forth in it for the girl. I'm sure there was something, but I can't tell until I get back to my office and look at it. I'll let you know."

They agreed to meet in a couple of days; Marshall gave him his card before he headed back to his law office.

It was already evening. Marshall continued analyzing the crime scene in the hopes of finding at least a small piece of evidence that would to lead him to a reasonable conclusion. Whether it was a cold blooded murder or an interrupted burglary, he needed something that would get him closer to making some sense of it all.

He slowly and systematically retraced his steps, both inside and outside of the house. Walking the perimeter, looking up toward the roof and down toward the basement, he saw nothing. He wondered why there were no footprints inside or outside the house.

In his initial inspection of the house, there were no broken windows, no broken doors, so from his perspective, the intruder entered the house freely. Had the McGuires' known the assailant? Had they let the killer in?

As painstakingly as the forensic teams worked, they hadn't uncovered anything substantial yet. They informed Marshall there were no apparent fibers left on or near the bodies as far as they could see with the human eye. He requested they notify him if even the minutest evidence emerged from their analysis. He knew not to press his luck by pressuring them, but he couldn't comprehend there not being one shred of anything of value. The perpetrator had been excessively cautious; that was obvious.

Marshall deduced the blood smears were just that, smears. Whoever left them did so deliberately, but made sure there were no fingerprints, and that fact weighed heavily on Marshall's mind. Each detail that didn't make sense was too convenient for the perpetrator's well-being – meaning the perpetrator had set this up to benefit him to the fullest.

This appeared calculated; too many pieces just didn't fit. Why were there no signs of a struggle? Why was there no blood on the floor from the perpetrator's shoes or outside the residence? Why were there no fingerprints? Too many unanswered questions. Marshall wanted something, no matter how small, that would change his mind about it being a planned act of violence; he could not shake the feeling the murders weren't accidental, weren't a burglar interrupted.

But he had nothing other than that scenario to go on for the time being. Random or not, he knew there was a monster out there, a calculating devil of a man or men who needed to be found. He didn't even have a murder weapon, and he knew the odds of finding it were close to none.

By 7:30 p.m. Marshall concluded his search and told Officer Richards he was heading back to his office.

CHAPTER 5

MONEY, MONEY, MONEY

It was 6:50 on the evening of the murders when Garrett Sanders, shaken, bolted through his office door. He dashed past the reception area, seeing that Jill had already left for the day. He poured a cup of coffee, hands shaking, and went into his private office.

Sitting down in his overstuffed leather chair, holding his coffee cup, he stared at his desk, dreading the inevitable. His closest friend was dead, murdered, his throat slashed like an animal and by an animal.

After a few minutes, he stood up and shook himself to wake up from the nightmare he was in, if that were possible. He kept seeing the bloodied floor and carpet, and it would haunt him for some time.

He pulled the McGuire file, realizing the moment he did that he hadn't looked at it for years— the last entry had been five years ago. He set those papers aside; they didn't relate to the will anyway. He found several loose papers that hadn't been filed, which he set aside until he had time to review the will. The next group of legal documents were those pertaining to the last wishes of David and Janice.

Before going any further he left a note for Jill to hold all calls and change the next day's appointments and not disturb him. He explained on the note that the McGuires had been murdered. He wanted no interruptions. He would drop it off at her desk before leaving for the night. It would take him the rest of the evening and the next day to sort everything out.

He already knew David's estate was worth quite a bit. He just didn't know how much. To his amazement, he now saw David's estate value was astronomical. Periodically, over the years David would drop off various documents to be put in his file. He would tell him they were for safe keeping and that he didn't need to review them. So until this moment, Sanders had no idea what documents David's file contained.

Sanders, as executor and attorney, had his work cut out for him. His mission: to decipher all the documents David filed over the years relating to accounts, credit cards, life and general insurance companies; initiate closing the appropriate accounts, files, and processing claims, as well as take care of the residence.

Already feeling overwhelmed with this task Sanders had to further scrutinize the will to see what designations David and Janice had made for their monies and more importantly for the care of Glory, if any.

Soon he would have to call Lucen, locate any other relatives, and contact the coroner, the funeral home, and the church. He had a lot to digest and a lot to do; his head was starting to pound.

With the financial risk involved, his concentration settled into preparing a detailed and itemized report that would explain, in plain English, the designations of the will to Marshall.

He knew that in murder investigations, especially where money was concerned, references could be made to the will several times during an investigation, so he was meticulous. If the killers were ever caught and tried, the information pertaining to distribution of funds could be brought up.

The will was much more complex than the average person's but Sanders was astonished at the fine points that set the conditions for Glory's care. He had to read them over twice to comprehend exactly what was requested. Since he hadn't seen them in fifteen years he had forgotten the fine points.

He was tired. He wanted to get home. Mentally exhausted, he felt like his head would explode. He hadn't remembered signing up for this when he got his law degree. He left the note for Jill on her desk and headed home.

Arriving at his office early the next morning, even before Jill, Sanders sighed with the thought of the day's work ahead of him. Almost as if someone were chasing him, he made a straight shot for his office and closed the door.

Pulling the McGuire file again, he observed there were individuals who would benefit greatly as set forth by the McGuires' wishes. He called the bank, brokers, and insurance company for balances and designations. He looked at his watch a few minutes later and was surprised to see that three hours had elapsed since he first sat down. Jill must have come in, but she hadn't disturbed him.

The day was wearing on, and he hadn't taken a lunch break. He had vowed this morning that, after he compiled the information, he would call Marshall and not put off their meeting another day. He hoped Marshall could make more sense out of it all than he could.

Retrieving Marshall's cell number off his card, he dialed the number. Marshall answered.

"It looks like I'll need to meet with you sooner than we thought," Sanders said. "There is a lot of money involved here, a lot of property, and some individuals with a stake in the outcome of the will. I think it will be of interest you. How about meeting me at 10:15 tomorrow morning?"

"I'm up to his eyeballs on this case and have not started the report yet. Can't this wait until day after tomorrow?"

Sanders was adamant. "Marshall this is no time for waiting. The information I have you need to know. I don't want to put this off." They agreed on 10:15 the next morning.

Marshall closed his eyes for a moment, realizing this was his hardest assignment to date. Yes, he'd excelled in every test he'd ever taken, but this was different. He could not retake this test if he failed. This was not a class he could breeze through, but an eye-opening, hard-core murder. He had solved every scenario given to him at the academy, but that was not real life. This was.

Six or seven more hours in the day would have allowed him the time he needed. In all likelihood, it would be three days before he got a decent night's sleep; he doubted he'd see any shuteye today or tomorrow. "Well, I've spent days at a time cramming for exams, and that didn't seem to bother me," he murmured to himself. He knew the chief would be on his back for his initial report.

The chief was a hardnosed sixty-five-year-old with over thirty years in the department. He never allowed shenanigans on his watch. "By the book," he would always say.

Time was not Marshall's friend right now; it was slipping away. He poured what he thought was his twentieth cup of steaming black coffee, and began typing.

The next day, May 15th, at 10:15, he met with Garrett Sanders in his downtown office. Jill immediately ushered him into Sanders's office without knocking. Sanders extended his hand, indicating Marshall should sit as Jill left the room, closing the door behind her. As he turned back to his desk he punched the speaker box. "Jill, bring in two black coffees." He then faced Marshall.

"Make yourself comfortable. This will take awhile. I'm sure you'll have lots of questions for me later." Now expecting the worst, Marshall took off his jacket and did just that, got comfortable in one of the three leather recliners.

Within a few minutes, Jill was in with two black coffees and a thermos. "I thought you might need more than a cup." She took her time handing Marshall his cup. Their hands touched briefly as he reached for it. She threw a big inviting smile his way, turned, and left the room.

Noticing the gesture with a smirk, Sanders said, "She seems a little smitten with you, Marshall."

Marshall had no time for that kind of malarkey. The reason he sat in this here was to find out why this information couldn't wait another day. "Get on with it, will you, Sanders? I've still got work to do."

Sanders began with the most important fact of the matter, the money. "The McGuires are worth a fortune, Marshall. We're talking millions here. Between the will and the life insurance policy, their estate has enough money to fund the government." He chuckled.

Marshall didn't see the humor.

Sanders saw this was not the time nor was this the man for jokes. He got serious. "But let me back up. First, the will states Glory is the goddaughter of David's brother and his wife, Lucen and Victoria. They live in Spalding, South Dakota. According to the will, they are to be paid twenty thousand dollars per year for her care, to cover anything she needs. This, of course, is only valid if something were to happen to David and Janice, which, as we both know, it did." He peered over his glasses to see if there would be a response. There was none.

He continued. "She'll have to go live with them."

As he rambled on, Marshall was trying to determine if he planned on taking a breath sometime soon. He rarely paused. It was as if he had so much to reveal that if he stopped for even a moment, he would forget something.

He could tell Sanders was trying to hide his underlying distress over the murders. It was a pretty good attempt to project his professional capacity as the McGuires' attorney.

"When Glory turns twenty-one, the South Dakota McGuires would be compensated with a lump sum of fifty thousand dollars. It's their reward for service as godparents. That money becomes their personal property to do with as they wish. Now, Marshall, this is where it may get a little complicated, so bear with me." As he looked up Marshall saw that small beads of sweat were forming on his forehead.

He's either out of breath or nearing heart failure, Marshall thought. "Got ya so far Sanders. Keep going." He leaned back with his palms together, tapping the fingers of one hand with the fingers of the other, waiting for the bombshell Sanders was going to deliver.

Sanders's manner was that of a game show host explaining the rules. "Now, let me be perfectly clear. If Glory were to die, the McGuires still get the lump sum, all of it. But, and I say *but*, not until the date of her twenty-first birthday. Understand that one?"

"Yeah, loud and clear. Go on," Marshall said as he leaned forward, anxious to hear more.

"If she leaves their home before she is twenty-one, let's say as soon as she is of age, eighteen, then the twenty thousand per year will go directly to her. Now, more coffee?"

"No thanks, Sanders, get on with it. This is getting good."

"Okay, if Glory marries before she is twenty-one, the allotment is still paid directly to her. She is still not to know, until she is actually twenty-one, of the millions she will inherit at that age. But if she dies before her twenty-first birthday, the millions go to, are you ready … ?" He didn't wait for a response. "To her nearest living relative, a husband, a child, Lucen, Victoria, get it? Once she is twenty-one and given the inheritance, she has full control and can spend it any way she wishes."

"Yeah, I got it." Marshall thought that schedule of payment a bit odd, but it was David and Janice, not him, who set it up. He thought it was good forethought of David and Janice not to expect someone else to use their own funds to support their child. David obviously wanted to ensure his daughter was well cared for, whether by her godparents or on her own. No one can know when they will die; he respected their early planning for her care.

Sanders tapped the desk with one finger to make his point clear as he said, "Glory is to know nothing of the will's contents, with the exception of the allotment to the South Dakota McGuires and to her if she is on her own."

He leaned straight forward on his desk as far as he could, extending his body to make a point. "Now, Marshall, listen closely. Glory is to be told she is to meet me when she reaches the age of twenty-one. She is not to know why, but the why is ..." He paused. "That's when I tell her she inherits everything; all her parents' money and holdings. We're talking in the millions here, Marshall, I mean in the millions of millions."

Sanders inhaled deeply and continued. "The will is to be openly read and discussed with her at that time; nothing is to be disclosed beforehand. Only David, Janice, and I were aware of the contents, which I'd forgotten about until now. Lucen and Victoria will be told only of the allotment, nothing more. And now you know." He sat back in his chair, exhaled deeply, and stared at Marshall.

"It's a great deal of money. Enough so they would not have to support Glory with their own funds. And enough to kill for, don't you think, Marshall? Enough to kill for?"

Marshall replied, "I'll be the detective on this, Mr. Sanders. You take care of the paperwork. I don't actually see a connection related to the money anyway. You need to concentrate on the attorney side of this matter. Don't go getting all Dick Tracey on me."

Sanders wasn't finished yet. "Further, Lucen was sent a copy of the will with a stamped seal on it sixteen years ago with explicit instructions not to open it. His instructions were to put it in a safe place or a safety deposit box until he received further direction."

Sanders talked rapidly as if he might explode if he were not liberated from the information. Marshall figured he'd bet a hundred bucks that

Sanders could hold his breath underwater for five or six minutes.

"The fact is that Lucen and Victoria accepted their status as godparents during a phone conversation I had with Lucen back then. David and I talked about it and, though they didn't get along, they only had each other if anything arose that they needed a family member. David asked me to not only send Lucen the papers but to call him. I'm sure this was forgotten about all these years since. Who knew, at the writing of the will, that David would make it big? That he would become a millionaire? No one, that's who, no one. So what do you think?" Jutting his head forward as if he were a turtle coming out of hiding, he stared at Marshall.

"I think that is crazy, and these murders are crazy, and there is something here that doesn't mesh. I just don't know what it is right now, but I have an uneasy feeling about this whole thing." If Marshall thought of this as a burglary, then this will information wouldn't be related. Unless Lucen had in fact opened the will and saw the contents or unless he had shared that information with someone else. From what Sanders indicated, Lucen had simply filed had his copy away. After all, Sanders implied the brothers had a tiff and had no real contact since Lucen left. Marshall's guess was that Lucen didn't open it.

Marshall and Sanders looked at each with an expression of anticipation, as if either one of them could voice all the answers to all the questions if they just thought about it a little longer.

Sanders announced firmly, "Total confidentially on this information, Marshall, except the allotment for Glory's care, of course. I'm only telling you this to see if there is something you can use. I want the ones who committed this crime caught and hung high." The tension rose in his voice as he spoke.

He took a sip of his coffee, trying to calm down, but he grimaced when he realized his coffee had gone cold. He whispered, "No one is to know the worth of David McGuire until it is revealed to Glory. I will also be compensated for my time at the same time the fifty thousand is disbursed to the McGuires, just for your information."

Sanders began a journey back in time. "Since David and I were friends, I must have agreed to these provision sixteen years ago. I didn't remember much about it until opening the will and reading it again. I had trust in David. Like I said, he was a great guy, so I must have believed at that time he made the right decision regarding his estate."

He sat back, relieved the information was off his shoulders. "I am to be the executor of all property, pensions, retirement, and any funds or investments at the time of the McGuires' death and secured and/or invested until Glory turns twenty-one."

Marshall inquired as to the legality of the will. "Can information be withheld from the beneficiaries? Isn't that a strange way to write a will? Oh, I'm not talking about the part about the care of the child. I mean the part concerning the inheritance and that no one is to know of it until Glory reaches twenty-one. Is that legal?"

Sanders sat up straight in his chair, and his chest heaved. "Yes, it's legal. Whatever is written in a will is legal, though I admit it is strange. The possible beneficiaries could take it to court to see if a judge would release the information, but I doubt it would fly. Guess you'd have to have pretty nasty relatives to pursue it further, but it's been known to happen."

He jotted a few notes then continued. "David probably didn't even realize how much he would be worth. Sometimes when people write wills, they are satisfied with the fact one was written at all. They forget about them, never go back and revise them. I am sure if David had known what would happen to him, he would have gone back and made some revisions." He paused.

"When I read the will, I will have to interpret it a little on my own, explaining to the concerned parties that I am in charge of all affairs related to the financial side of the will until Glory is twenty-one. No further funds information, except for the allotment, can be revealed until that time. I am not sure how but I will have to make my explanation work. I really don't want to be dragged into a court of law because I failed to disclose information. David was my friend, and I will do what I have to do to protect him, his daughter, and his money."

Marshall didn't have any further questions for Sanders. He had heard enough.

When Sanders called Lucen on the afternoon of May 16th to inform him of his brother and sister-in-law's murder. He told Lucen that he and

Victoria were the designated godparents of Glory. "This position is effective immediately. That is, if you are you capable and prepared to care for her until she is of age."

Lucen had a simple reply. "Yes."

Sanders told him about the arrangements for Glory to be on a plane in four weeks and detailed her travel itinerary. He also asked him to consider being in charge of the funeral arrangements.

His answer was straight forward with no hesitation, Lucen said, "No."

Sanders said, "I can set the funeral up for three days from now. Will you be able to get here by then?"

Again, a straight-forward answer came. "No. We won't be coming."

Sanders continued. "David allocated an allotment of twenty thousand dollars per year for the care of Glory for the time she lives with a guardian."

Lucen firmly and defiantly bellowed, "We don't need it; we can take care of her on our own."

Sanders simply said, "The allotment is part of David and Janice's wishes. It is important Glory's needs are met while she is with you. I am sure you are able to care for her, but this will make it easier on your family and on Glory. Lucen, she's been through a rough time."

After a few moments, Lucen replied, "Yeah, okay."

Sanders chose to only tell Lucen what was pertenient to the current day. He would receive the twenty thousand dollars each year for Glory's care. Sanders remembered Lucen from their school days and that the less information shared with Lucen, the less conversation you had with him, the better. Lucen was always confrontational back then. Though generally a quiet man, if given a subject he didn't agree with he could argue his point until the sun burned out. Sanders felt he'd told him enough already and wanted to end the conversation. He implored Lucen to keep the allotment information confidential, only between him and Victoria. He reminded Lucen about his copy of the will and that it should remain sealed until he himself instructed otherwise.

"When we were appointed godparents of Glory, David told me that stuff in a letter," Lucien said. "I guess he never changed it, and yeah, I agree. David was always the detail guy, dotting all his I's and crossing all his Ts."

Still reeling from the abundance of information Sanders had laid on him, Marshall drove straight to the bank where David had been president. In the conference room, he questioned the bank employees individually: tellers, loan officers, the security guard, and others associated with David. His questions were brief but focused on anything in the past few weeks that seemed unusual. All said the same thing: nothing out of the ordinary. All the bank employees were astonished by what had happened; no one could imagine why anyone would want to hurt either of the McGuires.

He continued his questioning at Jackson Elementary School, where Janice tutored. Principal

Thompson said he'd had no reason to be concerned for Janice's safety; everything was normal as far as he knew. "Janice was well liked," he said, "and there were no problems during her employment of four years. The students as well as the other teachers adored her."

Marshall located the McGuires' gardener, Albert Simpson, and asked him about his whereabouts and relationship with the family. "I groom the yard once a week, on Fridays. I talk to Mrs. McGuire. Mr. McGuire didn't give instructions about the yard. I never saw her any other day of the week. I keep busy with other yards."

"Where were you on May 13th?"

Simpson looked at his calendar. "I was at the Thompsons'. They live near the mall."

Marshall got Thompsons' telephone number, thanked Simpson, and got back in his car. He called the number, and Mr. Thompson confirmed Simpson had been there all day, except over the lunch hour.

To Marshall, it was obvious on his initial search of the McGuire home that he was dealing with a professional, someone who knew how not to leave a trace of evidence. The perp had time to come and leave the scene without suspicion, time to disrupt the contents of the rooms, time to kill, time to clean up after himself—evidently too much time.

Marshall resolved to fly to South Dakota to speak to Lucen, Victoria, and their son as soon as possible. He knew any interview with a person who had even the slightest connection to David and

Janice, whether near or far, was essential. He was grasping at straws for a lead.

His trip would wait until after Glory arrived and settled in at South Dakota. This would give him a chance to check on her welfare at the same time.

That afternoon, Marshall stopped by the Corner Shelter to check on her. He reminded her that his plan was to find the person or persons responsible for her parents' deaths.

He told Glory he had spoken to many people regarding her parents which basically gave him no insight into anything abnormal in the McGuires' lives at all. He felt it important to advise Glory of his progress and that, more importantly to let her know her parents had no enemies. He didn't want her to lose the pride she had in them. To allow her to think there was someone who may have had a vendetta toward her parents would not set right with him. The circumstances of her parents' will and the basics of his earlier meeting with Garrett Sanders was also discussed in general terms.

"Glory, are you aware of your parents' will?"

"No."

"Well, I met with Garrett Sanders this morning. He was a good friend of your father and your parents' attorney. I want to tell you part of the information I got from him. Don't discuss it with anyone. I can only give you a little information now.

"Your parents thought, years ago, when you were just a baby, of your well-being and addressed that in their will. They gave instructions for your care in the unfortunate event something should happen to them. They wanted you to always be protected." He paused. Now he had to explain the most difficult part. "The will says that you'll have to travel to South Dakota. You'll be living with your father's brother, Lucen, and his wife, Victoria. They were named your godparents when you were a small child. They are now responsible for your care until you're of age, which is eighteen or married. Do you understand so far?"

Glory noticed Marshall's nervousness and wondered why this was so difficult for him. "Yes, I understand, Marshall. That was like my father, the protector. He always made sure mom and I were well taken care of. But, you know, I don't think my dad liked my uncle very much."

Marshall replied, "That may have been true a long time ago, but your father must have trusted your uncle enough to designate him and his wife as your godparents."

"Yeah but it scares me. I don't know them. I never met them. Do you think my uncle is like my dad?"

"He probably is, after all they were brothers, grew up together. I think, from what I've been told, they just had different life styles but they are still brothers at heart."

Glory felt a little comfort with those words from Marshall.

"They will be given an allotment, a sort of payment, that will cover your expenses while you are with them. Whatever you need, they will see you have it. When you leave their home, the allotment will be sent directly to you. This will help you get started on your own."

She didn't respond one way or the other. Marshall knew this was a great deal of information for her to accept in her state. He again tried to make sure she understood that he and Garrett Sanders and Glory must work together.

"I don't care about the money," she said. "I want to know who killed my parents and why they would do it." Marshall thought her to be more mature than her sixteen years.

"I'll do everything in my power to find the ones responsible," he said. "I'll also keep in touch with you whether you're in Orlando or South Dakota. I won't be more than a phone call away. You understand that I'm just a phone call away? As soon as I have any information, I'll let you know." He left shortly thereafter.

Again, sitting in his car, Marshall rehashed the will. Was there a link between the millions and the murders? Red flags flew when he had heard this information from Sanders but he didn't want Sanders to know his thoughts. Sanders himself seemed to think there was a connection but Marshall didn't want to reassure him he might be right. He was a little annoyed at Sanders thinking he knew the possible motive, and did not want him involved in the investigation.

Marshall thought the questions was not so much about the yearly allotment as it was about the lump sum of fifty thousand dollars to Lucen and Victoria at settlement time, which was actually only a few years away.

He even tried the scenario that one or both of Glory's parents were threatened. He had heard of a case where the bank president's wife had been taken hostage until the bank president retrieved a vast amount of money from the bank, as her ransom. He rejected the thought that was a probable scenario with David and Janice. Somehow that just didn't fit.

He ran details and information through his mind over and over, trying to get it to settle in one place. *The will was written so long ago and never changed. That's not odd; people do that all the time. Money was allocated to others besides Glory receiving her fortune at age twenty-one.*

Marshall wondered if anyone else had known how much David McGuire was actually worth. How would they get their hands on the money if they did know? Did Lucen and Victoria find out about the fifty thousand? If anything happens to Glory, someone else gets the millions, but who would know that? No evidence, no murder weapon, and millions at stake. Marshall was admittedly baffled.

He felt it unlikely, but somehow knew there was more to this story than what he had so far. *Really, it could have just been a burglary,* he thought. *Better to lie on the side of caution.*

Then he thought further. Having aced the academy, he was well versed in the art of burglary and the actions of burglars. Burglars are not generally assassins as well; they want no confrontations. The typical burglar cases a joint, making sure no one is around. No, Marshall realized, it was not likely an intruder, a burglar, not likely. Nor was it random. Would a burglar be clever enough not to leave a trace of evidence after a murder? He thought not.

He was convinced the McGuires had not been surprised by someone in their home, but he was not about to let anyone know it yet. As his mind went back to no weapon, no evidence, no suspect, and no motive, anger began to swell in his chest. "No damn nothin'!"

The coroner called Marshall with his report while faxing a copy directly to Marshall's office. It was a straight forward autopsy report with cause of death for both parties named as "homicide."

The report analysis showed the same for each. "David's and Janice's throats both had a wide incision, approximately nine and a quarter inches across on David and eight and a fourth inches across for Janice, halfway between the chin and the start of the shoulders, extending from one ear to the other ear. The incisions were completed with one swift movement. There were no excessive tears or pulls of the skin, and no jagged edges.

"The knife was sharp. He or she probably used a nine- to ten-inch knife, such as the kind one would use for hunting. The person using the knife was right-handed. This fact was evident because the incision was deeper on the left side of the necks, at entry, and less deep on the right side of the necks, at the exit point."

The cuts were further explained by the coroner, though Marshall already knew the answer. "If it had been a kitchen knife, the incision would have been narrower. A hunting knife has a thicker blade and therefore leaves a wider gap. Both of the McGuires, after the attack, had been gently laid down where they had stood. No further significant movements of the bodies; there were no bruises, contusions, or litigation marks establishing that there appeared to be no struggle. Though death was not immediate, it was within seconds; neither one had moved since being placed on the floor."

He then reported the time of death for Janice, 8:45 a.m., and for David shortly after, at approximately 8:50 a.m..

Shortly thereafter Marshall called Allen Springfield at the Orlando Forensic Laboratory. He apologized for the rush but wanted to know if anything had been found in their search. Allen told him they were still in the testing process, but there was one odd test result. "The blood found on the bedspread, dresser, and counter was that of David McGuire. No blood from Mrs. McGuire was found anywhere other than at her body site."

"How about the evidence and fingerprints collected at the sight?" Marshall inquired.

"We are still testing, but at this point it looks like your perp was smart. No odd fibers, no prints, nothing more. I'll let you know if we find more, but it doesn't look like I'll be calling you."

Marshall thanked Allen, with a sense of hopelessness.

CHAPTER 6

FEAR OF THE UNKNOWN

Garrett Sanders offered her plane fare, but Glory insisted he secure train passage for her.

Sanders called Lucen McGuire with the new travel arrangements. "Now write this down Lucen. I have travel booked on the Silver Star Train Lines. She'll arrive June 13, 10:30 in the morning."

"I'll be there, Sanders."

Glory wasn't mentally prepared to meet anyone, especially not strangers—and without her parents. Especially people she would now live with, the McGuire's; people she'd never even spoken to, let alone met. As if what happened to her parents hadn't changed her whole life enough already. The fact was, she didn't know just how much it would change.

Having never been on a train before, she found the traveling a bit boring. After the first hundred miles or so, she climbed into the sleeper bunk to find peace. Sleep helped keep the memories at bay. South Dakota was a long way from Florida, so she slept a lot.

As the train stopped at the station, she was apprehensive. She became fearful of stepping off the train, a place she considered a temporary safe haven from the outside world. It had been three weeks since the funeral and just days since she'd left Orlando.

Why did she keep prolonging this meeting she wondered, it was inevitable after all?

Before discovering her relatives, people she assumed to be hicks from the backwoods, and before being whisked off to another world, one she was positive she did not want to enter, her actions were all in slow motion.

At only sixteen, she didn't look like the same girl of a few short weeks ago; now she looked like a woman. Yet inside was still the little girl with little girl hurts.

After the long, boring journey she stepped onto the unpainted, dried-up wooden planked platform at the station that looked like a scene from an old western movie set. She looked left then right, taking her time to see if she could deduce who her new family might be. She tilted her head ever so slightly to keep the full view of her face masked.

She longed to jump back on the train. But surely someone would board the train searching for her if she did. Escape was not a viable option, and where she would go? Realizing how vulnerable she was caused her to think that being there may be a better alternative than running off and ending up in trouble or homeless altogether.

Her mind was full of uncertainty, her heart in a continual ache. This strangely new and definitely unwanted situation made her well aware of the fact that her current options were as close to zero as one can get. She swallowed hard and clenched her hands together, conscious that she must endure whatever life held in store for her.

Still on the platform of the station, she adjusted her wide-brimmed navy-blue hat, taken from her mother's closet. She cocked it just so, keeping a portion of her face hidden.

Straightening her flowered skirt and white blouse, also her mother's, she took a deep breath. Her hope was not to be recognized until she was ready; she felt this may be the last time she had any control of her life. She took the opportunity to survey the assembly of bystanders waiting there.

Everywhere were passengers being discharged, picked up, or just simply exiting the train to stretch their legs and have a cup of coffee. Soon some would board the train again, setting out for the next destination.

Her pace was slow and steady along the planks; upright and poised; her mother would have been proud of her calm demeanor; even though inside she struggled with a fear of these unknown people. The noisy planks barked relentlessly back at her heels with each step.

With close attentive to each and every person there, she first noticed an incredibly bulky woman in the unreasonably large, flower-print, green-and-pink dress that accentuated her girth by at least one more size. She was smiling while her tightly permed gray hair, a light shade of lavender, glittered in the sunlight. *No*, Glory thought. *It* can't *be her. Don't stop. Keep walking.*

Her eyes were drawn to a strappy middle-aged couple. Both wore gray tweed coats, designer shoes, and wool, satin-banded hats. Their brand-name luggage sat beside them on the dirty platform. They eyed her as she walked past.

These two gave her a momentary vision of her parents; this was how her father and mother looked when they traveled.

Close to the magnificent-looking couple danced a freckle-faced girl. She touted pink ribbons in her auburn hair, and the contrast was almost unbearable to Glory. Her feet were shuffling to unheard music, probably to keep from collapsing from boredom, Glory thought.

Her neatly primped, red-haired mother was holding her hand, letting her own arm wave as the dance continued. Thoughts of a time when she and her mother had held hands everywhere they went came into view but then quickly disappeared. Glory's head bowed as tears came to her eyes.

A little further down the platform she paused. *These people probably think I'm from some exciting place like New York, just stopping off to stretch my legs before boarding again on my travels.* Chuckling to herself as these thoughts floated through her head, she pretended to be someone other than Glory McGuire.

Taking a rapid glimpse past the train station, she had a partial view of what she guessed to be a town. It appeared to be nothing more than a few wooden-fronted shops and stores, some with faded awnings.

Spalding was indeed a remote spot on the map. She eagerly looked forward to the day of escape. Even after being there only half an hour, she had figured that out. She only had one semester of school left and in less than two years, she would turn eighteen. *Adios, Spalding.*

She stopped short and stared at a very tall and thin man. His body was out of proportion for his frame, and from his upper torso sprouted short, wiry arms. But that was not the reason she stopped so abruptly.

There was something about him that made her focus completely on him from under the side brim of her fancy hat. Was it his posture? The way he stood as erect as a ten-story building? Something was familiar to her, recognizable, but she couldn't put her finger on what it was.

He wasn't smiling; he actually had no expression on his face. He wore a red and black plaid shirt and a somewhat tattered and worn gray jacket. His hat was a faded green and yellow John Deere. His boots were scuffed and brown, and he wore faded Levis.

The woman beside him was quite a bit shorter. Pretty, in a very country peasant sort of way. Her natural graying hair was pulled back and wrapped in a bun. She wore a modest green dress, cut just below the knees, with a little white band at the bottom of each sleeve. Over her shoulders a white sweater casually draped with the arms loosely tied around her neck—preppy looking, but older. Glory wasn't sure these people would have been her preference, but her choices were shrinking quickly as there were no other people on the platform now.

As she got near the couple, she observed the man more intently. His penetrating, sea-bottom green eyes intrigued her as they focused straight forward. His face was old, browned from the sun, worn and wrinkled. It gave the impression he wore more years on his face than he actually was. She felt a chill, realizing there was something more behind his eyes, hidden far back inside.

As incredible as his eyes were, there was something uncanny about this man that she couldn't decode, he may remain a mystery forever. He frightened her. He seemed to say, "Don't get too close; you won't like what you see." Was she reading him wrong?

She wondered if anyone could have so much misery in their life that it would surfaced in their face. Then she realized the answer to that: yes, the loss of one's parents.

Suddenly she knew these two were waiting for her. It was Lucen and Victoria, the ones Sanders had informed her of, the ones who would take care of her. A quick thought came to her: she could leave them as soon as she turned eighteen. *Hoorah!*

Before approaching the couple, she took one last glance around the platform, praying maybe someone else was there for her. No one else was.

She slowly walked up to the couple, and tipping the brim of her hat upward, she spoke while extending her hand. "Are you Lucen and Victoria? I'm Glory."

The old man just stared at her with those eyes. But the woman instantly smiled. "Yes, yes, I'm Victoria, and this is Lucen. We're sorry for your loss, but honey, I think you will be happy here."

The man still uttered not a word. He did nod his browned and wrinkled brow toward her as his face turned directly toward hers. She wondered why he was peering at her so, his sea-bottom eyes penetrating her very soul. But she knew she didn't like it. What was he thinking about this girl who was intruding on them? Was he speculating how long she would stay, or was he just looking right through her.

Victoria chatted on. "We're parked just over here. Lucen will get your luggage, and we'll drive you through town, show you the school, and then be on our way home. Come, let's go." Glory remained quiet but thought, "*Home? How I miss that right now and my mother and father. Home is gone. Everything is gone.*"

That Glory would end up here, at the end of the world, in another time, another place, was unbearable to her. She hoped again that it was all a bad dream. And she was reasonably sure she would not wake up.

She had to accept this as her fate.

CHAPTER 7

LOST LOVE

Glory had been extremely curious about the South Dakota McGuires ever since Marshall had told her she would be living with them.

She had been wise to anticipate a tough transition into their family. Knowing it certainly would not be easy, based on what her mother had told her about her uncle, she braced herself for the worst.

However at the same she hoped Lucen would resemble her father in some way. Her father was a wonderful man. As hectic as his professional life had been, he had always made time for her. Would Victoria be anything like her mother? Janice was full of laughter and believed in enjoying every moment of life; she was outgoing and energetic.

Her father had talked very little about Lucen and Victoria. Her respect for her parents had caused her not to pursue further questions. She did know her dad's only brother had been estranged from him for many many years.

A few years ago, at Thanksgiving, Glory had asked her father why they spent the holidays alone, why other family members had not joined them. Her had tensed and informing her, in a voice firm enough to set the Leaning Tower of Pisa back up straight, that Lucen, his wife, and his son, the only family members he had left, had moved to Spalding, South Dakota, a cold and desolate area. They didn't want anyone to bother them. He said after Lucen left, the two couples broke communication. Glory had wanted to know more, but was confident this was not the time to ask.

David's and Janice's parents were dead and so basically, this was the family, the three of them. There were no family holiday celebrations, other than the three of them—no letters, no cards from or with anyone other family. It was as if they never existed.

Her mother said, in the strictest of confidence, more about Lucen and David. She didn't want David to know she told too much to Glory. Until then Glory's only knowledge of them was that the two boys had grown up in the same house.

Her mother had explained that David was focused on success. Lucen focused on a carefree, simple life. David had been captain of the basketball and baseball teams and active in many organizations in school as well as the drama club.

Lucen had trouble making Ds in school; he cared little for education. His ideal day was going to the local lake with a hoagie sandwich from the 7-Eleven and a Wal-Mart fishing pole, staying until dark and usually alone. He loved the outdoors. David was extroverted; Lucen was introverted.

David stayed in Orlando and started at the bank just out of high school. He had worked his way up the ladder while going to college, taking business and finance classes, ending up as president and CEO of the largest group of banks in Florida, Orlando Central Banking System, in a short time. He wanted to stay in the beautiful weather to enjoy the beaches and activities galore, and to take family vacations to Yellowstone, Niagara Falls, Disney World, and of course, the Alamo, but never South Dakota.

There weren't any picture of Lucen, Victoria, or Tanner in her house, except a few pictures from her dad's yearbook. There were only a few photos of David in school activities and one photo of Lucen at the school lunch table.

She had often wondered if she would ever meet Tanner, her cousin, who was three years older than her.

Janice had further explained to her daughter that David met her during his fifth year at the bank. A feud between David and Lucen began when David was dating Victoria. Lucen also adored her; he would follow her around school and around town on the weekends, hoping to get a chance to speak to her. That didn't happen often.

Victoria chose to be at David's side every chance she got. They had a simple friendship—as far as David was concerned, anyway. As soon as David met Janice, he stopped seeing Victoria, who was devastated. She loved him, and when he could not reciprocate her feelings, she went into a deep depression. Lucen picked up the pieces and soon after the breakup, he and Victoria married.

Lucen and Victoria avoided spending time with the other couple. Janice could only assume the reason; it was too hard on Victoria. Within a month, Lucen and Victoria moved to South Dakota. Later that year, they had a baby boy they named Tanner.

Soon after that, Janice married David. Glory was born about three years later. Janice thought Lucen decided to get Victoria away to ensure no further contact would break her heart. He really loved Victoria.

Victoria's parents were furious at her marriage to Lucen. They referred to him as "no good" and disowned her, which may have been another reason they moved away.

Victoria's parents were an average couple with big expectations for their only daughter. Their hope for her was that she would continue to college and become a teacher or nurse. Those dreams, for their little girl, were shattered when she chose a life with Lucen, on a farm thousands of miles away. So the contacts were broken and had never been mended, as far as Janice knew.

When Glory was born, birth announcements were sent to everyone they knew. But even then, they didn't hear from Lucen and Victoria. They had written in their announcement that they would like Lucen and Victoria to be Glory's godparents. After all, there were no other relatives for them to consider.

They never heard from Lucen; he had spoken to David's attorney and confirmed he would do it. It hurt David, after hearing the request to be godparents, taken pride in David's decision to name him such, that his brother hadn't contacted him directly. When Lucen left he was short on his goodbyes and David understood his desire to get away from Florida. He had hoped when the attorney called Lucen it might break the ice and Lucen would call. He did not.

Janice had told Glory of meeting David for the first time. He was having lunch at the Chance Restaurant, and just by chance, Janice and some of her close friends were lunching there as well. David noticed her right away, even though he was in a booth on the other side of the restaurant.

Later he had told Janice that he had watched her interactions with her friends; she possessed an outgoing personality, and smiled all the while. He just had to meet her. He simply walked over to her table and introduced himself. "I'd love to take you to dinner tonight, if you're free." Janice, taken aback with his boldness, hesitated. They spoke for a few minutes, and she agreed to join him for dinner. They had fallen instantly in love.

After they married, David had given her all he had promised. She really hadn't a care in the world; her life was good with charity work, tutoring, and keeping her husband and baby happy.

Glory had been enthralled with the romantic story of her parents' meeting. They were not only her parents but two of the coolest people she knew. Glory's dream was much as her mother's had been:

to live a comfortable, secure life. Like her parents, she wanted to travel. She planned to head for the beach one day and the mountains the next, to eat seafood one day and elk the next.

She hoped to find a nice man, like her father, to marry, and to have wonderful children. *Three,* she thought.

Glory was definitely introverted, which made her a curiosity to many, though everyone liked her. She did not go out of her way to join groups in school but instead concentrated on her studies. She had decided early on not to hang around with groups of kids, because she knew better than to let others influence her lifestyle. She had seen the destruction broken friendships could bring as she watched her classmates over the years. "Hanging out with the rowdy crowd, you get rowdy; hang out with the nerds, you become a nerd." So she remained friendly with everyone. Her grades were above average, and she was pretty.

Privilege allowed her a lot in life. She had a curfew and rules in the house, a few minor chores to do, but that was all. She was a good girl who gave her parents no trouble.

CHAPTER 8

THE LAST GOOD-BYE

Shortly after her arrival on June 13, Glory, Lucen and Victoria climbed into a grimy 1972 Ford Ranger. She believed it was possibly green in color or blue, but she wasn't sure because it was faded so badly.

God, she prayed, *don't prolong this agony. Somehow you need to get me out of here.*

Lucen threw her bags in the bed of the dusty old truck. And they squeezed onto the ragged cloth-covered front seat.

Victoria bubbled with excitement. "You know we have a boy, Tanner, just a few years older than you. He's a mechanic, and a darn good one. We'll drive by his shop, and stop to see if he's in."

Lucen said in a matter-of-fact manner, "She can meet the boy later. Let's get home."

"Okay, Glory, you can meet him at supper."

Oh great, Glory thought. *Supper. Does this include pig's feet and goat or grits and bacon?*

They drove by a grocery store, a general practitioner's office, a vet's office, a post office, a beauty/barber shop, a café, a service station—and that was it. Most of the stores and shops were clean and had a western motif—nothing fancy, no elaborate adornments, mostly just plain wood buildings that needed paint.

As they drove by the service station Victoria pointed out with pride, "That's Tanner's station there."

Lucen suddenly pressed harder on the accelerator, leaving Tanner's station in his dust. So Glory had seen it all, the highlights of Spalding's "Main Street."

They headed up a paved road a few miles. The pickup bounced and bumped with every small bit of irregular crumbled asphalt on the narrow road. Suddenly they turned west onto a graveled, one-lane road.

Glory had to admit the drive to the McGuires was gorgeous. As they headed up a small incline, a few miles north of town, toward the base of majestic tree-covered mountains, Glory was in awe.

The pine trees lining the road were quite spectacular. This was certainly nothing like what she had seen before in Florida, a sharp contrast to her usual view of palm trees. Pine needles lay on the ground making a perfect hiding place for little creatures. She kept expecting a deer or a possum to jump out from between the trees and put their journey to a screeching halt.

Suddenly the sun shimmered through the tree branches like the arms of God reaching down to let her know she would be safe. Right there, right then at that very moment, she truly felt safe.

She looked to her left, directly at Lucen's shoulder. He sat much taller than she did, so she began inching her head upward until she saw his face. He bent his head and gazed at her with those piercing green eyes.

She instantly dropped her head and turned it so she faced straight ahead. She vowed to herself not to move her head again until the truck stopped and she was on solid ground.

Five more minutes into the trip, they drove into a clearing. She was stunned to set her eyes on a charming house at the heart of it. There were a few buildings to the side of the house, but her eyes were fixed on the house itself. A feeling besieged her that the house was a direct reflection of Victoria's character. She had created a breathtaking vision, like a postcard scene. There stood a little cottage surrounded by flowers and greenery. From the newly painted, white picket fence to the dark-coffee plantation shutters lining each long, six-paned window of the house, it was a sight to behold. The olive green of the house complemented the shutters, echoing, "Come on in."

Maybe Victoria reads Good Housekeeping *or one of those designer books. This is magnificent; obviously she didn't get the inspiration for this from Lucen.* The thought raced through Glory's head as she quietly chuckled to herself. She was amazed further when she saw the front door, the deepest of crimson colors. The door blended splendidly with the house with shutters.

Flowers of all colors, shapes, and sizes adorned the fence line, and flowering bushes formed a short hedge planted from the fence line to the front door, creating a unwritten "Welcome" sign. Glory could tell a lot of thought and love went into this setting. She felt alive in this yard; she even felt like dancing.

After seeing Lucen's attitude, sneers, and actions, Glory assumed he used the back door. The sight of Lucen gleefully prancing through the flowered path darted through her mind.

Glory's impression of Victoria changed in that instant. She transformed from the plain peasant woman at the station platform to a woman full of love who knew true beauty, much like her mother. She could tell Victoria loved the outdoors and loved living where she did. There was something special about her, and Glory decided to make an effort to get to know this woman better.

As she entered the house, she was not at all surprised to see it neat and tidy, and as well decorated as the yard. Victoria plainly paid great attention to the home's interior yet kept it masculine in comfort and furnishings.

The living room's colors were inspired by nature, predominately browns and beiges. A tall, brass lamp stood mightily behind a worn brown recliner, which she took to be Lucen's. The oversized shade had a hand-painted scene of deer and trees. A oblong russet rug lay in the center of the wood floor, giving the room warmth and coziness. A few neutral-colored pillows were on the gray-blue couch. Magazines and colorful sets of books sat three high on the coffee table. On top of the books was a single, artificial, yellow flower. A small statue of a girl plated in a bronze tone sat by the end table near a tan ceramic lamp.

There was a small, red brick fireplace at the end of the room. A few pictures of Tanner and Victoria had been carefully placed in the center of the mantel; the rest of it was filled with knick knacks.

Victoria grasped Glory's hand, steering her through the hallway to her new room. The room was small, but it had all the space Glory needed. It apparently had been cleared out and cleaned for her arrival. There was one bed, one dresser, a nightstand with a lamp, and a small closet to the side.

The room had a fresh coat of pale pink paint. The bed was made and covered with three pink pillows, big fluffy blankets and a pink comforter. Glory wondered if this was all new, because she could not imagine Tanner having ever slept in a room with pink walls and a pink comforter.

Victoria turned to leave the room. Gripping the doorknob, she said, "Dinner will be at noon sharp. Tanner eats in town, so it will just be us three but supper is at six sharp, so be prompt for that too. Enjoy the rest of the day. Take a nap. I know you're probably tired from traveling. See you later, Glory."

Despite having slept most of the way on the train, Glory decided to do just that. She haphazardly put her things away and was pleased that everything in the room looked and smelled so nice. She lay on the bed, and her thoughts went back to the funeral and the last time she would ever see her parents.

The viewing had been a few days after her parents' deaths. The funeral was the day after the viewing. Garrett Sanders had employed the help of his wife, Jill from his office, David's bank, and the church auxiliary as well as PTA members to take care of the arrangements for the service and the reception. Luckily his wife was an organizer, and everything went according to her plans.

Sanders's main focus was Glory, for her peace of mind focusing on getting her through the move to the shelter, the funeral and ready her for her trip to South Dakota. He tried to keep her as distant as possible from the actual planning of the viewing and funeral proceedings. She had enough on her plate already, with more to come. The murder of his friend and his concern for Glory caused him great distress.

During her time at the shelter Glory was understandably distraught and hadn't been eating well. It was taking a visible emotional toll on her; she was getting thinner and her face drawn and hollow eyed. Of course, that was normal, considering what she had endured in addition to the uneasiness of not knowing what was next. She was grateful to have both Sanders and Marshall there to see her through the ordeal of the funeral and help her manage the torment she felt.

Sanders asked the coroner to do his examination and release of the bodies as quickly as possible. He explained that the funeral should be held as soon as possible for the girl's sake. The coroner had obliged. He knew the cause of death before departing the residence the day of the murders and was able to process his findings without delay.

It was one of the largest funerals ever in that community. The church was filled to capacity. People who couldn't get into the church stood on the porch and sidewalk outside, some hoping for a glimpse of the daughter. The pastor had set up a microphone and speakers so those outside could hear.

Sanders escorted Glory through the sympathizers, the curiosity seekers, and the press who had arrived to cover the funeral. Marshall viewed the press as vultures who, even at a funeral, would try to get a statement from the grievers. Sanders held on to Glory as she covered her face with her hands, trying to avoid direct eye contact with unfriendly gawkers.

Everyone in attendance extended their sympathies to Glory as she entered the church, proceeded down the aisle and led to the first pew. Some were seen cornering Mr. Sanders throughout the day asking questions about the murders. Sanders would excused himself promptly.

It was heart wrenching for both Marshall and Sanders to see Glory sitting with her parents' caskets just feet away and knowing this was their last good-bye.

The caskets were open. David wore a suit and a blue shirt and tie. Janice wore a pale blue, high-necked dress. A few associates from the bank spoke on behalf of David. Janice's best friend, Anna, spoke on what a loving and kind person she was.

The pastor concluded the service then conducted a gravesite ceremony.

Glory touched the edge of each casket before leaving the cemetery, murmuring, "This is the last time I can be with you. I love you, and I miss you. I will do the best I can, I promise." She took one last look at her mother's casket before the weight of the day became more than her body could handle. She shook, and then her legs gave way.

Marshall and Sanders were right beside her, and as she crumpled, they grabbed her arms before she hit the ground. They led her back to the nearest chair, where she sat composing herself once again. Her desire, at this point, was to escape the presence of everyone.

The whole ordeal, the murders, the wills, the funeral, and now seeing Glory so unstable was wearing on Sanders, but he did what he could to maintain his composure in support of her.

At the reception, when Glory and Marshall had a moment together, she asked in a barely audible voice, "Marshall, who could have done this? Who would want to kill my parents? Will you ever find them? What if they kill someone else? Who were they?"

Marshall understood her torment but knew better than to express too much emotion. "Don't worry, Glory. We'll find the people who did this, and they will pay. They will pay big time."

She wanted an explanation as to why Lucen and Victoria hadn't attended the funeral too. Sanders told him they chose not to.

Marshall swallowed hard. "Glory, sometimes people aren't able to make travel plans that quickly, or perhaps they did not have the funds. It had been so long since they had seen your parents. I'm sure their reasons were sound. They are happy you are coming to stay with them, so don't worry about it. It couldn't be helped." That seemed to satisfy her at the time.

Secretly she knew she would someday ask her aunt and uncle why.

When the reception concluded, Marshall instructed Officer Laura to escort Glory back to the shelter. Marshall and Sanders arrived there shortly after and were able to secure a private room used for counseling the women housed there. They both, individually and together, reminded Glory of her situation.

"Marshall already told me. I don't really want to go. Do I have to?"

Sanders spoke before Marshall had a chanceto respond. "You do, Glory. This is now a fact.

She looked at Marshall with what he now called "her puppy dog eyes." They were so big and beautiful, yet there was a deep sadness in them that couldn't be concealed. "Do I have to go? What if I don't want to go there? I don't even know those people."

Marshall reiterated exactly what Sanders had told her; since she was a minor, she had to respect her father's wishes. "You'll be eighteen before you know it, and then you can be on your own. You call me when you're ready, and I will help you go wherever you choose. Then when you're twenty-one, we'll go to Sanders together to get the rest of the information about your father's wishes. I promise I'll be there with you."

Because another of Sanders's tasks was to see to that all the McGuire family's belongings were taken care of, he told her that whatever she wanted to take to South Dakota was hers to take.

He explained that the house and all items inside were to be sold; all debts would be paid; and if anything was left, it would be invested. Any furnishings left would be put into storage for her when she turned twenty-one. That's all he was permitted to tell her, according to David's wishes.

Resisting giving her more information was the hard part for him. He wanted her to know she'd be well taken care of. She couldn't know that one million dollars would be held in trust until she turned twenty-one. She asked no further questions, and that was a relief to him. He loathed keeping secrets. How odd for an attorney, not wanting to keep secrets.

Glory assumed there were a lot of debts. After all, their family had so many possessions: automobiles, boats, three wheelers, skidoos, and the beautiful home. She speculated there wouldn't be much money left after the McGuires were paid to care for her.

Two days before her departure for South Dakota, Sanders and Glory went back to the house on Sycamore.

She retrieved items she wanted to keep, such as jewelry and a jewelry holder, a few clothes, her mother's hairbrush and mirror, a book, a hat, a wooden tray that had belonged to David. She also took her father's watch and a few incidental items that only she cared to have.

Sanders didn't take an inventory of these items, feeling there was no need.

CHAPTER 9

A POOR MAN'S FORTUNE

Glory rested a bit at her new home. A half-hour later, she got up, changed into a white T-shirt and a lightweight vest, blue jeans, and tennis shoes, then headed to the kitchen.

Just as Victoria had said, "noon sharp!"it was, on the nose. Victoria served a light lunch of home-made vegetable soup, homemade bread, a small dinner salad, and fresh milk. Somehow Glory had expected Victoria to prepare and serve this type of meal. She guessed Victoria would bestow the same loving care on her cooking as she did on her house and yard.

When she saw Glory, Victoria waved exuberantly then pointing down as if to introduce Glory to her chair.

Lucen, sitting at the head of the table, said not a word. Victoria arranged the table so that the majority of the food was within reach of Lucen. Glory's and Victoria's would be passed around.

Glory peeked up from bites of food every once in a while. Once, when she did, she was looking straight at Lucen, who had been looking intently at her. With those frozen, green eyes and forever frown on his brow, she wondered what he was thinking—and if he didn't want her in his house.

Actually, he was thinking of how much she reminded him of his brother. No one ever knew what Lucen was thinking, and Lucen liked it that way. He carefully observed Glory and the subtle traits she had that resembled her father. Only Lucen could detect them; he'd grown up with them after all.

He saw it in her smile and the way one side of her lip rose a little higher than the other. He saw it in her eyes, the color of the ocean, and they had an excitement for life, equivalent to David's zest for excitement. He saw the color of her hair; the golden wheat-kissed color was just like David's. Lucen remembered some better times between he and David. Not many, but a few.

Lucen had made his mind up years ago to keep his thoughts to himself. Speaking them out loud had gotten him in hot water too many times. In school, especially, it only bred trouble. His thoughts were unlike anyone else's; he had an odd outlook on life. Some even thought he was a simpleton. He always stood his ground but often was called names like *weirdo* and *geek*.

Even his own brother spent more time with buddies than with him, but Lucen felt he could live with that. When his feud with David erupted, that was the last straw. He decided then and there to leave, to get away from David, his friends, and the crowd at school. In his mind, that would be the last time anyone would consider him less than the man he felt he was.

After their meal, Lucen stood up and quietly walked out of the house. Glory helped clear the table and decided to explore her new surroundings.

Within minutes, Victoria joined her in the front yard. She almost danced as she gave Glory the grand tour of her magnificent front garden. She showed her each flower, naming each with pride. She walked the flowering shrub pathway, explaining how each was perfectly groomed so that they would either leaf or flower more abundantly. It was obvious she loved her garden and loved yard work in general.

"Glory, when you get your own house, we'll plant together. I'll show you all the ins and outs. You'll learn what grows and what doesn't out here."

"I'd love that, but it will be some time before I can get my own place. I appreciate your suggestion to help me learn."

As if she hadn't heard what Glory said, Victoria continued her chatting. "See how everything springs to life when a flower blooms?" She touched an impatiens with gentleness. "A new day, a new flower blossom. Isn't life a garden in itself?"

"Yes, life is good," Glory said, but inside she didn't feel like life was at all good. She knew Victoria meant well and would help her through this hard time. She felt better as she listened and began absorbing Victoria's excitement like a sponge.

Victoria turned to go back up the pathway to the house. "I've got things to do. You just look around a bit, and we'll talk later."

As Glory circled the house, about to turn the corner near the back door, Lucen was rounding the same corner from the opposite direction, closing in quickly. They ran into each other, their bodies making a thump, startling them both.

Glory took a quick step backward. Lucen did the same. Neither said a word. Glory took a big gulp of air and thought to herself, *You better try making the best of this situation.*

"Lucen, what do you do out here all day long?"

Lucen simply said, "Come on." He turned and headed away from the house toward the pine trees. She wasn't at all sure she wanted to trail behind him, but she did, reluctantly.

He took her past the enormous pine trees encircling the back yard. She had to look straight up to see the treetops.

They came over the first rise, and her mind absorbed the freshness of it all. "How beautiful, it is so peaceful here," she said, and received no response. Coming over the second rise, she saw a few mountains backed up into each other. She stopped for a moment in awe of their splendor.

The mountains appeared to have been in a race. When the first mountain halted, then like dominos, the next one ran into the first and so on until they were all clustered together. Each peak had its own height and its own color, from brown to gray to blue to lavender. All reached magnificently upward into the blue sky.

At the foothills of the mountains were several fields from a lush lime to olive green. To the other side of the base of the mountains were honey-colored fields. In one of the lighter hued green fields where cows and goats enjoying a long day of grassy meals and leisurely walks.

Lucen's thin arm slowly rose as he fanned the air, to show the vast expanse of his property. Glory chuckled within herself to see this gesture; the flow of his arm, it seemed so totally out of character for him.

Clearly aware of his attempt to present the great expanse of his land, the mountains securing its borders, and great open spaces and the animals he raised, she said, "Beautiful. Just beautiful."

"Yep, this is it. This is our land, our crops, our stock. We raise 'em, we sell 'em. And it's a good living. It keeps me busier than hell though, and I have to do it alone. Tanner just never took to farming."

She turned toward Lucen and was surprised to see an expression of joy and pride in his face, easing the wrinkles. Without warning, he turned and headed back in the direction they had just come. She waited, expecting him to say, "Let's go" or "Come on," but in his usual manner, he said nothing. She turned and followed him, fairly far behind, wondering, *Who is this man?*

When they got to the clearing at the house, Lucen continue walking past the house. *Well, I guess he's through talking to me,* Glory thought.

She started toward the back door then stopped short of the entrance. Looking around at the property, closer to the house, her eyes were immediately drawn to the faded red barn. It was a massive and strong barn, especially against the silhouette of the pine trees. She wondered what it must have looked like when it was new.

There was a red shed and beside that some wire cages. She could hear clucking but saw only feathers floating in the breeze. Then she spotted beaks and then romping chickens behind the wire.

It was then she began to slightly understand this mysterious man, Lucen. The independent man, the loner, the quiet man had something inside him that made all this possible. She understood his love of being self-sufficient, felt the joy he got from owning his own land, cultivating his crops, and raising his own food. She actually thought for a moment how satisfying this must be for him. He built it all, works it all and provides for his family—all with his own two hands.

What her mother had told her was true: Lucen liked his space. He would never fit into the city. This was a tranquil place to live and a very comfortable and satisfying way of life for him.

Her father couldn't have been more opposite of Lucen than the man in the moon to the sun. But she wished her father could see Lucen now. Maybe they would be friends, brothers again, once he saw who Lucen really was on the inside.

She spent the rest of the day in her room, rearranging her personal belongings, then lay on the bed. Memories crept up inside her. She took the box out of her suitcase that contained the items she had gathered from her home in Orlando before she left and sorted them.

They were her mother's hairbrush and mirror, a makeup kit, and a necklace Glory had given her mother. It included a tie she had given her father at Christmas, a book he used to read to her when she was small, his wooden jewelry holder that he would set cuff links and his watch in, and his watch. They were simple things, but things she felt a connection with. Someday she would go back and see what was left in storage.

At supper that night, at exactly six, there were just three plates on the table. Victoria said Tanner had called and said he had some repairs to finish up, so he'd grab a bite in town. Glory was disappointed; she was looking forward to meeting Tanner.

She told Glory about Tanner's small apartment in town, attached to the back of the station. "It's what you would call a studio apartment, I think. It's just one big room and a bathroom, but cute. I helped him decorate it."

Glory began to feel cooped up after a few days. She enjoyed her walks to the fields, where she had gone with Lucen the first day, but she felt isolated. Town was too far to walk to. One morning, she asked Victoria if she planned to go shopping any day soon. Victoria said she was going that very day, so Glory asked, "Mind if I tag along?"

"Hop in the car. We take off in ten." Twenty minutes later, after Victoria quit finally little things to do first; wash a glass and a cup in the sink, wipe down the table and find her purse they were headed to Spalding.

They parked in front of the grocery store. Victoria led her through the screened door of the store. Glory noticed two customers staring at her. Knowing they, as well as others in the community, had heard the story of her parents' deaths, she considered their feeling of both sympathy and curiosity, which were displayed on their faces.

Victoria introduced her to every person they ran into, including the store owners, Kyle and LaVern Parsons. She whispered to Glory, "If you want to know anything about anyone you meet, just ask me. I am a walking resident behavior encyclopedia. I know everything about everyone."

Both let loose in giggles. Again, Victoria's lightheartedness put Glory at ease. It was just what Glory needed to start her day.

The grocery store reminded her of a Laura Engels Wilder novel. There was a square card table at the entry that displayed sale items including candies, salt and pepper shakers, squash and darkened bananas.

Down the center aisle were oblong tables with displays of dishes and silverware, candle holders, cooking utensils, and at one end hammers, nails, screws, and hooks. Old, round barrels stood at either end of the tables, holding walnuts and peanuts.

Behind the counter, running the whole length of both sides of the store, were open, unpainted wooden shelves. Residing there was jewelry, more candy in glass containers, and bolts of fabric with nontraditional patterns. Canned goods were stacked three cans high in one section, dry goods in another: flour, sugar, and the like.

Odds and ends were scattered throughout the store. There was little rhyme or reason to the organizational concept but anything needed was in there somewhere.

At the far end of the store was a tall, glass-front refrigeration unit holding milk, juices, pop, eggs, and butter. Next to that was a butcher shop. But by no means had Glory ever seen anything like it. It was a mere three-foot counter with about half a dozen packages of meat. She assumed most meat was cut to customer order.

There was charm radiating in this small country store, and she liked it. *Almost like an era gone by. So quaint, yet so accommodating, like a mini Wal-Mart,* she thought.

Glory excused herself, saying she wanted to explore the town. She strolled along the sidewalk, peering into the windows she passed. To her surprise, people inside were staring right back at her; little went on in this small town without being noticed, and a newcomer was like a celebrity.

The laid-back atmosphere, the simplicity of it all, gave her both amusement and a sense of pleasure. She remembered the hustle and bustle of Orlando and liked the contrast. This was an unexpected and almost welcome change from her life back home.

When she reached the end of the block, she stopped in front of a service station. Within seconds, a young man ran out with arms outstretched—a happy looking character with a smile as big as the sky, stretching across his face with its boy-like features. His hair was blond and he was an average height. He didn't hesitate a moment before grabbing her and embraced her in a bear hug as if they had known each other all their lives.

He was hugging what he thought was the prettiest girl he'd ever seen: tall with shoulder-length blond hair, blue eyes, full lips, the most gorgeous of smiles, and put together perfectly.

"Hi, Glory, I'm Tanner." Glory was pleasantly surprised to think he would know her without an introduction. Like him, she felt an instant connection, and she appreciated his friendly gesture, which made her feel very welcome.

He invited her into the station, practically scooting her along. "It isn't much, but I'm proud of what I've got. I want you to meet my partner, Weber."

As they walked into the greasy little mechanics shop, he maintained a steady chatter like there was no tomorrow. She really didn't care where the oil cans and tools were stored, but she humored him because of his obvious excitement to show her everything.

As they entered the repair area, she saw a man in blue work overalls hunched under a car hood. He almost looked stuck.

"Hey, Weber, meet my cousin, Glory." As the man rose from inside the cavern of the car, Glory saw he was quite handsome, even with smudges on his face.

He was a few inches taller than she and had not an ounce of un-muscled mass. Through his filthy work shirt, she could see he had bulk, especially in his upper arms, and she thought maybe he was a wrestler. At least he lifted weights or worked out. She didn't think a man could look that good from working on cars. His hair was dark brown and longer than the city boys she was used to.

As he drew closer, she saw his blue eyes, which caught her off guard to the point that she stared openly at them. The blue was the deepest she had ever seen, and he had a smile to die for. *One that would melt a bucket of ice cream, or possibly a heart or two*, she thought.

He slowly walked over, wiping his hands on a greasy rag and openly staring back at her too. As he reached his hand out to her, she delightfully did the same. They shook, and then she noticed he had, ever so gallantly, exchanged a portion of the grease smudges on his hand to hers; the rag had been worthless. He appeared to be reserved, but there was a glint in his eye that captivated her.

"I'm surprised, you being a cousin to old Tanner and all. You must be the better-looking side of the family." With a slight snigger, he nudged Tanner on the shoulder. "Nice meeting you."

He turned and headed back to his work, once again burying his head under the darkness of the hood, paying no further attention to her or Tanner.

Tanner led Glory to the rear of the station to show off his "studio apartment." It was decorated in browns and tans with understated hints of blue on the pillows and bedspread, dishes, and curtains. Victoria once again had done her decorating well; it was a nice home.

After Tanner completed the tour, she excused herself, expressing her need to return to the store to meet Victoria.

When she was three doors down from the station she paused and turned her head to look toward the station. Tanner was still standing in front, gazing at her. She waved and he waved back, but he remained standing as if his feet were solidly planted.

Strange fellow, but I like him.

At supper that night, Tanner mentioned that Glory had met Weber. Then he smiled and began his usual chatter. "Yeah, he's a nice guy. That's Weber most of the time; he doesn't talk much, but once you get to know him, he's a barrel of fun and a hard worker. We grew up together, got in a little mischief too." Smiling, he glanced at Lucen. "Tell you about it sometime. Then we opened our station about two years ago. Sometimes he brags about getting his own station, but I say there isn't enough business for two stations.

"You're welcome to come visit me anytime, Glory. Are you going to go to school here? What are your plans? Do you like it here?"

My, my, Tanner, you sure like to babble on, she thought, even though she found it comical and charming. She said, "Right now I am just trying to settle in. I'll start school in August. I just want to get my bearings and maybe work a few hours after school, if I can find something."

Lucen was serene during the meal. Victoria mostly smiled, saying little, but Tanner and Glory continued talking about everything from schools to Orlando to camping. When the meal was over, Glory helped Victoria while Lucen and Tanner retreated to the back yard.

The next day Victoria took Glory to enroll in school. It was a very small country school only a block from Main Street. Glory had the distinct feeling she would have no difficulty completing her last semester. She was used to a large school with hundreds of students with a great deal of extra curricular activities to take.

The building was small; she could tell there was probably only one classroom for two grades. There were no outside activity centers like a track field, no tennis court or even a swing set. There was a jungle gym and monkey bars and a sand pit; she figured those were for the smaller children.

Back home this is what would be considered a country school.

The principal, Mrs. Baker, welcomed her, and they filled out the necessary paperwork to enroll Glory for the new school year, set to begin on August 25. Mrs. Baker set up Glory's schedule and gave her a copy. She then gave them a tour of the school, and even assigned Glory a locker and issued her the combination.

It was amusing to Glory how ill-equipped the school was; it had only the most basic course books. The study areas and library were small rooms. But she was excited to complete the enrollment process and get back in school.

They stopped at the post office, and Glory went in for Victoria. The postmaster announced there was a package for Glory. It was from Marshall.

Excitement filled her with anticipation as she attempted to guess the contents. She hadn't even considered it would be a cell phone with a charger. A note said, "Keep this with you at all times. My number is programmed in. If I need to talk to you, I will call you on Lucen's home phone or on the cell. Don't tell anyone you have this cell phone. I want to know you're okay, and if there are any problems, call me. Ever, Marshall."

She was pleased he was thinking of her, yet curious as to why he suggested she not tell anyone about the cell phone. Why so secretive? She'd ask him next time they talked. She stuck the phone in her purse and didn't mention it to Victoria.

After the post office, Glory requested Victoria stop by the café so she could apply for a job. "Oh, that is not necessary, dear," Victoria said. "You don't have to worry about a job now. Get settled in and start school; you'll have to work a job soon enough."

"I know, but it will help keep my mind occupied, instead of always thinking about the past."

Glory asked Victoria if she could give her rides to work. She hoped to get a car and her license someday, but until then she had to rely on Victoria. "As long as my old Lucen gets his breakfast, lunch, and supper on time, so I don't get billy-whipped, I'm free for you."

So Victoria drove her to the little café halfway down Main Street. As they entered, Victoria made her way to the counter and ordered coffee. Glory asked the woman behind the counter if she could speak to the manager.

Laughter rang out boisterously from the woman as she slapped her hand on the counter, and she said, "I'm Olivia and I'm it, honey." Olivia donned a white based floral shirt with blue flowers and a stained apron.

She appeared a little coarse and robust, but the flowers on her shirt soften her a little. Her apron was stained with what appeared to be eggs, gravy, and catsup, obviously unnoticed by this larger-than-life woman. Glory asked if there might be a part-time position open and said when she finished her classes, she could work full time.

"Well, we're only busy a couple of times a day, so I don't need nobody full time. You could work breakfast before school and maybe even supper a couple of times a week. Would that be okay? We're closed on Sundays, so maybe just lunch on Saturdays. We close at three on Saturday. What do you think?"

Glory was ecstatic, but not wanting to seem over-enthusiastic, she said, "Yes, that's perfect. When can I start?"

"How about tomorrow? We'll figure out the rest of the schedule when you get done with school. Do you want to know what the pay is? It isn't much."

"Yes, what does it pay."

"It pays six dollars and hour and all the tips you can make." Olivia stood back as if to portray this was big time pay.

"I'm fine with that. Thanks, Olivia." That was the only time Olivia had talked to someone about a job who didn't seem to care what the pay was and didn't try to con her out of more.

There were only a handful of customers in the café at the time, but Glory felt their eyes piercing her. She imagined them to be saying: "What do you suppose happened to that poor little girl's parents?" and "Poor girl, her mama or daddy were killed." Glory was uncomfortable, but she knew people would gawk at her until the story wore old for them.

She would just have to do what her school guidance counselor once told her. She had been teased in Phys Ed for not being able to make baskets. "Suck it up," she'd said. "There's nothing you can do about what somebody else is thinking. Mind your own thoughts, and you'll be okay."

Glory began her job the next day and loved every minute of it. People were delighted to see a new face and a clean apron. She quickly learned customers' names and what they liked. She fit right in, and Olivia was pleased with her work. The tips were meager but not that important to Glory. She would work most days until school started then cut back her hours.

During her second week on the job, Tanner found a 1987 Ford Escort for her. "Only five hundred dollar—it's a steal," he said. It was in fair condition, and he promised to keep it running. She was elated; this would allow her a little freedom. Victoria would have more free time, too, not having to drive her around. Lucen paid for it from the money allotted in the will.

CHAPTER 10

SUNFLOWER TOMORROWS

August 10 was her seventeenth birthday, her first since her parents' murders, and she wasn't sure she was up to dealing with it. Victoria was aware of how difficult this day and any other holiday would be, so she was determined to make this one a happy day for Glory. She began by soliciting Olivia's help to bake a chocolate fudge cake with vanilla icing. Victoria hung a Happy Birthday banner on the front door and tied balloons with ribbons to a chair designated for Glory.

Olivia and Weber joined them for the evening meal, along with Tanner. Victoria made fried chicken, mashed potatoes, gravy, corn and a small salad. As usual, very little conversation took place during the meal.

After the table was cleared, Victoria brought out the cake with huge candles in the form of a

1 and a 7 (evidently the largest candles Victoria could find and in bright pink).

"Are we trying to start a fire, Vic?" Lucen blurted out. Laughter encompassed the room, except Lucen, of course. At least he gave a little shrug, which could have been interpreted as the entree to a laugh.

Glory made a wish—a wish she knew would never come true—and blew out the candles. With the meal already settling in their stomachs, they stuff themselves with cake then went into the living room.

Topping the coffee table were presents, something Glory had not expected. The first to be unwrapped was papered in pink and white, so she knew it was from Victoria. It was a beautiful pink hat and mitten set. *Perhaps I should talk to Victoria about all this pink,* she thought, then, *No, that would only hurt her feelings.* Glory was especially pleased to see that both Lucen and Victoria had signed the card. She couldn't imagine the determination it took for Victoria to get Lucen to do that.

The next gift was wrapped in blue with a white bow; the card read simply "Tanner." The gift was a beautiful golden necklace with a cross hanging on a golden chain.

The next was wrapped in purple. *Only Olivia.* thought Glory. It was a set of three neon headbands.

And the last gift was from Weber, something she truly hadn't expected. It was wrapped in red paper with a pink bow. *Did greasy monkey hands wrap this?* she wondered.

What she found took her by surprise: a silver bracelet with tiny delicate silver hearts all the way along it. Overjoyed and a little embarrassed, she raised her head to thank him, only to find him staring directly at her with a huge smile and wide eyes. The stare penetrated her very being, and she lowered her head, thanking everyone in the room for the gifts. This had been an unexpectedly good day.

Even better was the next day when Glory and Victoria puttered in the front garden. The smell of the flowers was a welcome scent to Glory as she remembered the beautiful flowers of Florida.

Their day was one of relaxation and dirt, which Glory didn't mind, since Victoria told her how a green thumb develops: "You just gotta get dirty." That was something Glory had never done before. The thought of getting so dirty would have never entered her mind before this day. And she actually enjoyed every minute of it.

On August 25th, Glory hesitantly walked into the high school. Nervous most of the day, she soon fit into the routine with the rest of her classmates. It wasn't hard to adjust. She did her class work effortlessly

During the fourth week, Glory went to speak to Mrs. Baker. She said, "Since I am new here and just have one semester, I really don't want the hoopla of a graduation ceremony. So I plan not to go." She shyly stated she would prefer her diploma be given to her by Mrs. Baker. Only because of Glory's circumstances with the death of her parents and knowing Lucen and Victoria would be the only ones attending a graduation, Mrs. Baker accepted the request.

Glory didn't attempt to make friends because of the short time she would be attending school. She met a few nice girls, but shied away from them. Even when an invitation included a show and a sleepover, she declined.

She anticipated a return to Florida, and making friends in Spalding seemed unnecessary. She planned to leave Spalding as soon as possible.

One day after school, Glory rushed out of her last class looking for Victoria to pick her up, because her own car was in for repairs, new tires, and a tune-up. Victoria had agreed to taxi her around for a few days.

"Hey, Glory, over here." It was Weber.

He said Victoria had gone to Lambert and was running late. Because Tanner was out of the shop, she had begged Weber to pick Glory up and take her.

Glory wasn't at all disappointed. She hopped in his pickup truck, and they headed to McGuires'. The car was silent for a while, then Weber asked if she liked school.

"Yes, but it's hard to get to know anyone when you know you only have one semester."

"What are your plans after school?"

"I think I'll try to get a better-paying job in Lambert or go back to Orlando."

He smiled another of his to-die-for smiles. "I'm glad you're working at the café. I'll stop in for lunch sometime."

When they arrived, Glory hesitated a minute before she exiting the truck. "You know what happened to my parents, don't you?"

"Yeah, I heard."

She sat back and talked about her sense of loss, about how she'd thought for the first two weeks that she'd go insane. "I had such a good life, and then everything was turned upside down. Not that it isn't nice here; it is. It's just not the same, if you know what I mean." He nodded.

Unsure why it was so easy to talk to Weber, she was amazed at what a good listener Weber was, which was what she needed right then. With teary eyes, she said, "Oh, Weber, they cut my parents' throats. I can still hardly believe it. The blood was horrible. My poor mother. How could someone do such a thing?"

Without a second thought, Weber reached out his arm and put it on her shoulder. He squeezed with a strength that whispered, "It will be all right." Then she just let go for the first time since the funeral.

As she cried, Weber pulled her close to him but said nothing; he just held tight. As she began to calm down, she considered the tenderness of this grease monkey, a side of him she hadn't seen. She looked up and was again drawn to his piercing blue and comforting eyes. She knew there was something special about him besides being handsome. She wondered if maybe he saw her as a little sister.

When Weber started the truck again, he asked if she would like to go to a show in Lambert sometime. Unexpected excitement filled her. "Yeah!"

She leaped down from the truck, saying, "Thanks, Weber, I hope I didn't inconvenience you. Thanks for listening."

Weber nodded. "No problem, happy to do it."

A few weeks later they did go see a movie— *The Firm*, from a John Gresham book. Both loved movies, both loved mysteries. After the movie had been playing for a half an hour Weber reached over his hand to Glory's lap where her hands were folded. He grasped on hand and brought it over to his lap. Neither hand moved again until the end of the movie.

They dated two or three times a week after that.

Weber wasn't very talkative, but he did talk about his longing to expand the shop, hire another mechanic, settle down, and have a family. Though the town was small, he was confident people from all over would come to their shop. It had a good reputation, and soon word would spread and the business would grow.

She didn't have the heart to tell him Tanner had said the business was not big enough to open another shop or to expand this one. She also didn't want to come between Weber and Tanner.

Glory's attitude and view of life was becoming ever brighter. It was because of Weber. She felt exhilarated every time she thought of him and felt comfortable being with him. She thought good fortune was finally coming her way; she had a good job, a car, a boyfriend, and Victoria and Tanner.

The only time she felt the least bit uncomfortable was when she was with Lucen. She craved his interaction, even his affection. She needed to ask him about the problems between her father and him, ask him why they didn't come to the funeral.

She longed to tell him how she wished they had spent holidays together and how she wished they could have been connected as a family. She knew she could not discuss any of these concerns with him; there would most likely be no response from this frowning statue of a man.

She also still anticipated the day she could move on with her life and out from under the care of the McGuires.

Though she loved Victoria and it would sadden her to leave, she decided that if she returned to Florida and a holiday came, she would send them invitations to come to dinner, though she was relatively sure they wouldn't come. She had grown very fond of Weber, and he might quite possibly be the one reason she would choose to stay in Spalding.

CHAPTER II

NOT-SO-TYPICAL EVIL

He grew up like any typical kid in an Ozzie and Harriet kind of house hold. Everything appeared fine during his formative years. He wanted for nothing, had no aspirations other than just being a kid. He had nice clothes, an adequate house, and friends at school.

His parents always had their evening meals together. Though it was just the three of them, it was still considered "family time" by his mother. She made sure there was meat, potatoes, a vegetable, and a salad on the table, believing in balanced meals for her family; nothing less would do.

He adored his mother; she was always full of laughter and anxious to hear about everyone's day. She kept the house spotless, insisting a happy, sparkling home leads to a bright life. To her credit, her yard was immaculate as well.

The family went to church every Sunday and, though they weren't Bible thumpers, they did believe in God. His mother reminded him time and time again, "You reap what you sow" and "Be grateful for what God has blessed you with; never expect more than what you're willing to work for to acquire."

She doted on her little baby boy from the moment of his birth, and as he grew, she went out of her way in every aspect of his life. She helped him with schoolwork and even took the time to teach him how to cook. Though he was no Eisenstein, he was a good boy and managed to muddle through school by the smallest of margins. That was all she could hope for. As long as he gave it his all, she was proud. "It doesn't matter what you do with your life, as long as you do it well," she'd say.

His father was a hard worker and would by no means allow his family to do without. He came from the old school where men were men and women were women; they had their own sets of responsibilities.

So in love with his wife was he. But he did not and never would openly display any signs of affection.

Men from that era didn't want to appear as if they weren't the head of the household, and their word was final. He was a kind old soul who would do any favor for anyone in need, not a greedy man, but humble and purposeful.

In the summer, during his youth, the boy's father spent a good deal of his time with him, tossing an old worn out softball or a leather football back and forth in the yard. He hoped his son would be a star athlete, but he would have been satisfied if he'd chosen farming.

It was a classic family until the boy turned fourteen. Like most teenagers, his brainpower, or lack thereof, told him he knew more about life and the world than his parents. It wasn't until he was older that his parents fully understood his desire to be out from beneath their wings.

His rebellion started small: slamming doors, stomping his feet as he left a room, throwing his plate and silverware into the sink from across a room, or throwing books when he was frustrated with studying. They may have seemed like little things, but they were the beginning of a change in his mental state regarding what he considered to be an unsatisfactory life.

As time passed, his father became more distant. He knew why. His father had wanted him to carry on with the farm but the boy had other aspirations. Farming just didn't interest him at all. He had more important things on his mind than tending animals and raising crops.

His father wanted to be a good guide, a role model. He wanted to show his son that hard work could earn a person's living but also keep him from the taking the wrong path in life.

He felt his mother and father never understood his dreams; they always thought being grateful for what you had was enough, working hard for what you had was enough. He really didn't want to work that hard. He actually didn't care about any of that.

His father began detaching himself from his son after first trying to be stricter. He became quieter, less visible in the community while the young man became more aloof. A permanent wedge had developed between them.

His parents were not simple people; they were educated, though neither had gone to college. They soon realized their son's ideas about life and their ideas were quite different.

He wanted to see the world, wanted to take in all the sights the world had to offer. They were content to stay on the farm and live a menial existence. He never did let on to them that he had more ambition than they could ever fathom, much more.

Then came a time when he reached his limit. His family was stifling him; he felt he couldn't breathe another day under their roof. He was not sure when the change came, but when it did it hit him like a Mac truck. "No one is going to hold me back or stop me from getting a better life, a fun life."

And so it had been. Secure in knowing no one would ever find out his strategy to meet those ends, he knew he would be the king in the game.

When the opportunity presented itself, he grabbed it with all the gusto he could and ran with it. He had taken action and was on his way. His current undertaking was playing out just as he had designed it. It was his first major leap to making more of himself than just a good old country boy. It was a risk, and he'd taken risks before; he wasn't afraid.

He calculated every detail of his plan to the tiniest. The first small ones were leading him to the one major step he would need to take, which right now seemed light years away. Jubilant satisfaction consumed him in his pursuit of success. Now, as other options were falling on his plate, he scooped them up like a good meal.

This year, a chance opportunity presented itself, one that a person usually waits a lifetime for. There it had been, right in front of him, waiting to be discovered. And he and he alone discovered it.

"You reap what you sow." His mother had said it for years, and he saw himself reaping quite a bit. Luckily hc had also learned from his mother that patience is a virtue.

Frustration can creep in when you least expect it, and he found he could have both confidence and frustration at the same time. It wasn't easy to look in a mirror anymore. Seeing his own face made him realize he was actually capable of killing people.

But on the other hand, it wasn't easy for him to accept living in poverty the rest of his life. No, he wouldn't allow poverty; he wanted money, and he wanted it badly.

He had researched the McGuires' habits, determining whether it was a feasible plan or not and worthy of execution. He also realized it would not be an overnight or easy task. But from its inception of the idea, he felt good.

Waiting was a pet-peeve of his. If he wanted something, he wanted it yesterday. In this case, that would be impossible; he had no choice but to stay unruffled, suppressing his impulses to jump forward too quickly.

The death of the McGuires had set his future success in motion. Now it was just a matter of time.

He would have to start pretending now, to start showing he was a kind and friendly man, a loving and compassionate man. It was like being an actor, and this was to be the most important role of his life.

CHAPTER 12

KINDRED SPIRITS

Victoria and Glory spent many joyful hours together. The murders were never mentioned, not ever. Victoria knew Glory would spend some days agonizing over her past, so she did everything humanly possible to keep her cheered up and interested in other projects.

When Glory wasn't in school or working, Victoria taught her things like how the laundry smelled after waving in the fresh air for hours. Glory had always helped her mother fold clothes from the dryer, but those clothes—even though they smelled good—were warm and not fresh like line-dried clothes. When she pulled a sheet up next to her face at night, she noticed the difference; the aroma was like landing in a field of wildflowers.

"You know the way to a man's heart is thorough his stomach," Victoria had said. "That's what I've always heard, and I believe it too." Glory often laughed at her during the cooking lessons that began shortly after her arrival.

They made casseroles and cookies, and soon she learned to sew simple things. Victoria opened her eyes to self-sufficiency and new experiences. Glory appreciated the effort Victoria took to place these experiences before her. Within only a few months, Victoria became a surrogate mother to Glory.

Once Victoria confided in Glory how difficult it had been for her, just like for Glory, when she and Lucen first moved to Spalding. They knew no one, but Weber's parents had welcomed them.

Paul and Jean Arturo were good people, gentle people. Paul was a hard-working cattle man; Jean a stay-at-home mom caring for their son. Weber and Tanner were the same age. The Arturos had welcomed them with one of Jean's famous apple pies. From that evening on, they were all the best of friends.

"That's how Lucen learned about cattle, goats, and chickens," Victoria told Glory. "Oh, he already knew about living in the out of doors, but the animals were a new facet for him. Farming the land was a lot different than he had expected. Paul taught him, and Lucen took to it like a duck to water.

"Jean and I spent our time cooking up new recipes and cleaning while the two boys climbed and jumped or fell off everything in sight. Oh, Jean was a lot of fun. I miss her a lot. We confided our deepest secrets to each other. My goodness, they were scandalous things—some we'd dare not tell our husbands in a lifetime. Let me tell you, we had some whoppers.

"We were really blessed to have the Arturos in our lives. When they died my heart broke in two.

Even though Lucen said nothing, I sensed his devastation. He had lost his best friend. I felt so bad for him.

"I think that's when he started shutting down. He disliked Weber hanging around Tanner; I guess it brought back too many memories of Paul. Paul had kept Weber on a pretty short leash, and then Lucen introduced Tanner to the short leash. You know hindsight is 20-20. Lucen should have been more open, more understanding, but with Paul's death, he changed.

"I remember those little rascals causing havoc wherever they went for a while, when they were just little too. Once when they were in fourth grade, they skipped school. They went fishing at the creek. Tanner got the beating of his life. He will never forget that. He knew better than to raise the wrath of Lucen again.

"As teens, sometimes they'd stay out late. Once they knocked over Mrs. Gentry's back fence, just dumb stuff like that. There really wasn't any significant act that made Lucen worry unnecessarily about the boys. I know sometimes he questioned if Tanner was a bad influence on Weber or if Weber was the bad influence on Tanner. As we both know, Lucen doesn't like uncertainty.

"It was fun watching those boys grow up—ornery little beggars, but so funny. They are both handsome boys, and all the girls in school liked them. Funny, they seemed to break up with girls after a few dates. Neither one of them has had a long-term relationship. Tanner was basically a loner. Don't know if either of those boys will marry. How am I to have any grandchildren if Tanner doesn't marry?" She stomped her foot as if frustrated by her own question.

She continued. "I don't think there was a problem with Weber or Tanner really. They were kids doing kid stuff. Then, in their teen years, well, heck, even Tanner dealt us a fit for a while. He was a good boy but had to test his wings a few times, you know, see if he could fly. Lucen clipped 'em as often as he could. You know, boys will be boys.

"I suppose it was just real hard on Weber when his parents had their accident. He was depressed. He stopped most everything except drinking a little and puttering on cars.

"Well, his dad didn't talk about his personal life much, but Lucen told me once that Paul said he wished Weber would take more interest in the cattle and help him out a little. Weber was not at all interested in working the land, and neither was Tanner. The land was something both Paul and Lucen loved, so they were disappointed that both boys just wanted to work on cars."

Glory could see the hurt on Victoria's face as she talked about the Arturos; it was apparent she missed Jean very much. "When the Arturos died, we all had a hard time adjusting. Shortly after that, Tanner and Weber opened their station. It's been good for both of them; they both grew up a lot."

She paused for the longest time, but Glory deciding not to say anything and let Victoria get everything out. "I got some pretty good stories and someday I'll tell you about them." Of course that left Glory wondering, but she decided it best to wait until Victoria was ready to tell her.

Glory was pleased that Victoria had unselfishly shared so much with her about her and Lucen and the Arturos. It led her to a better understanding of Tanner and Weber, and she did understand Lucen's loss of his best friend.

Emotions were welling inside her for Lucen, losing his best friend. The two evidently had so much in common and once Paul was gone Lucen had become close to no one. She knew she wouldn't be able to share with him how she felt. She yearned to talk to him and tell him how she understood the loss of someone so close, but she knew it was impossible, not with Lucen.

She too felt the same emotion for Weber, she had told him so, after all they had both lost their parents, she knew what he felt inside with such a tremendous loss of the people who loved you most.

Olivia and Glory grew to be best of buddies. At first the only way Glory could think of Olivia was as "Sir Olivia"—often laughing and at the same time praying she wouldn't ever say it out loud. Time gave her insight to look through Olivia's gruff exterior and see a more secure and caring woman than she'd first thought. Glory felt blessed to have her as a friend.

Olivia was a good boss. It hadn't taken Glory long to catch on, and Olivia had never gotten on her case. Some afternoons, when the noon rush was over, and after cleanup was complete, they would restocked, then the two of them would unwind in a booth with their feet on the seat. Glory drank pop, but Olivia chose coffee with a little Baileys in it. It was a relaxing time as Glory listened to stories from Olivia. She could trust Olivia with even her deepest thoughts about life, love, and work.

Olivia had grown up in Spalding. Her grandfather had owned the cafe and his daughter (Olivia's mother) had wanted nothing to do with it.

When Olivia was only ten years old, she started working with her grandfather, puttering around the café, wiping off counters and tables, collecting dirty dishes—whatever Granddad needed.

"Granddad always paid me, but we never told anyone," Olivia told Glory one day. "He'd just put money into a jar in back of one of the shelves. I knew someday Granddad would give it to me. At ten years old, of course, I thought I may end up with a million zillion dollars, but by the time he actually gave it to me, when I was eighteen, there was eight thousand dollars in it.

"I spent the money on a car and to move out of my folk's house. I put a little down payment on the trailer I still live in. Both were good investments. Nobody knew Granddad had been saving for me." She kept a steady stream of information coming, seemingly wanting to tell Glory everything about her life.

"When I was twenty-five, my granddad had a heart attack and was gone. Grandma had been dead for a long time already. When the will was read, his wishes were that I should get the café. He willed my mom only a hundred dollars. She was furious; she pouted and screamed for days, sometimes throwing things directly at me. She thought she'd get the cafe and sell it. Money was always her one priority; I was second and sometimes third on the list. I knew I couldn't make much of the café, but if that's what Granddad wanted, then that's what I would do. And here I am."

So she had worked there from the time she was ten until the very day she told all this to Glory. "I had a couple of boyfriends along the way, but nothing ever panned out, but that's okay. I'm happy being single. Ain't nobody good enough for me in this town." She laughed vociferously, causing her apron to jiggle up and down.

In one of their conversations, Olivia got the nerve up to ask Glory about her parents. Glory recalled the gruesome details, telling her the story from beginning to end. And her tears flowed. She did find some comfort though; she was finding it easier to accept what had happened when she openly talked about it. It helped her confront the reality of it all when she talk about it.

After hearing the account of the murders, Olivia asked her, "What do you think that burglar was after, if he didn't take anything?"

Glory said she didn't know. "They think maybe he got scared when they found out my folks were home and decided not to take anything."

"There's more to it than that, little one. I watch all them cop shows on the telly, and I can tell you there's more to it than that. They may have been scared, but burglars don't leave without *something*."

"What do you mean?"

"I don't care how scared a burglar gets; he will always grab a ring or watch, a radio or one of them laptop computers, or something. Crooks are there 'cause they want something—maybe to pawn, maybe to sell the stuff for drugs. Those druggies are a mean bunch—damn thugs. They want something and they aren't about to leave without something in their hands."

Olivia may have been "backwoods," but she could smell a rat a mile away. She could read people and know their questions before they asked. She wasn't married for a simple reason: she had too much insight into people.

"They took inventory of everything in the house," Glory said. "It didn't look like anything was missing. I've racked my brain trying to figure it out. I don't know what they would have wanted."

Olivia looked up and raised an eyebrow. "Something was missing if it was a burglary, and the cops missed it. I know it. Like I said, I watch those shows, and something doesn't smell right, doesn't smell right at all. If your parents were already dead, the burglars had plenty a time to grab something, you know. I'm just saying." And with that she broke off the conversation.

Olivia's comments gave Glory further cause for alarm. If the burglars hadn't taken anything, then did they even want anything? That would mean they killed her parents for no reason. That would mean that was what they came for in the first place. The cold chill of fear entered her body once again.

CHAPTER 13

NOT MY BROTHER'S KEEPER

Detective Marshall kept his promise and kept in contact with Glory on Lucen's phone, calling once every two weeks. There was no new information to pass on that couldn't be done on Lucen's phone. Unbeknownst to her, the cell was mainly set up in case she had an emergency and needed to get ahold of Marshall.

His progress had been slow, but he reassured her that the department was doing its utmost to find the killer. With each passing week, there was less and less to report. He had done as much as he could but had so little to go on his hopes of success were dismal. He dreaded the calls that ended with disappointment in Glory's voice.

"Glory, can you think of anything you may have found missing?" Glory said she'd picked out a few things she wanted but didn't notice anything missing. Sanders had told her the house items had been inventoried and accounted for.

"Right now," Marshall said, "it looks like there was nothing out of the ordinary, nothing stolen, no funds transferred or misappropriated. There doesn't seem to be anyone who would want to harm your parents." To get out of that conversation as quickly as possible, he added, "So, Glory, tell me how you're doing."

She brought him up-to-date about her living arrangement and her job. She said Victoria was really nice but Lucen was a strange man, and she was unsure of herself around him. "He's real quiet and glares at me a lot."

"I intend to come down in a week," Marshall said, "on the first Saturday of September. I'll be asking some questions of the McGuires and anyone else who may have known the family."

With a heightened pitch, Glory said, "Why? You don't think a family member had anything to do with this, do you"?

"You know, Glory, when a murder is being investigated, everyone is a potential suspect. I don't mean to hurt your feelings, but we even had to verify what time you arrived at school, what you did during the day—"

"Me?"

"...And what time you left school. So even though you have a perfectly good alibi, we have to see who else might not. "

She understood. "Oh, I see. I'm sure there's nothing Lucen or Victoria can tell you. They didn't speak to my parents for years, or even wrote letters."

"I don't assume any of them is a suspect but I have to do my job, Glory. We checked our records, and no similar cases were reported here or in the state. I can only surmise this was a random act of burglary or someone wanted to hurt your parents. I don't want to alarm you, but if it's the second choice, well, then we have a very scrupulous individual to find."

She thanked him and asked when he would be there. "I should be there next Saturday. I am going to fly into Lambert and rent a car so I should be there by noon. I know you have to work, but if you could get the time away for the afternoon, I would appreciate it."

"I look forward to seeing you, Detective Marshall. I'll see what I can do".

"Call me Marshall, please, and don't hesitate to phone me. And Glory, take care of yourself." He had concerns for her welfare; there was a killer loose and Glory was still very vulnerable.

"Yes, but I don't understand why you want me to use the cell phone? I could call you from Lucens'"

"Glory, I want you to always be able to reach me. I still have great concern for your well being."

"No one will care if I have a phone. I just don't understand."

It was best that he kept his fears to himself; it was enough to let her know he was concerned for her well being; that wouldn't frighten her as much as if he told her he still believed she still might be in danger. "I don't expect any problem, that's not the case. It's just that, well, I want you to have access to me at all times. It's better during this investigation if our conversations are private. Please understand." She agreed.

At the McGuires' evening meal, Glory reluctantly told Lucen and Victoria she'd heard from Detective Marshall. "He'll be here on Tuesday to ask a few questions."

For the first time in weeks, Lucen said more than three words during a conversation. "What questions? Who is he going to question?"

Glory chose her words carefully. "He said he has to question everyone who knew my father and mother."

"What the devil can we tell him about something that happened thousands of miles away to someone we haven't spoken to in more than sixteen years?" His face changed from its normal pale ivory to a crimson red.

Glory's chest tightened; she gripped her napkin with one hand as if it were a life preserver keeping her from drowning. Lucen's voice was as harsh as his green eyes piercing her for answers. She dropped her fork and stared at him, afraid to say any more.

Victoria reached over and patted her. "Don't worry about it, honey. We have no problem answering the detective's questions, do we, Lucen?"

"Humph. " He rose and left the table.

Glory wondered why he seemed so troubled; hoping it wasn't related to the money for her care. She didn't want to create a rift in this family. Though Lucen and Victoria were awarded the allotment for her care, she was careful not to request any money unless she had to. She had a job and made her own money and only asked for a little here and there; she didn't need much. Victoria saw that she had some extra cash when they went to Lambert to shop.

Lucen and Victoria had been frugal all their married life. They had tried to instill the importance of accounting for each dollar to Glory, and she readily accepted. They never talked to Glory about the allotment; she knew it was there, and that was enough. The material things in life did not concern her, except a few clothes now and then. She knew life was too precious to bother much with such thing; that's one lesson she learned from losing her parents.

Marshall arrived at noon on Saturday, September 11. Glory had prearranged the day off with eager anticipation of his visit. She liked Marshall; he was a good man and, she hoped, a good detective.

He arrived as dapper as ever in his khaki pants and blue denim shirt with a navy V-neck sweater. Marshall was thin and tall and looked good no matter what he wore. He felt that a suit would alienate people in this small country community.

More than thrilled to see him, Glory tried to keep her composure. As she opened the McGuires' door to greet him, she offered him a casual handshake. He held on as long as respectable, not wanting to let go. Finally, he inquired as to Victoria and Lucen, and released Glory's hand.

Victoria entered the room, bubbly and pleased to see Marshall, but Lucen entered as abruptly as ever. Victoria showed Marshall to the living room in her usual delightful hostess manner and offered coffee. He had had enough on the plane, so he declined.

Marshall was conscious that he needed to be especially diplomatic on this visit. His goal was to extract as much information as possible from the McGuires and anyone else related to the family. The odds of anyone in Spalding knowing an iota of information that would help him were as remote as finding an alligator on the front porch when he left.

"I don't want you to jump to conclusions with my visit here. It is part of my job to question every-one in the family—you, Lucen, as David's brother, and Victoria as his sister-in-law. I want to make it perfectly clear this is just a routine visit with basic questions. You understand this, don't you?" There was no response. "I would appreciate your full cooperation and truthful answers. If I fail to cover any issue about which you can supply information, just let me know. Some of the questions may seem odd to you, but I have to cover every bit of ground I can. You understand, don't you, for Glory's sake?"

Victoria was the first and only to respond. "Of course."

He then asked Glory to leave the room. She looked puzzled but complied.

Marshall began the inquiry. "I need to know where both of you were on May 13 of this year."

Victoria remembered like it was yesterday. "I was here at home. I didn't even go to town that day. I remember the call coming in later that evening, telling us about David and Janice."

Lucen said, "I went to town, always do, and had coffee at the café. Then I went over to see Tanner about a rattle in my truck, which, by the way he ain't never fixed." He looked sternly at Victoria, as if it were her fault the truck hadn't been repaired. "I came home and a little later the call came about David."

Marshall was about to hit some bumpy ground, but was compelled to go on. "I understand you and your brother had not spoken to each other for years. Can you tell me why?"

Lucen's chest visibly inflated. His entire body rotated toward Marshall. His frown caused his eyebrows to meet in the middle. "Well, not that's it's any of your business, but we got into a disagreement a few years after graduation, so I just moved away."

Marshall refused to let it rest, with Lucen's answer being as clear as mud. "Sorry, Lucen, but I need a little more than that. What kind of disagreement did you have with David?"

"Oh, you know, normal kid stuff. Can't even remember what it was about now. What does it matter?"

"It's strange that you two never spoke after you moved here. I wondered why."

"Just because we didn't, that's about all there is to it. David and I weren't much alike, didn't really have anything in common."

"Do you remember receiving an envelope with a seal on it from your brother or his lawyer some years ago?"

"Yes, and it's hidden. No one knows where it is, and it's just like when I got it. I never touched it since the day I got it. Lawyer called me up and told me not to open it, so I didn't."

"Could anyone have found it?"

"No, not where I put it. It's as tight as a bug in a rug. I didn't look at it then and don't ever plan to."

Marshall still had an interest in the circumstances of the disagreement between him and David. "Lucen, let's go back to this disagreement. Would it have caused you to wish any harm to your brother?"

At that Lucen stood. Marshall rose up, too, thinking a fist might be coming his way.

"What the hell kind of guy do you take me for? I've never harmed a soul in my life, especially not my brother, for God's sake. I told you we moved because I couldn't stand to look at him anymore; it's that simple. I didn't hate him, well not enough to hurt him, and you're a dumb ass for asking." He promptly stomped out of the room, boots thumping with each step, and out the front door, but not without first slamming the door.

Marshall had underestimated the impact of his questions. He still had questions about the lack of communication between the brothers, but he would wait.

Victoria leaned toward Marshall and said softly, "I'm sorry, Detective. My husband is a little hotheaded. He does not like to be questioned about anything."

Marshall saw the embarrassment in her eyes. "Do you know what the disagreement was about?"

"No, I stay out of Lucen's business. I'm sure it was just a brother-to-brother argument. Probably nothing important. They were young and in school. David was real popular; Lucen wasn't popular at all. You know, possibly just competition between brothers."

"Do you think Lucen would hurt David?"

Victoria shifted in her chair uneasily. "No, never. Deep inside, he did love his brother. They just were two different people, totally different. In all these years he never even mentioned David's name. That night, after hearing the news, he sat in his recliner. He didn't watch TV, didn't look at the paper. He just sat there, all quiet like."

"Victoria, is there any reason you yourself would have any resentment toward David or Janice?"

Victoria's face took on a vivid pinkish color. "Of course not! They were wonderful people. We had a lot of fun in our younger days. David was a great guy and Janice a perfectly beautiful human being, and we were family. We never had anything against them. Just sometimes arguments cause people to do things they wished they hadn't."

"Like what?"

"Like move away from your family, people you love. Oh, we love it here, but I miss family." The color began returning to her face.

Marshall graciously thanked her and invited Glory to join him for the ride to town. It would go faster if she showed him around, he said.

His objective was to question the local residents of the area, as well as Tanner. Hidden inside him was also a craving to spend more time with Glory.

They first went to the café, where Glory introduced Marshall to Olivia. He noted that she was exactly as Glory had described her, a hearty, robust woman who would "tell it like it is."

There were very few customers, so Marshall asked Olivia if he could talk with her in the back. Olivia guided him through the swinging doors near the refrigeration unit into the kitchen.

"On May 13th of this year, the day of the crime, can you remember Lucen being here?"

Olivia put her thumbs through the ties on her apron. "Oh, sure he's here every morning for coffee. The only time I ever remember not seeing him was 'cause he was in the hospital twelve years ago with gall bladder or stones or something like that. Otherwise, like clockwork I see him every day, except on Sunday, a course. We're closed on Sundays."

Detective Marshall asked if Lucen ever mentioned David.

"Not that morning. I didn't even know Lucen had a brother until the day after the murders, when he came in for coffee. He told us his brother had been murdered the day before. What a shocking announcement that was to start a morning."

"What did Lucen actually say? How did he act?"

"He told the guys, 'My brother was murdered yesterday, in Orlando.' And that was it."

"After he told the men about his brother, what else did he say?"

"Nothin'."

Why anyone would convey the fact that his brother had been murdered and just halt the conversation was beyond Marshall's imagination. "Didn't anyone ask what happened? Didn't Lucen tell more about it than just that his brother had been murdered?"

Olivia saw that Glory was uncomfortable in this situation and asked her to go out front and see if anyone needed anything. Glory was relieved; all the questions made her uneasy.

Olivia straightened her posture, very upright then shifted her weight from one foot to the other with her hand on her hip but never moving from the spot she had planted herself to talk to Marshall. "Quite clearly, Detective, you don't know Lucen McGuire very well. If he tells you something, then you been told. You do not ask him questions. We all know better than that. Sure, we were curious, but ain't a one of us would ask him nothin'."

A slight smile crossed Marshall's face. "Oh yeah, I already know that."

"That night, I did go into my internet to read the headlines from Florida. I found out what happened, got all the details there. It was an awful murder, just awful. Who could have done something like that?"

"That's what I'm trying to find out. Did you tell anyone what you read?"

"Oh yeah, a few guys at coffee. But that was before Lucen came the next day. Oh, and Bertha at the beauty shop. Tanner came in later that morning. I said I was sorry to hear about his uncle, that it was a horrible way to die. Tanner just looked at me kind of odd like. Then the strangest thing happened. He said, 'Well, if you gotta die, I guess you don't have a choice how you're going to die, you just do.'" He ordered a hamburger and pop. I didn't say no more. Isn't that a funny thing to say?"

Marshall analyzed Tanner's statement for a moment, and said, "Well, yes, I guess it is." Then he asked, "Did Lucen act differently than normal when telling the men about the murders?"

"No, same old Lucen. No expression, no sorrow, no nothing, just words out of his mouth."

They left the café and drove directly to Tanner's station, just two blocks away. As usual, Tanner came out when he saw Glory get out of the car. He gave her a hug and asked, "What's up, cuz?'

Glory eagerly returned his hug. "This is Detective Marshall from Orlando, and he needs to ask you a few questions."

He looked down at the ground then back up but was visibly uptight but ready to answer his questions. Then he looked at Marshall and said, "Okay, shoot."

Marshall asked, "What were you doing the day of the murders, May 13th."

"I don't know. That was a long time ago. I don't remember every day. I'd have to look back at my receipts for that day. They're a mess, so it could take me a while."

With conviction in his voice, Marshall replied, "I've got plenty of time. I'll wait while you look."

He stomped inside the office, with Glory and Marshall following, and yanked open a desk drawer and started shuffling the papers inside with a fury.

Then he pulled out receipts and threw them on the desk. "There, I had a couple of repairs out on the road: three oil changes and a tire repair. Satisfied?"

Marshall noted Tanner's edginess. "Well, that can't have taken all day. What did you do the rest of the day?"

Tanner seemed annoyed at that question. "Me and Weber are pretty busy here most days. Some people don't even get charged, so it could be somebody got a repair there's no receipt for. I think we ate here that day, yep, pretty sure we did."

"What about the next day, Tanner? What did you do that day?"

"Same old, same old, I guess. The night before I went to my folks. They told me what happened."

"But the next day, after you heard about the murders, what did you do?"

"I did the usual stuff, nothing different. I fixed cars and tractors. That's what I always do. I wasn't too concerned because I didn't know Glory's folks. When I heard Glory was coming, I was happy about that."

"Why was that?" asked Marshall.

Tanner smiled at Glory. "Because other than my mom and dad, I don't have any family. Except Weber, he's like family. It was cool to know I'd meet my cousin."

"Why did you say to Olivia, 'Well, if you gotta die, I guess you don't have a choice how you're going to die, you just do'?"

"Well, that's the truth. You don't have a choice. Guess I was just making small talk, that's all. It didn't matter to me at that time."

Marshall's eyebrows rose. "Well, if not then, what about now?"

"Only care now because I know Glory and care about her. I care what happens to her, no other reason."

Marshall thanked Tanner. And he and Glory headed back to Lucen's.

Marshall was pleased that he had some "alone time" with Glory. He so wanted to tell her how beautiful he thought she was or that her voice was like an angel's and that he wished they were back in Florida where he could keep an eye on her; like a guardian.

He was the lead detective in a murder investigation, a professional in his twenties. She was just a teenager girl involved in a murder case. He knew he had no right thinking of Glory in any other light, but she had captivated him. He knew it was inappropriate in a number of ways to think of her in any other way. He would have to maintain the character of his upbringing; his professionalism as a law enforcement officer. He did feel a need to protect her from whatever was out there, he had empathy for her being cast into a life she wasn't accustom to. His feeling, well, he couldn't let it go but knew he wouldn't act on them either. *Maybe when she's eighteen and returns to Orlando, I could tell her then*, he thought.

When they arrived back at the house, Marshall thanked Glory for accompanying him, all the while hating to leave her. "This is really out in the middle of nowhere, isn't it? I had no idea how remote it was."

Glory replied sarcastically, "Yeah, right out of an old western, but right now its home, isn't it?" Immediately she felt bad for sounding ungrateful.

"Well, it won't be long until you are of the age you can go wherever you want."

"I know. I do miss my home. I miss the hustle and bustle of Orlando."

"Well, tell me about this boyfriend thing?"

She seemed to cheer up then. "Well, he's really not a boyfriend, just a boy and a friend. I do care about him, and he treats me nice. But you know I don't want to be a waitress forever."

He took her hand. "Remember, I am only a phone call away. Don't lose that cell phone."

She waved good-bye as he took off in his rental car.

This case had gotten more complicated and less decipherable with each passing day and each interview.

Marshall's list of suspects expanded then depleted with each interview. He felt he met resistance but he couldn't understand why. Anyone should be able to give a forthright answer to any of his questions without hesitation. Most interviewee had a reason to be interested in Glory's future and her money, but each had a plausible alibi and non seemed to be the murdering type, if there was a type and, each one seemed to have a genuine affection for her.

CHAPTER 14

BONDED BY DEATH

Glory was elated when the semester ended. It was nearing Christmas time. This coming year she would be eighteen; finally she could choose her own destiny.

On December 18, the last Friday of Glory's attendance before graduation, Mrs. Baker summoned her into her office. She congratulated her on her academic success and on finishing the year early. Mrs. Baker presented her with the diploma. Glory took it with pride.

Marshall continued to call Glory every two or three weeks. They chatted briefly only because she had nothing to tell him and he had no new information for her.

Not long after that, while Glory was on a date with Weber, he unexpectedly opened up to her about his parents. He evidently finally felt comfortable enough to talk about the circumstances of his parents' deaths four years earlier. She knew the time would come, and she had patiently waited.

Glory visualized the scene as he told the story: "They were out on Highway 44, which crosses the state east and west, nearing Cayuga Pass. It's a real hilly and winding road—dangerous, especially at night. They reached the top and began their decent into Jackson Township. Within a few miles, the power in the car went out, included power steering, brakes, everything. They simply lost all control." He hesitated as if trying to decide what else to tell her and to hold back his emotions.

"They couldn't have even opened the doors; they had automatically locked when the power went out." Glory cringed at the thought; they had been caught in a death trap with no way out.

"My folks went over a guard rail. At the bottom of the canyon, the car burst into flames. They had no chance at all." Glory saw the devastation on his face as he tried to control his flow of tears.

"The electrical system was faulty. It wasn't that old a car but the cops investigating it figured it was from wear and tear. They couldn't blame anyone, not the automaker or the guy that sold it to them. No one."

"Oh my God, Weber, I'm so sorry. It must have been awful for you."

"Yeah, it was. The insurance company paid on a measly little policy my folks had. Don't tell anyone, but I got twenty-thousand dollars for a settlement. I used a lot of it to bury my folks. But I got my old truck and went into business with Tanner. Then it was gone."

"So you didn't have enough to pay off the house?"

"Nah, the bank still owned it and the land. I didn't want to farm. Bankers are thieves, don't you know? That Beacon family with all the kids bought it. Guess he liked farming. Now I live paycheck to paycheck."

"Lucky you and Tanner are so close. I bet he helped you through that time."

"Yeah, we've been best buddies since we were kids, except for a few times we had a tussle or two. Tanner can get pretty pissed off sometimes, and you don't want to be near him then."

In Tanner's defense, Glory said, "Oh, I can't believe that. He's always so happy, well, except sometimes when he's around Lucen. I love being around him; he always cheers me up."

"Don't let that pretty face fool you. He can go off at any time. My guess is it's because his dad is such a butthead." They both burst into laughter.

She continued. "I think Lucen is mad at him for opening the station instead of helping him on the farm. I think Tanner's bad side is inherited from Lucen."

Weber looked at her as if he hadn't really heard what she was saying. "Glory, I think I understand your pain because your parents died like mine did. It's very hard living through an experience like that."

Glory smiled. He had unlocked his restricted heart enough to talk about his parents. Glory was thankful he trusted her now.

"Luckily I got back on my feet real quick like, thanks to Tanner. The station brought me back to life."

The next week, Weber and Glory sat together on the rickety unpainted porch swing at Lucen's, after returning from a trip to the movie house in Lambert.

Lucen loved that swing and felt the character would be diminished if it were painted. Victoria itched at the wanting to paint it to match the rest of her décor, but Lucen had put his foot down.

He leaned over and kissed her on the lips. Then he sat back and looked at her.

"Why do you keep staring, Weber? You're making me nervous."

"Glory, you are absolutely gorgeous. I was staring because you're all I ever think about. You've stolen my heart, you know?" The remark startled her a little; it was such an unexpected statement. Then, once more, he leaned over and kissed her.

She had to admit, Weber mesmerized her; he was a gentle and kind man and made her feel important and loved. Suddenly she realized just how much she did care for him. Her heart melted with a desire to rush into this relationship, but knowing better, she said, "I am not very experienced in relationships, Weber. I didn't date much back home. Let's not rush things too much." At the same time realizing how much she did care for Weber.

Weber halfheartedly agreed to take it slow, but he knew he wanted her in his life. He wasn't going to take no for an answer.

Three days later, as Glory prepared to finish the cleanup after her shift at the café, Weber's truck pulled in the front parking area. Olivia saw him and turned to glance at Glory. "What's with you two kids?"

"What do you mean?" Glory asked.

"You two in love?"

"No, just in real deep like right now. He's a good guy."

"Well, if you say so."

"What's that mean?"

"Well, just never saw Weber go with any girl very long. You must be something special, maybe what he was looking for all along. Is he good to you?" She smiled like the Cheshire cat.

"He's wonderful, Olivia. He cares about me a lot, and he does treat me special."

The dating continued. With each one, they grew closer. After all, they had a lot in common, both parentless and basically alone. One of the most admirable traits she saw in Weber was his easy-going nature. Considering what they both had experience, she felt that together they could make it through any turmoil.

Their interests were common as well. Both liked mystery movies and being outdoors. And she loved the quiet times with him, sitting on the porch and just talking. She was relying on him more and more, and realized he had become an important part of her life. Was she finally finding happiness? Her excitement mounted, and she had butterflies in her stomach whenever she knew she would see him.

GARDEN OF DEATH

She desperately tried not to think about little things she'd heard about his reckless behavior when he was a boy. After all, when you're a teen, you tend to act on crazy impulses; she knew that. But that was not Weber. No longer a little boy, he was mature now, all grown up and in a business. His parents' deaths had created a void in him, but she hoped she could at least partly fill it.

She considered Weber and Tanner to be her best friends. Both were always available to her and both seemed elated to see her. At the same time, the two were very different. Tanner was the chatter-box and had a great sense of humor. The only time Tanner was quiet was when they took their walks through the fields. Weber was more laid-back and didn't say much. She loved it when either of them showed up at the café or at Lucen's.

Glory missed the fun her parents created on hol-idays. The three of them would meander around the kitchen, competing to see who could come up with the most creative dish. On Christmas, after a hearty breakfast, they would open presents. After opening gifts they did or didn't need, they'd head into the living room supplied with a bowl of pop-corn and Christmas goodies. There they'd nestled together to watch movies.

With the exception of a few gifts and a nice meal, it could have been any day of the year at Lucens. But Weber was consistent with his atten-tions to Glory, and she liked that.

He saw her later that day and presented her with a silver watch with diamond-like stones around the face. On his budget, she presumed they weren't really diamonds. "This ring of diamonds represents my continuing love for you," he said.

She said nothing, surprised that he had put himself out there like that. She smiled, and they kissed.

Glory began putting in more shifts at the café. Now that she'd graduated, she had plenty of free time. The days flew by, each reminding her of her future, of what she could do when she turned eighteen. Each day gave a new scenario for her to contemplate. She liked Spalding now, though she still missed Orlando. Her reservations about staying in Spalding were becoming fewer and fewer because of Weber.

Marshall appeared in Spalding about every six months. He wished it could be more often, but there was no justification for the trip, because the case met an impasse, there was no further information or leads he could pursue. He wasn't about to give up though, he knew someday there would be a break in the McGuire case. Right now his concern was Glory's safty.

In late April, the sun finally made its debut, showering the garden with warmth. Glory spent what little free time she had with Victoria or Tanner—when she wasn't with Weber, of course.

She had also grown close to Tanner. He often stopped by after buttoning up the station or on Sundays for dinner. On several occasions they spent an afternoon in the fields just beyond the pine trees.

One Sunday after the noon meal, she insisted Tanner go walking through the fields with her to the base of the mountains she adored. He didn't hesitate, wanting to take advantage of every chance to spend time with his cousin. And though he hated farming, he loved the earth as much as she did. He also wanted to escape the unmistakable glares of Lucen for a few hours.

They walked hand in hand through the pine-lined yard, over the rises, and into the open fields experiencing kisses of a spring breeze. She thought of Lucen every time she walked there, since he had been the first one to introduce her to the vast expanse of beauty. She loved watching the progress of the changing colors of the seasons. Yet remembering Florida and the warmth all year long gave her a craving to return.

Their walked continued until they decided to rest at the last fence row. She realized their trek had taken them almost an hour.

Glory broke the silence with a sigh. Contentment bathed her in comfort as she regarded the spectacular touches of God's creations: the green open spaces; the wheat in the fields pushed back and forth by the gentle breeze that touched them; the pillow-soft white clouds gliding to and fro and up and down, touched by unseen forces high in the sky.

Her favorite site unquestionably was the beyond the fields. There rose the mountains up toward the heavens. On each one were majestic pine trees in shades from lavender to black. Further up the mountain, the trees were just dots.

Glory smiled as a pine cone lost its grip and fell softly to the earth, rolling down the incline and landing near her feet. She watched as the cows and goats gorged themselves in their unceasing green smorgasbord. She lay back on the grass, looked straight up, and thanked God for this place and the tranquility in her heart.

As the breeze hit her face and a breath of fresh air filled her lungs. She told Tanner how much this place meant to her, how much she loved the chance to talk to God and reflect on her life, her parents, and her future.

"I used to come out here a lot too," he said. "When I wanted to be alone and think, or just get away—especially when Dad got on my nerves. I'm glad you like it as much as I do."

"I hope in time you and Lucen will grow closer."

With his legs crossed, he picked at newly sprouting blades of grass. "Awe, we're close, in a crazy kind of way. He just doesn't talk much to me. He doesn't like me being gone from home. Actually, from the farm, I think; he would have scripted me to be a farmer. I just wasn't into that scene, you know? I needed my freedom. That's why I moved out when I was eighteen."

He stopped and concentrated on splitting the blades of grass; it took total concentration to pull the tiny stalks apart. "It wasn't like that when I was a little kid. Dad spent lots of time with me. I know he's glad he had a son; he probably couldn't have handled a girl. He's kind of a guy's guy, if you know what I mean. As I got older, we just got further apart. I never know what Dad really feels about *anything*.

"Why is that, Tanner? Why is he so quiet? And when he does talk, is it because he's mad?"

"I wish I knew what was going on in his head. It may be because of the death of Paul Arturo. He was his best friend. But he once said he wasn't close to his folks; he thought they gave his brother all the praise. That only came up one time. I never heard him say it again."

The conversation was beginning to make Glory uncomfortable. After all, that was her own father Tanner was talking about. "Tanner, just because they were brothers doesn't mean they had to be alike. Everyone has something special about themselves. I'm sure your dad's parents loved both the boys."

"Yeah, maybe. Sometimes I think my dad looks at me and wishes I would have been more like your dad—a success. Can't help who I am, now, can I, Glory?"

"I'm sure Lucen is proud of you. What's not to be proud of? You have a good business and you're making it on your own. And anyway, you are the only one that matters now. If you are proud of yourself, that should be enough. Parents always want something great for their kids, but not always what the kids want for themselves."

"Oh, I'm proud of what I've done, but someday it's going to be even better. Somebody I'll have stuff, and people won't think I'm just a grubby mechanic. I may be poor now, but I won't always be."

"Oh, Tanner, nobody thinks that. You've got a great personality and you're a hard worker. People respect that about you."

"Yeah, sure."

"What about your mom, Tanner? How do you get along with her? She's so wonderful."

His grimace changed to a smile. "Grant you that, Glory. Mom's always been there for me; she came to all my school stuff. She even came to all the teacher-parent meetings. I didn't do too well on my grades, but Mom didn't care. She just told me to do my best."

Again he turned the conversation back to Lucen. "Dad always seemed to have a reason not to come. Usually it was because he was too busy with the stock." His own words were depressing him. "That really hurt a lot; it was an excuse. Not sure why he always had to have an excuse, but he did."

"The farm had to have kept him busy," Glory said. "He was working it all alone. Surely you understand it was hard on him?"

"Yeah, I guess. I should helped him more. I don't think he liked me much when I grew up."

"Oh, Tanner, he loves you. From what I've seen, Lucen just doesn't show emotions. Maybe Lucen just doesn't want anyone to see he is as vunerable as anyone else. Don't be mad at him, Tanner. His heart is in the right place; he just doesn't know how to get it out of his chest."

"I'm not mad, just kind of bummed out. He's my dad, yet he's not much of a dad."

She could tell it was time to change the subject again. His relationship with Lucen may be the reason for his happiness with Glory; she had more of an interest in Tanner than his father did.

"My parents were really good to me," she said. "I miss them, but I am happy to have Victoria. I wish you could have met them. Oh, Tanner, you'd of liked them, I know you would have."

Tanner's gaze turned to sympathy as he looked at her. "I know I would have. I'm sorry your parents died. But I am glad you're in Spalding, Glory, real glad." She knew he was being sincere. "You're something special."

His wish was that she would not return to Florida, and she knew that. "It's always been my dream, since I got here, to go back to the things I love: swimming, hiking, biking, and sun all the time. The weather is so great there. But I'm just not sure what I want to do yet."

"If I were you, I'd probably go back to that fun life. I'd want to live that kind of life forever, not this boring day-to-day same old same old life. But I'd sure be miserable if you left. You and Weber are pretty close, too, and I know he wants you to stay." His eyebrows rose and he looked at her as if waiting for a question to be answered.

Her grin brightened her whole face. "Yes, I like Weber a lot. Just remember, no matter where you live, there are good days and bad, good people and bad. You just have to make the best of each situation, and that's what I'll do as long as I'm here."

They talked for another hour about nothing significant, then headed back to the house. For fun, they skipped halfway across the flatter fields and laughed as they held hands. Once in a while, one of them would fall in the grass, laughing more loudly and longer.

Back at the house, Tanner's arms encircled Glory, squeezing so tight she couldn't breathe. "I love you, Glory. I mean it."

CHAPTER 15

A COLD DAY IN HELL

Months went by. Glory continued at the café, becoming more acquainted with all the town folks and meeting their visiting relatives. It was easy, because there weren't that many residents. She soon learned who did what, with whom, and why. Victoria helped her sort out the collection of tittle-tattle she heard.

The gossip swirling around town regarding Glory's circumstances had finally stopped, and Mrs. Baker's new red Chrysler 300 was the new talk of the town.

Glory's tip jar was always nearly full at the end of her shift; yet with so few customers, she didn't understand how so much money ended up in it. "You're a welcome sight for sore eyes," she'd hear. Perhaps it was because it was someone other than "Mr. Olivia" serving coffee.

Her time with Victoria in the garden increased, though she couldn't quite get the hang of pruning.

As always, Victoria only asked for "her best." Mostly Glory spent time transferring dirt from one place to the other. They both laughed, knowing Glory was no kin to the earth. She never knew it to be so much work; her gardener in Florida had made it look so easy. She hoped someday, when she had her own place, she would actually get the hang of pruning, but until then, she'd just fake it.

Marshall still mulled over the facts of the murder case. He tried to reassure her as he continued to do investigative work on the case, but his eyes told her the truth. She could see the lack of confidence as he told her he wasn't going to give up finding the person or persons who killed her parents. She knew that he knew there was little possibility of success.

For the last two years Marshall visited Spalding on a regular basis. He would ask a few unimportant questions, still with little hope of getting a break in the case. No one had any further information for him, but the underlying reasons for his visits was his concern for Glory. He knew the visits were marked by the residents of the town and that as long as they knew he was coming there was a small chance no harm would come to Glory; if indeed there was anyone there wishing her harm.

Marshall had genuinely reached a dead end. His gut ached like never before. He had combed through every report written and created more than one script board to write the events in the order they occurred in an attempt to piece together the killer's route, his thoughts, his actions. He wrote in times, dates, locations, people, the money involved, the years until Glory turned twenty-one, every detail he could muster up.

There were too many blank spaces on the board that he couldn't fill in. His frustration grew each time he attempted to come up with a feasible explanation.

His instincts told him that the answers were right in front of him, declaring to him that he had a blind eye to them. His instincts had always been right; he had solved every case. But this time was different. Now the facts only told him there was a killer out there somewhere between Florida and South Dakota, and he was outwitting Marshall. He didn't take that well. He was the genius, after all; the one who should have all the answers.

Was it true, was there someone smarter and cleverer than Marshall. He doubted it but at this juncture it looked as if Marshall may have met his match.

Finding burglary suspects had been a cinch for him. A burglar is not normally a very smart criminal. They usually left prints. He remembered the 7-Eleven. The suspect came in, looked around, went to the cooler, opened it (prints), looked at a lighter (prints), picked up a lottery ticket (prints), and then robbed the place. Within twenty-four hours after the surveillance tape was on TV and forensics had the prints, the case was solved and the perpetrator was caught and caged. A neighbor had called to say a fellow down his street always wore a Chiefs sweatshirt.

Once Marshall had to investigate a hit and run. A six-year-old boy had been hit while riding his bike. Once again, witnesses described the pickup, got a partial on the plate, and said the driver had long, dark hair. Within six hours of running the partial plate number through the NCIC System, the perpetrator was caught. He had been drinking and had not even seen the young boy. The boy suffered a broken leg and the fear of God, but returned to get his bike fixed and ride again. The case had been simple.

Why is this one so hard to crack? Marshall asked himself. *Because, Marshall, there are no prints, there are no eye witnesses, there is nothing for you to go on. You're on your own, buddy boy.* His suspicions would be drawn in one direction, then he'd hit a roadblock. He redirected his suspicions until he hit another obstacle.

Once, on one of the shorter visits to Spalding, Glory blurted out, "My parent's case is cold now, isn't it, Marshall? Finding those awful people who killed my parents is a dream; it will never happen, will it?"

Taken aback by her bluntness, he was tempted to say, "Unfortunately you're right. It's a cold case. We don't have a damn thing to go on and there is no way we will find the killers. It will be a cold day in hell when we catch him, or them."

He found himself incredibly drawn to Glory for countless reason. He didn't want to let her down, and he vowed not to give up, a promise to himself. The reason he refused to let investigation stop was Glory, although it was his chief's inclination to stop immediately. The chief wanted him to focus his efforts on other cases, which he did. But every time the opportunity arose, he would reexamine the McGuire case, while trying to stay under the chief's radar.

"Glory, it's not over, and it won't be over until I have those thugs behind bars. Just hang in there, sweetie. Never say never, Glory. Tomorrow is always a new day." *Sweetie?* he thought. *Good God, this is a client, not a date. I can't believe I said that.*

"Thanks, Marshall, I know how hard you're working on it, and I understand, believe me, I do. I know there is a chance it will never be solved." Her maturity surprised him. Face-to-face with a tragedy, she had grown. Such a thing can do that to anyone.

Unhappiness hit her full force when he left town, but she didn't know why. Marshall was a good man, good to her, and she truly believed he could solve the case. She accepted the fact that in all probability it would never happen, but she was grateful for his attempts and appreciated his endurance.

Marshall was now pretty well acquainted with the locals, and they enjoyed his visits and his discussions of the "big city" whenever they gathered at the café. All except maybe Lucen.

Marshall tried to avoid Lucen as much as possible on his visits to Spalding. Lucen never took to Marshall. And Marshall thought he never really took to anyone outside of Victoria, and even that was questionable at times.

When Victoria heard Marshall was flying in, she joyously prepared a feast and begged him to come to supper. Just to appease Victoria, he made a point of stopping for a meal once only on each visits.

Usually the meal included Tanner and Weber. And as predicted, Lucen would say little. Minimal socializing took place wherever Lucen was present. Marshall dared not bring up information or questions about the investigation at these times, not in front of Lucen. He would leave with a bitter taste in his mouth and wondered why Lucen, Tanner, and sometimes even Weber clammed up when he came.

On Glory's eighteenth birthday, August 10, 2005, Victoria again intended to celebrate, since celebrations were few and far between. Only since Glory came had Victoria been able to justify a party. Lucen ho-hummed all kinds of celebrations from birthdays to Christmas and even hated to see the window decorations in town on Halloween. Now, with Glory there, she had a chance to have a party. What she considered was everyone's favorite was served: fried chicken with the works.

In the midst of the festivities, Victoria turned serious. "Glory, today you're eighteen. I hope you know you are welcome here, *always*. If you want to stay here, you can, and I hope you will choose that. I don't want you to return to Florida. I would be so happy if you stayed; you have brightened my life in more ways than I can say."

Lucen spontaneously jerked his body sideways, glaring at Victoria as if to imply, "What the hell does that mean?" But he uttered not one word. Of course, the glare didn't evade Victoria's notice.

"I mean, it's just, you're the daughter I never had, and I would be heartbroken to lose you." Even under the threat of more glares, she looked Lucen's way and smiled, implying, "I'll say what I want." Glory understood her meaning: she was family.

Glory replied, "Thank you. You mean the world to me to." And she took note of the interaction between Lucen and Victoria.

The gifts were small but each was a token of love: A heart charm to add to her bracelet from Weber. A pair of rubber shoes from Victoria. ("For gardening," Victoria piped in, just in case no one knew what rubber shoes were for). A movie pass for the Lambert Theatre from Tanner. The birthday cake and pie from Olivia.

She had grown extremely fond of Victoria and couldn't imagine life without her. Her friendship with Tanner developed into being best friends, and she couldn't envision being deprived of his incessant chatter. She actually had no one in Orlando— no one but Marshall. He had his own life, and once this case was over, she would most likely never see him again. She decided to take it day by day; there was no great rush to choose one way or the other.

When it came to dating, activities in Spalding and Lambert were limited. But since both Glory and Weber rose early in the morning, they didn't like to travel far and get home late. Most of the time, dates involved the Lambert Theater, holding hands, and sharing popcorn and a pop.

It felt so natural to her to have Weber by her side, holding hands. In the summer they drove to go to the lake or the river and had a picnic.

This night, when the movie ended, they decided not to stop and eat; popcorn had filled their bellies to capacity. Weber drove toward Spalding.

As they neared Spalding, just before entering Main Street, out of the blue and with a quick flick of his wrist, Weber tugged the steering wheel to the left, pulling off to the side of the road. He turned off the motor and swiveled his body toward Glory.

She tried to guess why he was stopping. Car trouble or a flat tire? If they drove just a little further, they would be in the heart of the city; there were lights there.

"Glory," he said, looking intently at her, "I know you are trying to decide what to do with your life. I know things have been hard for you here, not like your fancy life in Florida, but I hope you can find happiness here. I hope you won't leave."

"Weber, if it weren't for you and Tanner and Victoria, I don't know how I would have made it through it all. You are all so important to me".

Weber noticeably trembled as he took her hand. "I'm not so great at words, Glory, you know that, and I'm not a romantic type a guy, but I want to tell you how much I care for you." He paused, swallowing so hard he made a muffled gulping noise. He hoped for a response that would make it easier for him to go on, but there was none. Glory's eyes looked directly into his, with a hint of surprise at his urgency to tell her something.

"I know we haven't known each other but a couple of years, but I'm crazy about you. You're the prettiest girl I know and, well, Glory, I'd like to spend the rest of my life with you."

Mystified by this sudden outburst of affection, Glory was speechless. She gasped while trying to decipher his meaning. "Weber, I love being with you, I love when you hold me. You make me feel safe, but I am not sure exactly what you mean."

"Glory, I think we should get married. I don't make a lot of money, but someday I will. If you keep working at the café, I think we can make a good life together. There is a little house for rent, just behind the clinic, and I think it would be perfect for us. What do you think?"

She raised her hand so the palm would gently touch his face, and she felt a comfort. "How wonderful you are, and I do think we have a lot in common, but this is something I want to think about a while. Is that all right?"

Weber did not understand but told her he did and that if she said yes, he could wait until a later date. "Maybe at the end of next summer would be a good time to get married, when you're nineteen."

His face turned a pale pink, this time from being so outspoken. As he tensed up once more, waiting for her answer, she saw how difficult it was for him to express himself. He was, after all, a solo man—until they started dating.

She had sensed his lack of confidence as he spoke. "Oh, Glory, let me know as soon as you can. I can't stand waiting for you to say yes."

They sat cuddling in each other's embrace. Weber reached out one hand, turned her head toward his, and kissed her like never before—and with an intensity she had never experienced.

She thought back to her first meeting with Weber and knew she had been right; he could indeed melt a bucket of ice cream, and this kiss had melted her heart. She really cared for him, but not until this moment had she known how much.

Her experience in relationships was next to nil. Her father had been extremely protective of her, allowing her only minimal dating. He would let her go skating or to a movie in the afternoon on Saturdays, but never at night. He would say, "Honey, you've got your whole life to date. Just wait until you're seventeen at least before you date at night."

This romantic relationship that had developed with Weber was her first serious one—one that was overwhelming her with his desire to marry her and her desire to be with him.

He released her, started the truck, and headed back to Lucen's.

During the drive, she began to analyze her true feelings. He made her feel safe; she enjoyed spending time with him; he knew when she needed comfort, when to touch her face, and when to wipe away the tears. She perceived his love from the actions he took to make her comfortable and at ease at all times.

As they drove into Lucen's driveway, still holding hands, he stopped the truck. Again they stared into each other's eyes for what seemed an eternity.

Before separating for the night only in body but not in mind, they shared another simple kiss goodnight. Glory went into the house with a smile on her face, and Weber left with a smile on his.

Now she had to decide between college in Orlando and a wonderful man to spend her life with. She knew if she married Weber, she would probably never see Orlando again. This was a tough decision, because she missed "home" so much. She knew she'd have a good life with Weber, that he would take good care of her. They would make their own fun, as they had been doing. Lambert wasn't that far away if they wanted some time out of Spalding; if you can call Lambert a town, it is more like five Spaldings put together, but it did have a theater and restaurants, a motel with a swimming pool, a nice park, and even a miniature golf course. They could travel another sixty-five miles and be in an even bigger city than Lambert.

The next morning, after waiting for Lucen to start his chores, Glory approached Victoria about Weber's proposal. Victoria's look of surprise was unexpected. "Darling, you haven't known Weber very long, and I know how bad you want to go home to Florida. You better give this a lot of thought."

Glory did not understand her reluctant response. "We've known each long enough, and we spend all our free time together. He's really good to me."

"Honey, I like Weber, and I know he and Tanner are very close, but your happiness is what's important. Have you really thought about this?"

"Yes, I thought all night. Victoria, I feel safe with Weber. He is kind and gentle, and I know he loves me. He'll take good care of me, and I'll stay in Spalding."

A smile grew on Victoria's face, even though she still had concerns for Glory's happiness. She knew what a hard decision this must have been; one to return to your home, where you grew up and two to stay in this remote town. She knew the decision wasn't taken lightly, but she hoped it was the right one. She didn't want Glory to have any regrets later for not returning to Florida and going to college. "Do you love Weber?"

At that moment, knowing Weber like she did and that perhaps he was the man of her dreams, she said, "Yes, I do love him."

Serious concern transformed into joyous laughter as Victoria practically jumped out of her chair. Heading to the counter for another cup of coffee, she exclaimed, "I need to wake up; I think I'm dreaming. Now we are to plan a wedding. You are like a daughter to me. Oh, Glory, I am so happy for you. I am so thrilled you will be staying in Spalding. It means a great deal to me to have you close. Oh, my gosh, we have to tell Lucen. We'll have to break this to him gently; he doesn't like surprises, you know. Oh, gosh, I am rambling on, aren't I?"

And with that, Victoria got out a tablet and a pencil. "Okay, let's get started. These kinds of things take forever."

Glory couldn't understand the sudden change in Victoria's attitude, but she guessed that once

Victoria was assured she loved Weber, things were okay with her.

The fact is, Victoria had her reasons for doubting; history had proven that what you think you see is not always what you get. She was genuinely concerned that Glory was making the right decision for the right reasons. She couldn't tell Glory that—someday maybe, but not today.

"I haven't actually told Weber I'm accepting his proposal. Last night I told him I needed to think about it."

Victoria shrieked. "Well, call him. Call him now!" Glory assured her she would call him a little later, and she suddenly wondered what her father would think of her marrying a mechanic. He would have some objections, unless the mechanic owned his own lucrative business. He had always told her to be sure to marry a professional like a doctor, someone with a secure position. She tried not to think about that.

Victoria could hardly contain her enthusiasm. Her longing to bust out in song and dance was strong, but she quelled her desire to do so. Now her duty was to plan the best wedding celebration this town had ever seen—a wedding Victoria wished she could have had herself.

Victoria and Lucen were dirt poor back when they married. Lucen didn't make much money, and Victoria didn't have so much as a dime to her name. They married in a simple ceremony through a Justice of the Peace.

She thought about asking Garrett Sanders for the money to pay for the wedding but quickly decided not to. "The McGuires can handle their own. Glory would appreciate the wedding more if I put all my effort into it."

That evening Victoria approach Lucen on the front porch swing. "I need to talk, Lucen."

He grunted, as usual. "What's up?"

Shyly and with a built-up tension, she conveyed the message in the least disruptive way possible. "Well, you know Glory and Weber have been seeing a lot of each other and—"

"Did that girl go n' get herself in trouble, did she?"

Victoria laugh, and Lucen glared at her like she had a screw loose. "No, no, Lucen. Weber has proposed."

"Well, they haven't known each other that long to be thinking 'bout marriage."

"You know, Lucen, love cannot be timed; it just happens. And they want to marry this summer, I think." She paused. "Lucen, are you okay with this?"

Lucen thought for a few moments, lowering his brow in the way he did to make sure nobody knew what he was thinking. He looked up and said, "Yeah, okay, but you tell that girl if she makes her bed then she has to lie in it, for better or worse." End of the conversation, per Lucen.

Victoria knew better than to say or ask any more than she had on the subject. Lucen did not like small talk and did not want anyone rambling on about what he called "girl stuff."

Victoria ran into Glory's room and told her it was okay with Lucen, as if that really mattered to

Glory. If she wanted to marry Weber, she would with or without Lucen's blessings. Glory immediately called Weber. "Yes, Weber, I'll marry you."

He shouted "Hoorah! When, Glory, when?"

She didn't want to be pressured into setting a date just yet. "Maybe this summer would work, when I turn nineteen." That was enough for him. They said good night and hung up.

That night Glory called Marshall. She sounded so excited when she informed him of the happy news, he did not want to burst her bubble. He chose his words, carefully, not wanting his utter disappointment to be detected in his voice. "Tell me all about this lucky fellow."

For a moment, Glory said nothing. "He understands and cares about me, and he wants to take care of me. He is a good guy, Marshall. It's Weber."

Was there a bit of hesitation in her voice? "Let me know the date, and I'll be there," he said reluctantly.

She asked Marshall to contact Sanders and tell him that, since her care allotment wouldn't go to Victoria anymore after she's married, he should put the money into savings for her.

An unsettling question popped into Marshall's head: "You can have the money for yourself, you know?"

She was so quick to respond that doubts about the marriage rose in Marshall's mind. "No, I don't want to rely on anyone for anything. My husband and I should be able to make it on our own. If the time comes when I need it, I'll let you or Sanders know." She even surprised herself.

Glory wondered why had she spouted this off so quickly. Why hadn't she said that, yes, the money would help them get started. She just felt it to be the right thing to say.

Marshall was pleased to hear Glory was planning to make sure Weber stood on his own two feet to support them. *Good for her*. He told Glory he'd contact Sanders right away.

Later that night, Weber and Glory spent forty-five minutes on the phone, going over the main points of what needed to be done. Once they'd set the date for a few days after August 10th, which was her nineteenth birthday. They decided on August 19th. Now set, they both felt more relaxed.

He talked about a bungalow he found for rent and convinced her he would handle the rental. "I want the house to be a surprise for you, Glory, so don't be going over there to check it out; you can see it on our wedding day."

Glory thought this very gallant and flattering. "Thank you, Weber. I promise I won't peek at the house until then."

"I'm going to call Tanner right away and tell him, Glory. He'll be happy too." Enthusiasm burst out with each syllable he spoke.

"Okay, I called and told Marshall already."

"Okay, baby, I'll call you tomorrow." He was none too happy she had called Marshall about their wedding.

Weber called Tanner, who hardly had time to say hello before Weber blurted out, "Tanner, Glory and me are getting married!"

It took Tanner a moment to register that statement. "What? You're marrying my cousin? Is this a joke?"

"Heck no, man, I'm serious. We're getting married after her next birthday."

"That's great, Web." He wasn't being the least bit sincere.

"That's in August, not far off. Got to go. Just wanted to let you know she said yes."

"You treat her right, Web. She's my cousin, and you treat her right."

Fear gripped Tanner as he thought this may alienate him from Glory. *Maybe Weber won't like me hanging around so much.* He hoped not, because he didn't intend to let her out of his life. She was family, after all.

CHAPTER 16

AN EVIL OBSESSION

All aspects of his plan were evolving well. Glory was in Spalding, and she had developed a close relationship to all the family members: Lucen, Victoria, and Tanner. To his delight, she now had committed to stay in Spalding, thanks to the proposal. Satisfied with his great acting performance, he said to himself, "Am I really that good at this?"

He had some reservations about how well the final stage in his plan would be executed. Since its inception, he had decided to "Keep the Faith."

He attempted to formulate his words carefully to portray a desire to comfort. "How you doing there? Everything okay?"

Not much reassurance was received. "Okay, I guess. It's hard waiting for you to get this finished. How much longer?"

His moderate patience level was beginning to wear thin. He did not like being questioned and he did not like not having control. He had calculated every move so cautiously, and not being able to discuss openly the situation, other than by phone, made it more difficult.

His voice rose slightly. "Well, you've got to wait; you don't have a choice. You knew about waiting before I started this. You knew it would be difficult; it is not easy for me either. Damn it, didn't I tell you that at the beginning of this? Didn't I?"

The outburst was not appreciated. "Yeah, you did. It is just that it's getting harder every day. It's taking forever."

His head began to pound; his temples vibrated until the beating in his eyes became intense. Just one more word of doubt, and he may lose his composure altogether. "I don't like this situation either, but it will take time. Damn it, hold on. I am counting on you. If you don't think you can handle it, tell me now."

Those last words meant, "Tell me now because if you can't, you're dead today." After all, what was one more death to him? So the words came out in a fearful whisper "Okay, I can do it. I'm fine, really. Really I am."

"Talk to you later." And he hung up.

He sat alone, thinking. As days turned into months and months slowly crept into years, he had somehow held on, some days by only a thread. He wasn't alone in this, and that yielded more nervousness in him than the acts he had committed. Confident no slip ups would take place on his part, his worry was, *What about someone else?*

But there was nothing worse than being a skeptic. He had been precise in his planning, so skepticism was not his norm, and overcoming that emotion now was wearisome. It wasn't just him now. Someone else could, in a split second, interrupt the whole scheme.

His adrenaline pumped harder on days like this, brought on by a combination of satisfaction and fear, both equal in intensity.

In order not to create any suspicion, he led his life circumspectly, keeping his eye on each individual. Each word he spoke was calculated to benefit no one but himself.

He pretended to be whatever he anticipated someone else was expecting. He continued working hard, being cheerful, and thus manufacturing a persona of an easygoing guy. They had to believe he was worth believing in. He knew if he got too comfortable with himself and his actions, he would make a mistake. So he kept his eyes and ears ever ready for any sign that things may be amiss.

He dreamt of the money, the success, the years of fun, and a lavish lifestyle ahead of him. Once he was gone from Spalding, he could be himself again. Time was going by faster than he thought it would. In the end, there might be no one but him. It was a sad thought, but one he had to consider.

As each hour passed, he heaved a sigh of relief. Each day brought him one day closer to his goal. One wrong move and it could all go up in smoke. He couldn't let that happen.

Little did he know he was on the verge of losing control of his own thoughts, losing control of his composure. He didn't realize he had developed an egotistical mindset that he was invincible. He was creating in himself his own worst enemy.

He never much liked chess, but he viewed this undertaking as he would a game of chess. He, of course, would be the king, and all the players were pawns—and they were playing the game accordingly. Soon he would be able to say, "Checkmate."

"Trust me," he would say, and people did. He didn't frequent the bars, didn't run from town to town, but appeared to be more stable than ever, working hard to gain everyone's trust, and he did.

He tried to contrive a means of keeping Detective Marshall out of the picture. The only other time he envisioned the plan not working was when someone entered the picture who could blow him out of the water, like Marshall.

He didn't like Marshall anyway. He especially didn't like him being so close to Glory. Whenever she mentioned Marshall's name, he felt tense. If Glory ever said anything about him to Marshall that may cause him to question his "good intentions," he was up a creek minus a paddle. Marshall wasn't about to give this case up for "cold," he knew that.

If it came down to him or Marshall, he assured himself Marshall would be the one to go. In fact, if it came down to him and *anybody* else, he knew there would be no hesitation, on his part, to blow that person away, no matter who it was.

"The trap is set. Come to me, little mouse. You are so close." He was so obsessed with his scheme that he had begun playing games with his own mind. "No one's suspicious, and there's no way to connect the dots. Ha! Oh my, but I'm good. Stay focused, stay focused. The mouse is near the trap."

CHAPTER 17

A WILTED BOUQUET

Glory was not totally convinced she was prepared for marriage. A wedding may not be the solution she'd been searching for, the one to fill the void she felt. But she'd committed now, even with the hesitation in her heart. Weber indeed was a wonderful man who cared for her. But now Orlando was out of her sites, and that saddened her.

She tried convincing herself this was the right decision. "Wouldn't happiness be greater than anything else? Isn't having someone love you the ultimate goal in life?"

Glory just didn't have the enthusiasm she thought she should. Even when picking out her wedding dress, she had settled on simplicity. It was a beautiful dress, purchased in Lambert. Victoria had offered to take her into Sioux Falls, but Glory had declined, saying Lambert carried nice garments and she would find a pretty one there; and she had.

It had lovely, white, eyelet fabric with an empire waist, was slightly off the shoulder and cocktail length. Victoria made her a pink ribbon belt that accented it perfectly. It would be tied into a big bow to drape down the back of the dress skirt. It was certainly not the big, fancy, satin wedding dress she had dreamed of, the one with the flowing train like her mother had worn and all the brides' magazines displayed.

Victoria's flowers would be a centerpiece for the wedding. Her carefully groomed and pruned flowers would make a spectacular background for the celebration. Victoria bubbled with excitement.

Glory's bouquet was a combination of pink mums and white roses with various other colors scattered throughout. There were small white flowers in her golden hair as well as a small veil that came down just over her exquisite blue eyes.

She found a pair of satin shoes that she had dyed pink. *She will look like a garden herself,* Victoria thought with pride.

One weekend in July, Glory and Weber traveled to Lambert to pick out rings. Aware of the fact that Weber had little money, she wasn't expecting much.

As the rings were placed on the counter, sparkling in black velvet cases, she eyed a beautiful three-quarter-carat, three-diamond set. She nearly fainted from suspense, hoping those would be the rings he chose. To tout those glistening stars on her finger for the whole world to see would give her a feeling of being loved that diamonds often offer the bearer.

As she looked up, she saw Weber gazing at a pair of matching bands. Disappointment mounted as she realized that was what he could afford. Weber smiled, swelling with pride that he was able to get rings at all on his budget.

He asked the clerk, "Let's see those." They were a pair of gold bands with one small diamond stone centered in each. The clerk put them on the table. "Oh, those are great. What do you think Glory?"

Glory looked at the rings and saw a little label at the bottom that said "Zirconium" and a price tag of 250 dollars for the pair. "They're beautiful, Weber."

He told the clerk, "We'll take them." The clerk looked straight into Glory's eyes, as if to say, "Sorry, honey."

Glory mailed Marshall a short note confirming the date of August 19 for the wedding. She had tried to make it coincide with his next scheduled visit around that time. She wrote, "You have been so supportive over these last few years. You are my friend. It would mean a lot to me for you to attend. I know it's a long trip for you, but please try to come." She hoped he would come. But he was a busy man, a detective, always solving crimes and running investigations. She wondered if this wedding would be the last place he cared to be.

When dressed and ready to go to the church, Glory felt like she had just walked out of a magazine fashion spread. Soon after Victoria had put on her light blue crepe sheath dress, she had purchased through a J.C. Penny's catalog they headed for the church.

When they arrived Gory saw a rental car with Lambert Motors on the license plate, she knew in a minute it was Marshall. Her pulse increased as she stepped out of her car. The rental car door opened, and out he came, this time dressed in a suit. *How handsome he looks,* she thought. *How very very handsome.*

Without hesitation, she asked Victoria to go into the church and said she would following right behind her. She secured her footing in her pink heels and ran to Marshall. Her arms wrapped around him and then, realizing this was a little embarrassing for them both, she let go and backed up. "Oh, Marshall, I am so glad to see you. I never thought you'd be able to make it. Thank you so much for coming."

He smiled. "This is a special day for you, and I wouldn't have missed it for the world. Oh, by the way, happy birthday, Glory." He handed her a small box.

He hadn't brought a wedding gift, only a card, which he would leave in the basket inside the church. He was compelled to make sure she received a birthday gift but, because he was rather detached about this wedding he couldn't bring himself to celebrate it any more than he had to.

She asked him to stay after the wedding, hoping there would be time to talk. "I have a room in Lambert," he said, "but I'll only be able to stay one more day. If I don't get to talk to you today, maybe we can meet tomorrow."

She smiled and explained that she and Weber would only have one night in Lambert then be back to work. After they saved money, they would take a nice honeymoon. "Maybe the Bahamas. Maybe next year."

The wedding was at the local and only Lutheran Church. The McGuires and many of the town folks were in attendance, but none of her few friends from Florida were able to attend except Detective Marshall.

Flowers adorned every nook and cranny as well as each pew in the chapel, courtesy of Victoria's now empty garden. Victoria was overjoyed showing off her green thumb and her floral arrangements. Vibrant shades of pink, yellow, lavender, and green billowed from all corners. Flowers also lined the entrance to the aisle. And many exclaimed that the wedding bouquet was the most beautiful they had ever seen.

Into the church Glory went.

She had asked Tanner to walk her down the aisle, which he said he would do proudly. She had wanted to ask Lucen, but she knew he would just scoff at the idea, so she decided not even to approach him with the request.

The conversation she had with Tanner about walking her down the aisle had given her some doubt. "Glory, are you sure you want to settle in Spalding? To be married to a mechanic? You'll have to keep working, and you could have a better life. Weber's a good guy and all, but are you sure?

Are you *really*? What about your dreams and what about Florida?"

"Well, when you love someone, you're willing to give up a lot of dreams you may have had."

"I know, and I'm sorry, I just want to make sure Weber is the guy for you?"

Glory had swiftly turned her head until she faced Tanner eye to eye. *Why all this doubt?* she wondered. *Just a few days before the wedding, and he is asking questions about me making the right decision.* Before she knew it, she spoke in a whisper, "I think so."

"Then I'm happy for you. I really wanted you to stay here, really wanted that a lot."

After a short ceremony with no special vows exchanged, the pastor pronounced them man and wife, Glory and Weber Arturo.

Those in attendance applauded as Weber and Glory made their way back up the aisle. They left in Glory's car, while everyone prepared to meet again in the church basement for the reception. They drove around town twice and then parked for a few minutes at the café while the people in attendance had a chance to get to the reception area.

They entered the reception room and again there was applause. Of course, the first dance belonged to Weber and Glory. His arms wrapped tightly around her, holding her as if implying she was his now and would be his forever. Now she did feel more secure in her decision to marry him; this is what she wanted to know.

Olivia and Victoria had made the cake, a glorious three-tier white one with a plastic bride and groom at the top and little white icing dots all over.

Glory was visiting with the guests and emitting a great deal of happiness. As she glanced at the corner of the room, she was surprised to see Marshall sitting at a table for four, alone, watching everyone in the room, especially her. She excused herself from her guests and quickly walked over to his table and sat down.

She felt a strange connection to Marshall. Perhaps it was because he had worked so hard to help find out why her parents were murdered. Maybe it was because she knew she could always count on him. She looked at him and smiled, and he returned the gesture. *Her eyes are dancing,* he thought. *She must be happy.*

"What do you think of it all?" she asked.

"Oh, it's very nice." But he knew that if it was his wedding and he had a beautiful girl like Glory, a girl who turned heads everywhere she went, a girl whose voice could stir up a man's desire, there would be an orchestra playing. Gold and silver trimming and embellishments would be everywhere; crystal chandeliers would drape from the ceiling. It would be the wedding of a princess. He reminded himself not to go there. *She is happy, and that is that!*

She asked him to meet with her the next afternoon, and they arranged to meet at three, after her short shift at the café. Weber would be back at the bungalow, completing last-minute details before taking her there after her shift.

Marshall was delighted. He had thought he would leave the wedding and fly back without having any time with her. Now he was going to spend time with this magnificent woman—no longer the little girl he had met a few years earlier.

Extending her hand toward his, she said, "Let's dance, Marshall."

He laughed a hearty laugh. "Dancing is something I never majored in, Glory. You may be sorry."

She laughed and reached her hand further until his. "Who cares. Anyway, you just have to move back and forth. It's that easy." With that she jumped up from the table, threw her head back, and led him to the dance floor.

God, he thought, *she is gorgeous.* He followed her out to the dance floor for their first dance. And he took pleasure in having her so close to him. Thoughts of her beauty filled him with joy as he held her as tightly as he dared to. He momentarily closed his eyes, consumed by her scent, the smell of an angel. His heart raced.

Weber cut in, grabbing Glory's arm and with his other hand pushing at Marshall's chest forcefully. "You don't mind, Detective, if I dance with my wife?"

Marshall gave a short bow to Glory as he responded, "Of course, enjoy. Thank you, Glory, and congratulations to both of you." He walked back to his table.

As he watched the dancers, his eyes were of course drawn to Glory. He noticed, but didn't much like, the fact that Weber was holding her tighter than he had before. Her head nestled in his shoulder, just the way he wished he could have danced with her.

Weber's eyes were glazed over with apparent fury. He also had an awkward, crooked smile. It made Marshall uneasy. He felt it a perfect time to leave; it was getting late, and he wanted to get to his motel and review his notes. He went outside and drove to his motel in Lambert.

In anticipation of the coming day, when he could see Glory again, filled his mind, he forgot about his notes. He lay on the bed with visions of her swirling in his head.

Glory was somewhat apprehensive about her wedding night. She knew nothing about lovemaking, except what she had read in a few magazines like *Cosmo.*

She had been grateful Weber never pressured her into sex before they were married. Simple kisses and touches were it. She hoped he would be patient and help her through it now.

She was not old enough to drink, but when they got to their hotel in Lambert, after unloading their suitcases Weber insisted on going down to the hotel bar for a nightcap. She had hoped they would stay in their room, but she decided to make the best of it. After all, this was a celebration.

She ordered a Shirley Temple and Weber a Whiskey Coke. She had seen him drink on several occasions, but only a few beers. He had already drunk quite a bit at the reception, so she hoped this would be the last drink of the night. They sat across from each other, and she waited for him to take her hand or raise a toast. He didn't. He just drank, more than she had ever seen him consume before.

She wondered why he didn't seem to be conscious of the amount he was drinking. *After all, this is our wedding night. Doesn't he want to go back to the room with me? He is older, more experienced. Surely he knows his limitations.* She consoled herself with those facts while she waited and waited for him to say, "Let's go to our room."

Finally, setting his glass down hard enough to rattle the ice, he said, "Let's go." He took her by the hand, and she had to scurry to keep up.

Through the door and into the room they went. He took off his shoes, peeled off his jacket, and jumped backward on the queen-size bed so hard that his body bounced. He lay still and flat on his back.

"Come here, baby," he said as he reached out his arms.

She hesitated. "Just a minute. I've got something special for this night. I'll go put it on for you." With that, she locked the room's door and entered the spacious bathroom.

She changed from her eyelet dress to an off-white, silk, low-cut negligee with lace covering the bust area. Then she washed her face, brushed her teeth and combed through her long, blond hair. She looked at herself in the big mirror and smiled. She did indeed make a beautiful bride.

She opened the bathroom door and froze as she stared at the bed. Weber was still fully clothed, sprawled out flat on his back, mouth open, in a deep sleep and snoring loudly.

She sat down on the cushioned chair next to the bed and whispered, "Weber? Weber, are you awake?" He didn't answer. Tears began to well in her eyes. She tried again, a little louder this time. "Weber, can you hear me?" Still no response.

Then a flood-gate opened from her eyes. She suddenly felt alone. As tears streaming down her face, the drops landed on the lace negligee that she so wanted Weber to see. She brought her knees up to her chin and wrapped her arms around her legs in a fetal position.

When her eyes had almost swollen shut, she crawled into bed. She could pull the covers only as far as her shoulders. Weber had positioned himself diagonally on the bed, and it was impossible to move the blankets from under him. She turned away from her new husband on their first night together, their wedding night. And after some time, she found rest.

Glory woke to the sound of the shower running and no one beside her. She contemplated pretending to be asleep a bit longer, but just then Weber opened the bathroom door. His lower body was wrapped with a large white motel towel tucked in around his middle, his six-pack gleaming with water droplets.

He walked toward her, smiled gingerly, then came over to sit on her side of the bed. In a husky and sexy voice full of caring and love, he said, "Oh baby, I am so sorry. It was such an exciting day, I just celebrated too much. Will you forgive me?" With his face only inches from her, the fresh smell of him sent her pulse racing, as he stared right into her soul. His arms slide under and around her shoulders, and the towel dropped. He crawled into bed beside her.

They made love but it was not at all what she had expected. *Cosmo* had not prepared her for this. Wasn't there supposed to be a build-up to a special excitement for both people? Wasn't there supposed to be a hunger rising from a basic need? Wasn't there supposed to be a prerequisite to a climax that would send both their hearts racing? She had looked forward to those experiences: the excitement, the hunger, the need that could only be quenched by two people becoming one and lingering in a blissful euphoria. It didn't happen that way.

He kissed her for what only seemed like a minute. His caresses were short-lived too. Suddenly he was on top of her, his weight almost unbearable. She felt like a trapped animal with no means of escape.

What happened to the long kisses they enjoyed before being married, the gentle, easy touching? She anticipated the special thirst between two lovers. She waited for him to tell her what to do, to guide her. He did not talk. She did feel his need to quench his thirst, but it left her far from the water's edge.

It took great effort on her part to hold back a scream. "Wait, wait!" All she could mutter was, "Weber, this is my first time." As he moved and moaned, he kept repeating, "You're doing fine, baby, just fine." Then it was over. He rolled off her and closed his eyes. She lay dazed and confused.

Wasn't she supposed to feel something more, and weren't they supposed to talk and cuddle now? *Well,* she thought, *here I am and here he is, and this is who I married.* She wanted to be a good wife, but this was just wrong, and she knew it.

Soon he opened his eyes. "We have to check out by ten and get you back to work at noon, so better get dressed and pack up."

They dressed and went down for breakfast. There wasn't much talk at breakfast or in the car afterward. Although he did mention he would take her on a honeymoon as soon as he saved up enough money, she listened for more. She smiled and nodded, but inside she was bursting.

How many emotions can one person hold at a time, she wondered. Sorrow, hate, love, anxiety, disappointment—each one nested in her heart at that moment.

He dropped her off at work with a quick kiss and said everything would be ready for her at the bungalow when she came home from work.

She hadn't told him about the meeting with Marshall that afternoon. She felt a little guilty about it because she was fairly sure Weber did not like Marshall very much. As he dropped her off she said, "I'll see you around five."

"I can't wait, baby. I'll see you then."

He does sound sincere, she thought.

CHAPTER 18

A NEW BEGINNING

Glory was excited that Weber had planned this surprise for her and was anxious to see what he had done with the bungalow, but her heart was still heavy. At this point, the bungalow was the only excitement to look forward to in her marriage.

Once inside the café, she began putting her purse away and remembered the box Marshall had given her the day before. She reached into her purse and took it out. It was a small glossy mahogany box with a spring that made it easy to open and close. Inside was a necklace, a silver heart with an arrow through it, and a lifetime pass to Orlando's playground Disney world. It was both beautiful and funny, an odd combination. She wondered if she would ever get back to Orlando to use the pass.

She was maybe more excited than she should be about Marshall's arrival at the café. So much so that she had trouble keeping her mind on her service. She realized she forgot a cup of coffee for Walter, but after serving it, she forgot Clarence's coconut cream pie. She even served Anna and Albert Walker their hamburgers but forgot to order their fries. "Oh my gosh, what am I doing?" she said to herself.

Whenever Marshall was due to visit, she had glowed. But why? True, they had grown close after speaking every few weeks or at least once a month. She considered them good friends, but she questioned if her feelings were normal. She thought it best not to ask anyone, just in case they weren't.

She had been watching for it since two when Marshall's car pulled up. Out Marshall stepped, again dressed casually in kakis and a polo shirt.

He walked through the café door just as Glory was removing her apron. She quickly retrieved her purse and met him there at the door.

She assumed the customers would start yakking up a storm. After all, she was just married yesterday to that nice mechanic down the road, and here she is meeting another man in the middle of the afternoon. *Too late to change the situation now,* she thought. *There are no redos.*

She moved quickly to get them on their way and away from the café as soon as possible. "Let's take a walk."

Walking beside Marshall's large frame made her oblivious to the pain her heart had suffered earlier that day. He was tall and strong, the kind of man who you knew always had your back. She thanked him for the gifts, but said no more about them.

They walk two blocks and enter the small parking area near the play ground. They sat on a picnic bench, facing each other. He coveted peering into her blue eyes. Afraid he may get too caught up in them, he diverted his gaze.

Marshall asked if she had learned anything further about the conditions of her financial care, thinking maybe after this much time either Sanders or Lucen had revealed something.

"I know when I'm twenty-one I'll get the rest of the stuff in the will, when I meet with Sanders. I've never discussed it with Lucen or Victoria. It really doesn't matter what's in it, Marshall. My parents are gone." The old hurts rose inside her. "Marshall, have you gotten any further with my case. Has anything led you to believe you might find the killer?"

He hesitated, positive his answer would not please her. "I think the intruder was there for a burglary, not expecting anyone to be home. He was taken by surprise at the presence of your parents. This is probably why nothing seems to have been taken; he got scared and left. If he ran away, leaving no prints or evidence, it impedes our investigation, and we have little to go on."

Marshall had a few ideas completely opposite to what he had just told her, but he didn't want to elaborate. His thoughts would be cause for alarm, and he didn't want to subject her to that. He had combed the documents, fine-tuning every bit of information he had until he knew all the data by heart. He knew he was missing something still. But his gut still told him he may be closer to the answer than he knew. He had a personal vendetta now that he felt he had to satisfy.

"I made an appointment with Lucen and Victoria for later this afternoon while I was at your wedding. I doubt there is anything more they can tell me, but I want no surprises later."

Glory and Marshall talked briefly—her trying desperately to reassure him of her happiness as a new bride and him trying to figure out if she was really happy or not. The spark he had seen yesterday wasn't there today.

"I'll walk home from here," she said. "When will you be back?"

He rose from the table and gently put his arms around her for a brief hug. No sense anyone seeing that and starting more rumors. "It won't be long. Call if you need me."

Glory sat in the park for nearly an hour before heading home. She'd told Weber she'd be home around five, and she didn't think it a good idea to get there any earlier.

During her time alone in the park, her mind raced back to her arrival in Spalding. She recalled her first meeting with Weber, the wedding, her wedding night, and what Marshall had said about the murders. She felt alone, yet she wasn't; she was hurting and happy at the same time. She'd have to shake off her doubts before reaching the bungalow.

Marshall drove to Lucen's home as previously arranged. Both Victoria and Lucen were waiting for him, and Victoria, in her usual upbeat manner, invited him in. Lucen was in the living room. It was almost as if he had been in that chair in the same position since last time Marshall had visited.

"Though the investigation has gone somewhat stale, I am still looking for answers," Marshall said. "I know there is something out there we've missed, and I won't rest until it's found. I told Glory I thought it was a botched burglary. It appeared the McGuires were home or they came home shortly after the perpetrators were in the house. Truthfully, I'm not so sure it happened that way at all." The room remained quiet.

After the uncomfortable moment of silence, he began again. "I'd appreciate it if you would not mention what I am going to tell you to Glory. No need for her to worry. I think this case hits closer to home, not that I'm accusing anyone, but I think someone knows more than they are willing to tell me." He paused for a few seconds. No response.

"Bear with me. I'm hoping there may be something I missed in my questioning before. Hopefully this will be the last time you'll be hit with any questions, so I apologize now." Lucen stared at him, and Victoria smiled and nodded.

Lucen mumbled, "You seem to spend an awful lot of time here. Do you think it's someone here? Marshall, are you going to find that killer?"

A lump formed in Marshall's throat. That was a question he asked himself day in and day out. He didn't want to sound pessimistic and didn't want his frustration to be apparent.

"Lucen, Victoria, it has been a couple of years since the murders. That's a long time in the crime world when there are no leads. It's virtually impossible to solve a case after that long without something substantial showing up. Now, it may seem to most people this is unsolvable, a cold case, but to me it's not. As I mention before, a clue is waiting to be discovered. I intend to discover it, and until then, as far as I am concerned, this case remains open and under my investigation."

He didn't let anyone get a word in edgewise and hadn't intended to until he finish his spiel. "Is there anything else you can think that you may have forgotten to tell me earlier? You've been here for many years; is there anyone here or anyone you remember from Orlando who would have a reason to dislike the McGuires?"

Victoria immediately blurted out, "Of course not, not here. I never kept in contact with anyone in Orlando, so I really can't tell you about anything that went on there. But here, no, no one here really knows much about our family. Well, until Glory came. I wish to God we had something to give you, but we just don't."

She paused, and said, "What do you think happened to the McGuires, Marshall?"

"You'll be the first to know when I know. I can't speculate; I'm looking for the truth. Sorry, Victoria."

Focusing on Lucen now, he continued. "What about you? Is there anything you can tell me about anyone you know?"

"Like I told you before, I haven't talked to anyone from Florida for years. I don't know anything."

"I appreciate both of you for trying to help."

Then with an air of authority, he continued on another subject. "Lucen, I was with Garrett Sanders when he notified you about the will. You are aware that Glory's allotment ceases when she moves out?"

"Yeah, I know. It's not a problem. We get along just fine and so will she."

Matter-of-factly Marshall said, "Now, I do have a concern about her car, an old Ford Escort that looks like it needs some work. I have asked Garrett Sanders to give you whatever money you need to go find a decent car for Glory. I don't think Weber can afford one, and I know she won't ask for the money herself. You'll find just the right one for her, I'm sure. I'm going to count on you to do this for me, so we both know she has a dependable car to drive. How about it?"

With no change in his facial expression, Lucen mumbled, "Sure, yeah, I can do that, get right on it." Marshall thanked him.

Marshall could sense minor aggravation in his response, though nothing had been said to agitate him.

Lucen rose from his chair and headed for the back door, turned for just a moment, and said, "You done with me?"

"Yes, thanks, Lucen." Then without further hesitation, Lucen walked out, slamming the door loudly.

Marshall glanced at Victoria. There was a look of puzzlement on her face. "Detective Marshall, we love Glory; we help her whenever we can. We try to give her what she needs, like her parents did. Now that she is married, I am sure Weber will see she's taken care of. He loves her very much. I wish we could be of more help to you, for Glory's sake, but we just don't know anything. I just don't think those killers are to be found."

He waivered at whether his next statement should be made but bit the bullet. "Victoria, are you aware that in a couple of years Glory will be twenty-one and you and Lucen will be receiving a settlement for caring for Glory before she was married?"

"Oh, not anymore. The allotment stops, remember?"

"I'm not talking about the allotment, Victoria. I'm talking about a settlement, a lump sum of cash."

"What, what are you talking about?"

"Please keep this to yourself. It's confidential. You needn't even tell Lucen I told you. David's will specified that if Glory were to go to her godparents for care, when she turned twenty-one, they would receive a lump sum settlement for her care. That is in just two years." He waited for a response.

"No, I didn't know and I'm not sure Lucen knows. He doesn't share a lot with me, you know."

Marshall asked her not to repeat his lack of confidentiality. "No one." He emphasized. "Especially Tanner or Weber." He thanked Victoria for her time and asked her to thank Lucen too. "Try to make Lucen understand it is important we get to the bottom of this, and I don't want to leave any stone unturned. And I don't particularly care if it takes twenty years to solve; I assure you, I will get to the bottom of it."

"You know, it is best I don't mention this stuff to Lucen anymore; no sense riling him up again."

"Well, don't let him forget about the car."

Marshall headed for Tanner's station. Luckily Tanner was in and remembered him immediately from a previous interview and the wedding. Marshall asked, "Got a few minutes, Tanner?" To which he replied, "Sure."

As Marshall questioned him, he asked who else worked there with him. "That would be Weber, Glory's husband. He's off today, getting his house ready for her."

"Do you know about the care your parents gave Glory until she married?"

"Well, not much. I know my folks are her godparents, and I just assumed those are the people to care for her if her parents die, right?"

"That's right. Did Glory get what she needed?"

"Well, sure, I think they took good care of her. My mom dotes on her a bunch. She works at the café so she makes a little money there. I keep her car running well, and Weber will take good care of her. I'm sure of that, and if there is anything else she needs, I'll make sure she gets it."

"Tanner, did you ever get to meet Glory's parents?"

"Heck no. When would I have done that? They lived in Florida."

"Have you ever been to Florida?"

"Jeez, no. Why would I ever go to Florida?"

"Maybe you went to meet the McGuire's, maybe to meet your cousin."

"I haven't ever been there so just forget that. We've never been anywhere but here in this dump."

"Why do you think you never went there to visit?"

"I don't know. I guess my dad and his brother didn't get along much. Anyway, that's what my ma told me, but she didn't say why. Guess I knew better than to ask."

Marshall assumed Tanner was telling the truth. He obviously wasn't aware of the monetary arrangements David had made.

Marshall did sense a growing tension as Tanner answered his questions about Florida. Too bad he had to leave the kid in the dark, but conditions are conditions, rules are rules. If Tanner knew about the allotment, it could stir up jealousy, and that would be a problem, Marshall hoped he never found out.

Tanner reiterated, "Now that she's married to Weber, you don't need to worry about her so much. He'll see to her." A slap in the face never hit harder than those words to Marshall.

"I'll do what needs to be done, Tanner. No need to tell me my job."

CHAPTER 19

HOME SWEET HOME

Weber had rented the little bungalow the day after Glory had accepted his proposal. He had made a compromise with the owner so it would be held until they married. He only had to pay fifty dollars a month until they moved in, then the rent would be 150. He wanted to secure a good home for Glory, and it gave him plenty of time to get it cleaned up. He promised Glory he would fix it up for her, and he didn't want to break that promise.

In his spare time, Weber had painted and cleaned every nook and cranny. He wanted it suitable for his new bride. What a surprise this would be for her when she got home that day.

Glory had resisted the temptation to stop by and peek through the windows when in town. It seemed to have meant so much to Weber to have her wait, so she kept her promise as well.

The yard was a disaster. She planned to ask Victoria to help her bring it to life, as she had done her own. Glory knew Victoria, with her green thumb, could make it look like paradise, just like her own place. Well, maybe not quite that nice.

She slowly walked up to the bungalow that afternoon. Weber was waiting at the door with a smile and two wine glasses. Handing her a glass, he took her hand. "Welcome home, wifey." She smiled as she walked through the door. It was much bigger than it had looked on the outside.

Weber had done a nice job of decorating, for a man. It was cozy. Glory did see a few things she'd have to change. He had gotten some ill-matched, but attractive, furniture. Though he didn't have the knack for decorating, she was proud of his efforts.

He led her to the refrigerator and opened the door; it was jam-packed with food. He walked her over to the dining room table; candles and a tray of meat, cheese, and crackers sat in the middle of the table with a bottle of wine on the side.

"Oh, Weber, this is beautiful." She raised her glass toward her husband in the toast. "I'm not old enough to drink."

"You were old enough to get married yesterday, so you are old enough to drink today." He held his glass toward her. "To us, to the future." She sipped at the wine, noticing the bottle was almost empty; he had started without her.

"Another toast, to a beautiful wife." Smiling at each other, they each took a drink. She wasn't sure wine was her cup of tea. It was bitter, but after she swallowed it, she became aware of a hint of sweetness.

Weber put his arm around her waist, guided her to the couch, and invited her to sit. "Someday things will be better; we can go places and get a nicer house. Just have faith in me, baby."

"Oh, I do Weber. I do have faith in you, and I love the house." He had done so much to make this home theirs, and she knew she should acknowledge his work.

He took her in his arms and began kissing her, stirring an excitement inside her. She feared another disappointment but loved feeling his warmth next to her.

She began to succumb to his kisses. His hands touched her lightly, sending tingles throughout her body. She stood up, closed the drapes, and removed her uniform. Semi-darkness was comfortable for a newlywed still shy and self-conscious.

He took his time caressing her from head to toe, stopping at her neck to nibble and then up to her ear lobe. Down her neck the kisses ensued until his lips were on her breasts, kissing and fondling them with his tongue.

His fingers then began a search of her body, tracing each curve for the first time. Her breathing began to quicken, as did his. Her body moved closer to him with each heartbeat until there was almost no space between them.

His hand caressed her thighs with a pressure that caused her to feel a new desire, and soon his hands touched her delicately in the places where desires linger. She released a satisfying sigh as her arms wrapped themselves around his shoulders to contain the shudders welling up inside her. This was certainly nothing like what she had experienced earlier.

He pressed closer to her, kissing her lips more passionately, his tongue running along the outlines of her mouth, tantalizing her. Again his kisses reached downward; the searching led him to new-found zones he could kiss as he nestling his head into each. She detected the hunger in his kisses, detected his wanting of her. He exhibited a masculinity she had not seen before, and her embrace tightened.

She felt herself lose all control and craved his manliness. They made love, both with hungers that left them breathless. This time there was pleasure within her. When their bodies untwined, she was spent. This was a feeling she wanted never to leave.

Upon rising, he kissed her on the forehead, pulled on his pants, got his wine glass, and filled it again. "That was great, baby." His final words led toward the bedroom, and both to a peaceful night's sleep.

The next day Victoria came to the bungalow after Glory's shift at the café. Her exhilaration poured out as she spoke. "I'm sorry but I couldn't wait to see your place. Oh my, this is as cute as a bug's ear, honey, except for that yard. You can't live here and have the yard look like that. We have some planting to do."

"I'd love that, but what in the world will we put in that weedy mess. Those are weeds, aren't they?"

Victoria broke out in boisterous laughter. "Of course they are. You're getting better. I'll teach you which ones are weeds, and before you know it, you'll be teaching classes." A wide smile illumined her face.

From that day, Glory looked forward to Victoria's visits. They would share tales often of Lucen and Weber. As Victoria talked about Lucen, Glory thought there must be something very special about him. *But darned if I can see it.*

Victoria visited every few weeks to help her rake, hoe, and dig holes for planting. Glory knew this was one task she couldn't do on her own. Victoria told her that, unlike in Florida, the cold can destroy what a person so hardily cultivates, unless the right plants are used. Glory knew she needed a full-scale instructional program to get it done right.

Victoria was kind enough to bring some plants from her garden then had stopped at the local grocery store to pick up a basket of marigolds seeds. "No matter how bad a gardener you are, marigolds will grow. They grow for anyone." That was a relief to Glory's ears.

As they played and planted, their faces took on a hue of brown earth; their clothes became brown with hand prints from wiping off their hands. The garden began to take shape. Glory prayed she would develop a green thumb and that the garden wouldn't fill with weeds before she could get to it again.

Victoria explained that because winter was coming soon, and everything needed to be in place before the first frost. "Then in the spring, we'll get to work again. Oh, it'll be fun, Glory. And with every year that passes, the garden will become more beautiful." Glory looked forward to the day her new yard would smell of blossoms like the yards back home on Sycamore South.

A few days after Victoria's visit, there was a knock at the bungalow's door. Glory's first thought was that Victoria was back to do more gardening. When she opened the door, she was greeted by a good-looking woman in her forties with a pastry dish in her hand. "Hi, I'm Marie Hansen. I live next door. I wanted to give you a few weeks to get settled and then bring you a homemade peach pie and welcome you to the neighborhood. I hope I'm not interrupting you."

Glory liked the small-town courtesy. "Come on in, I'll make us some coffee." They chatted while eating a fresh, hot, peach pie.

Marie told her she had lived in the house next door for thirty years. The house had been left to her by her parents. She married and had a daughter, Elizabeth, who was now about Glory's age. Shortly after her daughter's birth, Marie's husband had died in a boating accident, so it had been just her and Liz. She said she would bring Liz by to meet Glory in a few days. "She works in Lambert, but will be home this weekend."

"I'll look forward to it."

Glory went to Lambert a few times a month, sometimes alone, sometimes with Victoria. Today she was trying to find a hobby. After working and taking care of Weber, she found she still had free time; she needed something more to do.

Stopping at a fabric store, she picked up crochet thread and a hook and found a beginner's how-to book. So while Weber slept or worked, she crocheted or read a book.

Glory took pleasure in cooking and trying new recipes on Weber. He wasn't the keenest on this idea. He had grown up on meat and potatoes, so he thought that's what everyone should eat.

He knew it meant a lot to her, so he encouraged her to keep trying new foods. He ate most of her trial-and-errors, but a few went straight to the garbage. When she and Victoria would discuss some of these recipes and describe the reactions of Lucen, Tanner, or Weber, they'd break out in laughter. Some things were better never baked again.

Hours were spent in the yard, pulling weeds with Victoria. "I've never seen a yard with more weeds than this," Victoria said, "never in all my days. They just keep growing out of nowhere. Guess we'll have to plant more marigolds; they keep the weeds down."

"Holy cow," Glory said, "my garden is cursed! It's just cursed. This garden will be the death of me." And they laughed. Glory loved being with Victoria; she kept everything so lighthearted and never seemed to worry about anything.

"Things can always be fixed or tossed and new ones bought, so why worry," she would say. She reminded Glory of her mother.

The weeks after the cursed garden had been planted and replanted, and after Glory's shift at the café, Marie came over. Behind her was a lovely girl with brown hair and brown eyes, brilliant auburn hair and a beautiful smile. "Glory, this is Elizabeth, my daughter."

The girl beamed. "Hi, you can call me Liz."

Glory welcomed them in to sit in the small living room of the bungalow. Liz said, "I saw you during high school and thought you were beautiful. I was afraid to talk to you, you were so quiet. People knew what happened to your family."

"Yes, I do remember you. I was only there a semester, so I didn't try to make any friends. I guess Victoria, Weber, and Tanner were about the only people I am very close to. I'm sorry."

"Oh, no, don't be sorry. I understand. Maybe now we can get to know each other."

Glory liked the idea of having someone her own age as a friend. "That would be nice."

Marie chimed in, "Glory is married to Weber Arturo. Wasn't that Weber boy the one you dated?"

Liz bowed her head in embarrassment that her mother would bring it up. "Well, not really dated; we went out a couple of times. He was too old for me back then. I dated Tanner a couple of times, too, but I like boys closer to my own age."

"Do you have a boyfriend now, Liz?" Glory asked.

Liz said coyly, "Well, no, I work at the grocery store a lot and come here on weekends, so I've not met my prince charming yet, but someday I will, and I will live happily ever after." With that, all three giggled.

Glory found Liz to be a vibrant and energetic girl. She looked forward to spending time with her.

With Glory resigned to the fact that her day-to-day life was not as exactly what she had planned for herself, she knew she'd have to make the best of it. She had no great expectations of what was to come.

She spent as much time with Victoria and Liz as she could or worked on her sewing projects and crafts. When Liz came to Spalding, they would shop or just stay at Glory's for pop. Once in a while, they traveled to Victoria's and picked flowers for Liz's studio apartment.

Glory was always careful to be home or free from company before Weber came home. She had to time her visits with his work schedule just like Victoria did with Lucen.

The first time Glory and Victoria were invited to Liz's apartment, fall was in the air. Glory loved traveling to Lambert and taking in the fabulous colors of the season. They stopped at the one and only Lambert grocery store, where they found Liz. Liz's shift was over within the next few minutes, and she begged them to come to her apartment for coffee. They agreed to wait.

They followed Liz to her apartment and were surprised to see a rather rundown brick building with perhaps ten apartments. There was little parking and none for them. They parked about half a block away.

Liz apologized upon their arrival. "I am sorry you had to park so far away. It's like that here with two or three people in the apartments, and they all have their own cars."

Glory said, "No apology necessary. We're just glad to see your apartment."

As they entered the apartment, they were both surprised at how tiny it was. It was definitely a studio apartment. It was clean and neat and arranged nicely for the space allowed, which wasn't more than 450 square feet.

There was a love seat, two small chairs, and one coffee table in the center of the main living area. A small kitchen covered one end of the room, made up of one counter about four feet long with a small microwave, and a stove and refrigerator. The sink was in the middle of the counter.

A full-size bed completed the room at the far end with a cushy green comforter on top and shams to match. There was a small bathroom, just barely big enough to get one person in. Glory noticed two razors on the bathroom sink. But she had no second thoughts; she often took one razor out before discarding the other.

There was no dining-room table; none could fit into the space. They shared coffee and their usual girl-talk on the couch.

When it began to get late, Victoria said, "We better hit the road, or Lucen won't get his supper, and you know he'll be a grouch for two day."

With each visit, Liz and Glory grew closer. A few months after Glory had seen the apartment for the first time, she was in Lambert making a point of stopping to see Liz. Liz did not invite her in, but instead came out to the landing to talk to her.

"Sorry, Glory, but I have a friend inside. Not that I don't want you to meet him, but it's nothing serious yet, it's nothing special. So there's no point, is there?" Glory understood she needed her privacy.

"Well, if it does become serious I want to be the first to meet your new man."

They continued with small talk, then Glory said, "I better go so you can get back to your friend."

Liz hesitated, as if she had no desire to return to her apartment but would rather stay and chat with Glory. Then Liz got serious. "How's married life treating you, Glory? Is it as good as they say it is? I'm sure being in love has got to be great. I can hardly wait to get married and have a family."

The question puzzled Glory. She thought Liz should get back to her company. "Well, it's a little harder than I thought it would be, keeping up with a man's demands. Housework is still new to me, but I've managed it. Marriage is fine." *Why doesn't she just go back in with lover boy,* Glory thought. *Maybe he isn't so special.*

"But it is neat, isn't it, I mean, being married and all. My father died when I was young, so it was just me and Mom. I didn't have a real family like you had. Oh, I'm sorry I brought that up. I just mean I can hardly wait."

"Yes, it's neat, a family is nice." This once again reminded her of her mother and father—the family she desperately missed.

"Well, how's Tanner then?"

"Oh, he's fine. I saw him a couple of days ago. He is such a great guy and a chatterbox, but I love him dearly."

Glory found Liz to be extremely entertaining because she never knew what she would come out of her mouth. "Is he still stalking you?"

Glory laughed. "What? He doesn't stalk me. Where did you come up with that?"

Liz looked down and then straight up and directly into Glory's eyes. "I think he has a crush on you. I think he's always had one since you moved to Spalding. What do you think?"

Glory laughed, almost the point of tears. "I think you're just being silly, Liz. Tanner and I are very close, you know that. We spend time together because we enjoy each other's company, but we're cousins, after all."

"Well, it sure seems like he hangs around you a lot. Course, I understand that. I'd love it if you were my cousin."

Glory found Liz to be especially silly today but also a little irritating. After all, she had someone in her apartment waiting for her. "Thanks, Liz, but Tanner and I are family, for goodness sake! I better go now."

Glory realized that Liz did question her about him a lot. *Maybe secretly she likes him,* she thought.

Liz's final good-bye was, "Please stop whenever you can, Glory, and let me know everything that's happening in Spalding. I sure miss being there." Glory assured her she would.

CHAPTER 20

PATIENCE IS A VIRTUE

Like a web, angling left, right, up, and down, the ruse was nearing completion. Comparing the two, one would uncover few differences. The spider spins a web of entrapment to catch its prey; the man spins a web of deceit to catch his prey. Both the spider and the man need the prey alive for as long as it was necessary then…kill it. Both kill: the spider to feast, the man to play.

"It's going well. My freedom is within reach. Good God, these people are stupid. Who would have thought I could pull this off? Sweet Glory in Spalding, who unfortunately won't ever see the light of day in Orlando again. I'll be traveling all over the world, anywhere I want, in a fancy car with fancy clothes. No one is going to look down on me again or say I'm poor or a no-good, not anyone."

His agitation rose as he considered how much longer both of them could hold out without a slipup, how much longer he would have to wait to make his move. He had concocted this plan and determined to see it through. No turning back now.

There was less and less time with just the two of them alone together, out of hearing distance of others. He made contact only by phone now, when he wanted to discuss his scheme. It was too risky when they were together to mention a word of it out loud.

"Hey, it's me."

"Are you coming to the house?"

"No, we'll talk on the phone. We're getting closer. Are we still on the same page?"

"Is everything all right? Are you getting nervous?"

"Of course not! I don't get nervous. Damn it, you should know that by now. I'm not afraid of anything or anybody."

"I know, I know, but can you please come to the house and talk to me?"

"Better not. We'll see each other later, but don't mention anything, you hear me? Everything is perfect, I told you." He had a tendency to become impatient with these phone calls, but it was the only way he could keep them both on track.

"I'm tired of waiting, really tired. How much longer?"

"Not long. Hold on, you're doing fine. I'm proud of you."

"*Doing fine, my ass.*" he thought.

He wondered, in his twisted little mind, if he would have to take care of more than just Glory's parents. Maybe his cohort was getting a little to antsy. He knew it wasn't something he wanted to do, but if he had to, he would. He had no qualms about it. He wasn't about to let anything or anybody jeopardize his future.

"I'm a little scared. What if something goes wrong?"

"Nothing's going to go wrong. Get that out of your damn head. You get scared and you'll screw up. Just calm down; everything's going to be all right. Just keep doing your part, just doing what you are doing. Okay, got to go."

"All right but—"

Click.

CHAPTER 21

PERILOUS CLIMB

Well into the first half of her wedded year, Glory thought she had settled into married life quite well for a nineteen-year-old. She still struggled with thoughts of her spring garden, but she kept her hopes high. *Someday, I'll get it. I'll have a garden like Victoria's.*

It was the middle of December when she asked Weber to change the light bulbs in the garage because she needed to get the gardening tools sorted and ready for the spring.

She knew it wouldn't be long before Victoria would be over for more weed lessons; spring would be exploding its warmth and colors before you know it. If she prepared her pots now, and set up her garden tools, fertilizer and potting soils she could take an inventory to see what else she might need to get. She had decided to paint the pots of different sizes and shapes in the garage and set them in the front yard for more color accents. She would put plants in them later. She though

Victoria would be excited to see she did some decorating before she came over to help plant.

A few days later, she reminded Weber again. "Yeah, yeah, I'll get the ladder out and do it." He didn't.

A week went by. There wasn't really a rush; it was still cold out. As an organizer, she wanted to get all the tools and pots ready to go when spring and Victoria came.

She gave it one more try. "Weber, would you mind changing the bulbs in the garage so I can get started on my plant pots?"

His reaction made her body stiffen. "I told you I'd get the ladder out and do it, just give me a few minutes, will you?" She went about her cleaning, finishing the laundry. At the end of the day, after supper and when the dishes were done and put away, she walked out to the garage. Still no lights; she couldn't work on her pots. Disappointed, she decided the next morning she would change the bulbs herself.

Morning came. As soon as Weber left for work, she went to the garage, found the light bulbs, and got the ladder out. She set the ladder directly under the florescent light fixture and set a light bulb on the edge of the workbench. She began to climb.

Jeez, it wasn't like I asked him to put a new roof on. It was just a simple light bulb, she thought. *Such a small task, and I've asked him more than once. I should have done it myself in the first place.* She was more than a little irritated.

Just when her foot set down on the fifth rung, the ladder began to shake. It was a slow, unthreatening shake at first, then it began to vibrate relentlessly. In less than a second, one side of the ladder leaned to the left and just as quickly leaned to the right, then crumbled out from under her, throwing her off. She tried to grab the edge of the workbench, but it was just out of reach.

Down she went, her body twisting on the way. She saw her head aiming for the corner of the workbench. As hard as she tried to avoid it, she hit it full force. At the same time her foot slipped between two ladder rungs and, upon everything falling off the workbench, the ladder landed on top of her. She was now lying flat on the concrete garage floor.

The excruciating pain radiating from head to toe disoriented her. She had landed flat, except for her leg, which was twisted in the ladder rung. She lay there for a second or two, unsure whether she had been knocked out for a while. Groggy and confused, she thought, *I better get up and see how bad this is.*

Now aware that she had hit her head, she put her hand to her hairline just in front of the top of her ear, and it felt wet. She pulled her hand back and saw blood covering her fingers.

She pushed the ladder with her arms and at the same time tried to get her leg out from between the rungs, but the pain was unbearable. She wished she had just waited for Weber to change the bulb, but she always wanted to get things done even if she had to do them herself. How foolish she felt now.

She decided to sit for just a minute and get her wits about her before she tried again to get free of the ladder. She glanced down where her foot was between the rungs, and at one side of the ladder, where the leg supports are, she saw a clean, not jagged, break of the aluminum leg of the ladder. Her first thought was, *Weber had better take that ladder back to whoever he bought it from. It's crap.*

She again tried to pull her foot out. She knew to do so would involve enduring unwanted pain. She bit her lip so hard it began to bleed while at the same time twisting her foot so that it would slide out from between the rungs. She let go of her lip and cried out in so much pain, it was unimaginable. At least she had succeeded in getting her leg free. She lay back before trying to get up, taking large gasps of air. The pain was so intense it had knocked the wind out of her.

She could feel not only the heat but the pulsating in her foot and knew it was beginning to swell. Her head throbbed. She was not capable of standing up so she got on her hands and knees and began a baby crawl to the house.

Now what? she thought. Who should she call now? Weber would be mad if he had to leave work, and he said he had a call between there and Lambert anyway. She hoped he wouldn't get mad that she broke his ladder and the light bulb. "This stuff doesn't grow on trees, you know," he'd always her remind.

If she called Tanner, he'd call Weber, she was positive of that. So she chose to call Victoria. Lucen answered the phone with his usual "yep." She asked for Victoria.

"She's not here, went to Lambert for the day."

"Lucen, I'm sorry to bother you, but I've been hurt. I think I need to see a doctor. My leg is injured; I can't walk. Would you be able to help me this one time, please? I need to go to the hospital Lucen."

Glory almost began to cry when she heard Lucen's response; it was without hesitation. "Be right there." And he hung up the phone.

Lucen arrived within minutes, which was amazing since he was the slowest driver she had ever seen, and it was quite a distance from his house to hers.

He lumbered into the house. At once he saw Glory sitting on the floor with the phone in her lap. Blood was running down her face, and one foot with no shoe on it was red and swollen. "Reckon you do need a doctor." He bent over, grasped her arms, and helped her up, then placed one arm around her shoulder then under the opposite arm and helped her to his truck. She clung to him as if her life depended on it, and at that moment it seemed to.

"What the hell happened?" *Always so gruff and tough,* she thought. And she still feared is demeanor and standoffishness a little.

She told him the ladder broke when she was trying to change a light bulb. She had fallen.

He got back out of the truck and headed for the garage. She wondered why. He knew she needed a doctor quickly. He walked in the open side door of the garage and saw the ladder on the floor. He went over, picked it up, and leaned it against the wall then came back to the truck. Glory wondered why he had gone back into the garage, but because of the excruciating pain throughout her body, it really didn't matter to her right then.

Doctor Batton saw her right way. She required six stitches in her head, and he said she had nothing broken but the ankle had been twisted badly. He wrapped it tightly and instructed her not to sleep for at least two hours to make sure she didn't have a concussion and to stay off the foot for at least four days.

He scheduled an appointment for one week later and gave her a pair of crutches to use. Lucen helped her out to the truck and took her home. As he helped her into the house, she thanked him. He nodded, left the house, and after a few minutes of sitting in his truck, drove away.

Exhausted, she lay on the couch trying not to fall asleep.

When Weber got home that night, he walked in the front door to see her asleep on the couch with a bandage on her head and a wrap around her foot, sitting on an elevated on a pillow. He practically ran to her and knelt down. "Glory, baby, what happened?" She awoke and told him the story of the ladder.

"Why didn't you call me?" he asked.

"I knew you had a busy day, and Lucen helped me." A little white lie couldn't hurt, could it? Why tell him the real reason: the fear of telling him at all. She knew his temper about money and now with a doctor bill, a broken ladder, and a second doctor's appointment in a week, it just wasn't worth it to call him. He asked where the ladder was, and she said it was still in the garage.

He said he'd be right back and went to the garage, saw that the ladder was standing up in its original place, and checked the legs. One was broken—a clean break—and two of the rungs were bent. He returned to the house.

"I didn't cook anything; I have to stay off my foot for a few days," she said apologetically. He went into the kitchen, opened the refrigerator, made a sandwich, got a bag of potato chips and a beer, and sat at the kitchen table, eating.

She watched in bewilderment, wondering why it didn't cross his mind that perhaps she was hungry too. He watched TV for a while and then went to her.

"Oh, baby, I'm sorry about your accident. You just rest up on the couch for a few days." He kissed her on the forehead and said he was going to bed. And he did.

She lay curled on the couch and then tried to get up. It was not easy. She had to get down on her hands and knees and crawl to the kitchen. The crutches were not well fitted, and she was too unsteady on them. Besides that, they would make too much noise and wake Weber, who had to get up early.

She grabbed the ham and bread from the refrigerator, slapped it together, grabbed a pop, and crawled back into the living room, where she ate in silence. Setting her dish down on the coffee table, she laid her head on the pillow and fell into a deep sleep.

She had a dream that started with a knock at the door. She got up off the couch, and her foot didn't hurt at all anymore. She walked to the front door, opened it, and there stood her mother and father. She lunged forward to hug them both, then backed away and began sobbing. "Where have you been?" He father said they had taken a little vacation.

Then her father's shirt started to get a red stain in the collar area, then it ran down his shirt. She looked at her mother; her blouse was soaked in red. Glory started to scream, waking herself up.

Beads of sweat ran down her forehead. She looked around, realizing it was all a dream. She wept. This exquisite dream, seeing her parents, had turned into a horrid nightmare.

She thought about how she should have gone back to Florida. Weber had seduced her with his charm, a charm that was losing ground now. He had been so good to her at first, understanding the loss of her parents. Oh, as handsome as he was, she could tolerate quite a bit, but his indifference made her shudder. How did he change from one minute to the next?

It took Glory a week to get back to normal; she was isolated most of the time. Weber didn't come home for lunch, and several nights he came home late with liquor on his breath.

She knew Weber didn't like to be around sick people, and that's why he didn't show up till it was time to go to bed. She knew sick people weren't much fun, so she let it go; she didn't want to start whining or start an argument. She wasn't able to see Liz. She felt lonesome.

Victoria came over several times to see how she was doing. It was always a pleasant surprise to see her. One time she brought a pecan pie, which was immediately cut and shared with a pot of steaming black coffee. She brought macaroni casserole on Friday. On Saturday, after Weber closed the station at noon, he headed straight home and ate half of it; he loved Victoria's cooking. He must have seen it the night before and thought about it all the next morning.

Tanner would stop about every third day. They'd talk about his most recent repairs. Glory always found him so entertaining. She thought, *Well, I hear about his repairs. Maybe he'd like to hear about my café customer's favorite dishes.* That made her chuckle to herself, knowing that it would never happen.

She loved Tanner. He had a small-town boy way about him that she adored. She felt bad that he and Lucen didn't have a closer relationship.

Lucen was old, beyond his years; you could see it in his face. Glory still had doubts about Lucen, even though she understood his need for the solitude he chose.

Marshall kept up his pursuit to find the killer of the McGuires. He rehashed and rehashed his records and then decided to contact the Lambert sheriff's department for the official police report on the death of the Arturos, Weber's parents, and a rap sheet on Weber, Tanner, Lucen, and Victoria. Why hadn't he thought to get their rap sheets earlier?

Later that day the accident report was faxed to Marshall's office. He quickly skimmed it hoping something would pop out at him that would be useful. He did not like what he saw.

The only rap sheet that was not sent to him was Victoria's; she had no priors. Tanner had no apparent past problems except a few truancies and smoking in school that was reported to the police, and he and Weber had been out target shooting and shot a few of Mr. Murphy's chickens. No prosecution took place, but Tanner was required to pay for the loss of the chickens.

It was reported that Lucen had several heated arguments with people in the area but nothing of a violent nature. The police were called on one occasion on Lucen because of the severity of problem. He was arrested for aggravated assault, but that was ten years ago, and it was over the ownership of a tractor. Lucen had hit the man in the midsection when he refused to release the tractor to him. Lucen had parked it just off his property on the other side of his gate, and the other man had decided to take ownership of it. In the end, Lucen won.

Like Tanner, Weber had more than a few truancies as well as verbal arguments with his parents and teachers. Police were dispatched but no criminal action was taken. One fight ended with a kid a year older than him getting punched and getting a small cut by his eye.

Another section of the report related to Weber liking a girl and her refusal to date him. She had started dating someone else, so Weber pushed the kid around a little and punched him. He had been arrested and spent four weekends in jail and paid medical restitution to the other guy, about 125 dollars.

It was obvious that Weber and Lucen had tempers.

Tanner was easy going but did have some orneriness issues. Maybe those could be attributed to Weber, or maybe it was in his blood.

Lucen's blood was as cold as anyone Marshall had ever known. Tanner could have inherited that trait from him. Was Tanner too easygoing, trying to cover who he really was?

Marshall had his work cut out for him. Even with this new information, he was no closer to solving the case than he had been that morning.

He paused after reading the reports and put his head in his hands, supporting it with his elbows on the desk. With one hand, he started thumping the side of his head, trying to knock some sense into it. But to no avail; the only thing he gained from that practice was a throbbing headache.

The chief was losing patience with Marshall. He had asked him on more than one occasion to drop the case and file it as cold. Marshall knew he couldn't do that. Even if the chief took him off the case, he would somehow find a way to wiggle back into it.

He was not about to let Glory down, and he sure as hell wouldn't let himself down, as the professional he considered himself to be.

This investigation was ripping him to shreds. There was no way he would let go, not now. He didn't like the fact that Glory had been hurt, even if it was an accident. But what if it wasn't?

CHAPTER 22

YOU BELONG TO ME

Spring came in like a lamb, and by May both Victoria and Glory were taking the opportunity to spend the days outside working in the garden. Glory loved the sunshine; it reminded her of home and that getting through the winters in South Dakota was an experience all its own.

Though she didn't have to work at the café, it was her release from sitting at home. She compared it to therapy, like gardening was. She enjoyed the visits with the locals, loved to hear their stories, their gossip, and their laughter. With her working, she and Weber were making it without help from anyone, and she liked that fact. They weren't saving any money, but they weren't having any financial difficulties either.

Glory felt confident except for her feelings for Weber. In all, they got along, but they were merely cordial to each other. Weber was always busy running here and there to fix cars. She hoped the summer would give them more time together.

She wished her marriage was more consistent; there were so many ups and downs with Weber. She remained patient. Marriage was not what she had expected, though she thought it was like that for most people. When no one else was around, Weber could be a prince, but at other times his bear side kept her on her toes at all times.

Right from the beginning, she had her doubts but didn't discuss them with anyone, especially after what Lucen said: "You make your bed, you lie in it." Those words kept resonating in her head.

The idyllic life she had envisioned with Weber had not come to pass, but she vowed she wouldn't give up.

She cared deeply for Weber and thought he would change in time. If he would open up talk to her like he did when they were dating, she would be elated. She tried to understand the reasoning for some of his actions, or lack thereof. She assumed he had been on his own for so long it was hard for him to have someone else always in tow.

It was difficult to get close to him, and their sporadic lovemaking took on more of a hunger on his part and became less of a blend of two people in love. She wanted, actually craved that intimacy with him.

She vowed to do everything possible to maintain her job and the house, and to make sure his needs were met.

Glory also had an uneasy feeling that maybe she shouldn't keep analyzing this relationship; being held by love and fear at the same time was boggling her mind. Try as she may, the thoughts were relentless. She wanted a baby and she wanted a house, and she couldn't bring herself to accept the fact that neither were in her near future.

Glory deemed it best not to tell Victoria everything. Why should she worry her? And she didn't want to be known as a whiner. It seemed best not to let Victoria know there might be any despair in her little corner of the world.

Victoria, just like Glory's mother, always seemed to see the bright side of everything that sprung up; Glory hoped she could be like that someday.

Lucen wouldn't like it if he knew of her doubts; he was not at all receptive to misery. He would most likely say, "It's your problem; you deal with it."

How did those two make it all these years, Glory wondered. They had married a long time but didn't seem to connect; she guessed she'd never know.

After her twentieth birthday and into the next year, things ran smoothly, at least well enough for Glory to get by, to keep her sanity. There was no significant improvement in their time together or in their lovemaking. More often than not, she felt she was just there for his pleasure.

She remembered that magnificent day they had moved into the bungalow and made love so passionately; there had never been another day like that one. She did her best not to let Weber know of her disappointments; she staying ready for him whenever he was ready for her. That was okay with her; it was now to the point she initiated nothing.

Most of the time, he was so tired from working that he ate and went to bed. Their outings dwindled to almost nothing, but the few times they did plan something, it was fun just to get out, like going to a movie. Every time they went to a movie she remembered the first time they went. He held her hand. He didn't do that anymore. She missed Orlando; the theater, the nights out to dinner, and the Sundays with Victoria.

Her desire for him was decreasing, but she felt a deep obligation to him. After all they were both orphans. She had wanted to exemplify her parent and had hoped her marriage would be much like theirs.

She wished she could share with Marshall; he understood her, but the confession of such intimate problems would have embarrassed her. And what could he have done about it? He would have been disappointed in her, and she didn't want that.

Weber liked Glory to be with him wherever he went. She questioned if it was a trust issue or if he actually enjoyed her quiet company. On most occasions, she declined his invitations to "ride along with me, baby."

He had a roving eye that sent shivers up her spine whenever they did go somewhere. He had a bad habit of not just looking at other girls and women, but actually straining his neck to gawk. He never made a comment or whistled, and it never seemed like he had time to cheat. But she became angry, though she desperately tried to ignore his behavior.

She refused to mention her feelings to him; that it made her uncomfortable. Men liked to stare at pretty girls, she assumed, and he was a complex man, so she accepted it.

As far as he was concerned, she needed watching. He accused her of being overly friendly with the male customers at the café, saying she paid too much attention to them. It was the first time she had seen a jealous side of him, except for the time when she danced with Marshall at the wedding reception, which she found endearing, at the time. She tried to explain it was her job to be nice to people, men and women alike. He seemed to think the service went beyond the café.

She said, "If I'm not at the café, I'm home, Weber, or with Liz or Victoria. You know that. Why do you do that?"

He turned toward her and stared at her with fire in his eyes. She had quit speaking back to him, because he got angry. She had seen this hateful look before. *He is about to lose it,* she thought. It scared her, and she said not another word. She thought Weber must love her a great deal, or why would he worry so much about her finding someone else? She longed to say, "You've got to remember we're in Spalding, South Dakota. The prospects here are not the greatest."

From that point on, whenever he came into the café, waiting for her to finish her shift, she switched from her normal jovial self to a waitress serving food with no small talk; she was a fast learner.

His temper was unpredictable; his manner was mild most of time. Something could set him off for no reason. Usually it was little things. He would start his rants, something like throwing magazines and once a coffee cup at the wall. These times made her nervous, but again she said nothing.

Marriage was not quite the fairy tale she had always dreamed of, but there were few good times, too, like the few times they went camping just down the road to Walder's Lake for the weekend or hiked in the mountains.

All in all, Weber was kind and good. She loved his quietness and how once in a while they would sit on the couch, watching a movie. He'd wrap his arm around her shoulder, and they'd just eat popcorn, saying nothing until the movie was over. Those times were few and far between. He slept a lot—at the campground or even during a movie.

Weber took his job seriously and everyone liked his work, she had to give him credit for that. But at home, he slept, watched TV, and ate, but very little else.

Once Liz had asked her, "When are you two going to have a kid?"

But she just said, "Weber wants to get settled and get us a nice house first."

"Oh, well, I guess that's best," Liz replied.

Now reminded of that conversation, sadness filled Glory as she ached for a child, a full family, like most families. She had wanted one from the day they married. She knew now children would have to wait, if indeed a child was to be born at all. Weber was firm on the matter. She had asked him twice about it, and he had adamantly announced it wasn't the right time.

She knew they could afford a down payment on a house, but kept putting it on the back burner. In this, too, she had to respect her husband. Her mother had once told her, "I don't like your father to golf all day, but he doesn't like me to shop all day, so we compromise—he golfs and I shop." She wished she had her mother here now for advice.

One afternoon, Tanner said to Weber, "I think this detective guy is a little too interested in Glory. He hangs around too much when his work is in Orlando. Gosh, he comes here every few months and just stirs Glory's emotions up about the murders. I don't like him much either."

Weber said, "Yeah, that's what I think; the guy gets on my nerves, always looking at Glory. Crap, the case has got to be cold as a stone by now. Heck, there isn't a thing to find after three or four years. I'd like to tell him to stay in Florida; we don't need him here."

"Well, he's always poking around. I wish he'd stay away. Gets me mad. Hey, maybe he's worried about the twenty thousand dollars and he just keeps coming here 'cause of that."

Weber turned to face Tanner with his eyes ablaze. "What twenty thousand dollars?"

Tanner thought for a second that Weber was going to pounce on him. "Hold on, Weber, it was a slip of the tongue."

Again Weber came nose to nose with Tanner. "*What* twenty thousand dollars?"

"You mean you really don't know?"

"Know what? Damn it, Tanner, what is it?"

"Well, I heard Dad and Mom talking once. They got twenty thousand dollars a year to take care of Glory. You know, as godparents and all. Well, after you all got engaged, they said the money would be going to Glory, and Lucen said he was glad because he didn't want to mess with it anymore."

Weber thought about that for a while. "Well, I'll be damned. I'll ask Glory about it tonight."

"Weber, no." Fright covered his face. "My dad will kill me if he knew I heard. Please, Weber, keep it to yourself. Don't say anything; I don't want any trouble from my dad."

"Okay, okay, I'll keep my mouth shut. I'm sure she'll tell me in her own time. Gosh, Tanner, I trust her. She's a terrific girl, and she'll tell me about it."

That same week, Glory speculated that a child would not only result in her and Weber growing closer but also in her having someone who would love her unconditionally. With Weber gone so much of the time, it would be good for her. She thought she'd spend less time with Victoria and Liz and maybe even less at the café.

She knew Weber loved her; it was just that when he did talk about his feelings, it was hard for him and always had been. She just knew that if they had a baby it would change things a lot.

They didn't need much money. She knew she could draw on her twenty thousand to support a baby, to buy a house, or whatever they needed, but Weber seemed determined to provide for them. So she wasn't sure he should be told about the money quite yet. It may be too easy to count on the extra money all the time. She felt they needed to make it on their own. She could even stay at the café and maybe have Victoria watch the baby while she worked.

Glory decided to once again approach Weber with the idea. If he said yes, she would tell him about the money and that they could easily support themselves and a baby with that extra cash.

That night she prepared a nice meal, his favorite: fried chicken, mashed potatoes and gravy, and a salad. She set the table, lit candles, put on a sexy blouse, and waited.

When not called out of town, Weber usually came home around six. But at eight she guessed he had hit the bar again. Disappointed and depressed, she put away the food and washed the emptied dishes used to fres up the table. She blew out the candles.

But in about ten minutes, Weber walked through the door. She asked if he was hungry. He was. She got everything back out, heated it in the microwave, and sat while he ate. After she cleaned up, she went into the living room, where he was watching TV.

She asked, "Weber, can I talk to you for a minute?"

He said, "Sure," without diverting his eyes from the TV.

"Weber, I think it's about time to talk about having a baby again."

He immediately turned to look at her as if she had just hit him with a brick. "No, not yet. I want to be able to give you a place of your own, a home

GARDEN OF DEATH

you can be proud of, and put a little money aside before we have a baby." Did she detect a hint of anger in his voice?

She lightheartedly remarked, "You know what they say Weber: if you wait to have a baby until you can afford one, you'll never have one." She prayed this would get a positive response from him. If he said yes, she would tell him about the money.

He walked over to her, got down on his knees and took her hand in his. "No, not yet. It just isn't good timing. It is not about money and affording it; it's that we need to wait, enjoy our life together a little longer. Once we have a baby, we'll have less time for each other. Maybe in another year." His tone was sweet but definitely firm.

She had no choice; she had to agree. She hoped he was sincere in wanting to give her a nice home first and then having a baby. She thought she could take extra money from tips and start buying little things she would need for the baby and a new house. That would give her some hope.

CHAPTER 23

A NOT-SO-SUNNY DAY

In November, Glory began feeling sick to her stomach at different times of the day, whether at work or home. Olivia right away assumed the obvious. "You're pregnant ain't cha."

"No, that's impossible. Maybe I'm coming down with the flu."

Her problems continued for a few days, and on the fourth day she called in sick at the café. That day she lay around the house feeling miserable. She had severe cramps and a terrible headache, which just seemed to increase in intensity as the day wore on.

In the afternoon she began having cold sweats. She couldn't eat. She thought she should have something in her stomach, so she drank a few glasses of orange juice, thinking vitamin C would help, but soon afterward she start vomiting. The vomiting exhausted her, and her throat throbbed in scratchy, dry pain.

She returned to the couch and lay down. The cramps increased in severity. After half an hour, it was more than she could bear.

She called Weber at the station, saying something was wrong and she needed to see a doctor. He got home about a half an hour later to find Glory writhing in pain. He helped her to his truck and drove her to Doc Batton's.

Doc took one look at her and noted the color of her skin, white as a sheet, and her body in a cold sweat. She moaned with each new contraction, feeling like a sharp knife was cutting her from the inside out.

Doc administered medication that caused an instant rumbling within her, and she began throwing up. He gave her a pregnancy test, which was negative.

She continued to vomit and found some relief. Her abdomen was burning as if full of hot coals. Doc gave her another medication used to coat the stomach, hoping it would ease her pain. He then monitored her for half an hour.

He scheduled an ultrasound, knowing if she wasn't better soon, she'd have to be taken to the hospital in Lambert. The pains began to subside along with the vomiting.

Doc attributed her illness to a case of stomach flu, saying she may have eaten something a little moldy or spoiled. He recommended that she consider what she had eaten in the last few days. She could think of nothing out of the ordinary. He sent her home with some medication and instructed her to return in a few days.

Weber drove her home, helped her into the house, and put her to bed. She continued moaning, so Weber decided it best for him to sleep on the couch that night.

The next day, she still felt pretty rough, but managed to get through the day fairly well. The medication made her mouth dry. She opened the refrigerator door and saw the orange juice. As she poured a glass, the thought hit her that it might be bad. It smelled all right, though, and the expiration date was still okay, so she did drink half a glass. She also drank a lot of water but ate only crackers.

A few hours later, the pains in her abdomen began again. She scurried into the bathroom to force herself to throw up. She called Weber, and he said, "Before we go to the hospital, let's wait and see how you feel."

She did seem to get a little better after she threw up, but she was sweating profusely and another bad headache had taken hold. She decided to take some ibuprofen, lie on the bed, drink nothing more.

Maybe I'd better throw that orange juice out, just in case. She knew everything else in the refrigerator was fresh. She quickly fell asleep.

The next morning, she went for ice water in the refrigerator and noticed the orange juice was gone. She asked Weber if he drank it, and he said, "Yeah, had it for breakfast. Sorry, baby, didn't think you'd want anything to drink."

"You must have been thirsty; there was quite a bit left. Can you pick some more up today?"

He looked at her, smiled, and nodded his head "Sure. I'm glad you're feeling better baby."

The next afternoon Marshall called to tell her he wanted to touch base with her. She lied, telling him everything was fine. She asked, "Anything new?"

"No, it's been three years, Glory. It's now regarded as a cold case by the chief here." He explained they had questioned dozens of people and gone over every shred of evidential material they could get their hands, on hoping something would show up. He said it still baffled him why there was not a shred of evidence—no prints, no hairs, no shoe prints, absolutely nothing—that linked this crime with anyone.

One of the things he knew better than to relay to her was that forensics had found the blood smears to be strictly David's. None of Janice's blood was present anywhere else in the house. He did not want to scare her more than she already had been, but he knew this was one of the odd things he could use when trying to locate suspects. No potential suspect, if innocent, knew this fact.

He was angry at himself that he wasn't able to do more. "I can't tell you how unhappy it makes me not to be able to give you good news, but I want you to know it is still my promise to you that I will never give up trying to solve this case. I have to be truthful with you; it's almost a perfect crime." He disliked using the word *murder,* knowing the pain she felt when he said it.

She knew he was sincere, and she was grateful he hadn't forgotten her. She knew she could call him anytime. Though the calls back and forth between them every few months were generally just casual, they were a reassuring comfort to her. For Marshall they were much more. In his wildest dreams, he hoped Weber and Glory's marriage wouldn't make it.

Marshall had never had a long-term relationship with a woman. He had been so engrossed in completing school and landing a dream job. And usually his dates were with a group of law students. Once and only once, there was a young lady who gave him special benefits. It was not love, not even close to like. They were just there for each other when needed. They departed ways when left to pursue their own careers. He longed for a real love connection with a woman, but was willing to wait for the right one. Now that he had found her, he couldn't have her.

Each day of Glory's life was the same as the last. She expected nothing more than what was in front of her. Her shift at the café and coming home to prepare dinner for Weber was what she loved. Sometimes, depending on his arrival time, the food was a little well done and some nights stone cold. She longed for a decent schedule, like Lucen and Victoria had; it would have been so much easier.

When the monotony got to be too much, she traveled to Lambert with Victoria or went to see Liz. And when Marshall came, she found comfort in his presence and enjoyed talking to someone from the "big city."

If she had only known what Marshall was thinking about her, it might have made a difference in her way of thinking too.

Lucen had procrastinated in his search for a car for Glory. The time came when he knew he couldn't wait any longer. The Escort was needing repairs more than once a month, and soon it would be in the crush pile at the dump. He was a sharp shopper; he wasn't about to let one of salesmen pull the wool over his eyes. He found a couple of decent vehicles, but after having them checked over, he felt they weren't safe enough or the price was too high. He continued his search.

One afternoon, two cars pulled up in front of Glory's house. One was driven by Victoria. Lucen stepped out of the deep green Ford Taurus. Glory went out the door to meet Victoria as she was coming up the walk.

"Lucen went to Lambert and got this for you. Mr. Sanders okayed it for you. We have to take the Escort back to them for the trade-in."

Glory asked, "Why in the world would Lucen do that?"

"Ask me no questions and I'll tell you no lies. But don't let anyone know it came from Lucen. You get it licensed and plated right away, and if anyone asks, just say your lawyer from the estate said it was in the budget. Or say nothing. Or say you saved your wages for it. Agreed?"

Glory deduced that Marshall had something to do with this. She didn't question her any further but went to the side of car where Lucen was standing, and said, "Lucen, thank you for being so thoughtful. I was worried the Escort wouldn't make it much longer. "

Lucen's response was simply, as usual. "Me too." He turned and got into Victoria's car. Glory got the keys to the Escort and gave them to Victoria, then she signed the title over then gave her a quick hug and kiss on the cheek.

When Weber came home, he bounced in like he had just won the lottery. "Hey, baby, whose car?" he said. He knew full well whose it was, because Lucen had stopped by the shop to have Tanner and Weber check it over before he signed the purchase agreement.

Glory said, "Oh, Weber isn't it beautiful? Lucen found it for me, paid for it with money that was leftover from my parent's estate, and Lucen knew I needed a car. Isn't it great?"

"Yeah, that's great, baby." Weber acted happy for her, and they broke out the wine, each having only one glass. But he was fiercely jealous that he had not been the one to buy Glory a car himself.

Even more perturbing was the fact that it was probably out of her twenty-thousand-dollar allotment that she so casually failed to tell him about. He had a difficult time understanding why she hadn't yet told him about the money. He knew she wasn't the greedy sort, but still she kept the money a secret from him.

He didn't like her keeping secrets, but he had promised Tanner he wouldn't say anything about the money. He was her husband, for God's sake. He decided to let it go. No sense starting an argument.

He knew someday he'd be better off than today, and he needed to keep his promise to Tanner and to Glory. He would have to be careful so he didn't make it obvious how he felt about the car.

Tanner stopped to visit often, and they conversed about Florida, the world in general, current events, or car repairs.

"Tanner, when are you going to fall in love and get married?" Glory asked him one day.

"As soon as you stop being my cousin, I'll find someone. There isn't anyone else like you, Glory."

Glory chuckled to herself and reassured him his day would come. "You'll find someone that's just right for you, Tanner. She's out there somewhere."

"Well, she isn't in Spalding, South Dakota, USA, I'll guarantee you that. But if that's true, she will have to meet your approval. You're the best." Tanner paused and asked, "Are you happy, Glory?"

She had to think for a moment about all he'd said. She felt flattered but wished he wouldn't send so much credit her way. She was proud of herself, but she wished she wasn't so passive. Swearing, drinking, and smoking were not in her character, though she took a small drink of wine once in a while. She was a positive, hard-working young girl. She had learned from Victoria that seeing the positive was the way to share happiness with others.

Happy, yes she was as happy as she could be, she guessed. "Sure, Tanner, things are great."

"I just want to make sure you're not going to just jump up and leave us. We want you here."

"Stop that silly talk. I'm not going anywhere. You are my family. Your mother is really one of a kind, and we're very close, you know. And I have Weber and my friend Liz."

"Oh yeah, I know. It's good you had somewhere to go after your folks and all, I mean, like here. Ma is real keen on you too. She talks about you all the time. Guess she should of had a girl."

"Oh, Tanner, she's crazy about you. You're her son. You're special; everyone knows that."

"I still hope you never leave here. I'd be lost without you." She rubbed the top of his head and laughed.

Glory got an idea. "Hey, how about Liz, my friend from Lambert? She's real nice, and pretty too."

"Nah, she's not my type, too clingy and always dreaming big dreams. I'd have to be a much better businessman to win her over anyway." After a moment, he added, "Besides that, she talks about herself all the time. I don't think she knows nothing about me. Nope, not interested."

"How about I fix you up. We can double date?"

"Nope. Don't need any setting up."

"Okay, then be on your way, Tanner, and have a great afternoon."

Glory liked spending time with Liz. They did simple things, neither having a great deal of money to burn. Often it was just window shop which gave them a chance to daydream about things they both wanted. They would drive around in the exclusive neighborhoods and look at the fancy houses and fancy cars. Liz would say, "When I marry my prince charming, I am going to have a house like that, maybe even a maid, and a fancy, fast, red sports car. Of course I'll have a gardener. You work too hard in your garden, by the way." She paused. "Is Tanner still hanging around you all the time?"

"He doesn't hang around me all the time, and I enjoy his company, and my time in the garden is like therapy. I love nature and being outdoors."

"Oh, yes he does, he hangs on your every word; I've watched him. It's like he's fascinated with you. Strange, don't you think? I hate getting dirty; no, I think I'll have to have my own gardener."

Glory quickly responded, red faced and starting to get perturb at Liz's insistence. "I think you are reading more into it than what's there. Tanner and I are good friends and cousins, that is all. Now Liz, please don't bring that up again."

"If you say so, but I'd keep my eye on him if I were you," Liz sarcastically replied.

"Liz, I'm sure Tanner has grown up a lot since you were in high school. Would you consider dating him again? I can set it up, like a double date with me and Weber."

"You've got to be kidding. Tanner is not even close to my type. He's a goofball. Besides, I don't plan on settling in Spalding married to a mechanic, and that's where Tanner will always be. Oh, sorry Glory." Glory figured there was no sense in pursuing it further; evidently neither one of them was too keen on the other.

With Victoria and Liz, Glory was able to open up about her life and her dreams, but never about Weber. The knowledge that they both had such good hearts gave her the freedom to vent when needed. They all three needed down time from their day-to-day routines, and their men.

Glory cleaned out her purse that afternoon and unconsciously left the cell phone on the dresser. When Weber found it, he went ballistic. "You kept this a secret for years. I don't understand it. I'm your husband." It was a reaction she hadn't anticipated at all.

She had promised Marshall to keep it from everyone. Now she knew that the idea she needed "privacy" was infuriating to him.

"Why would you hide it from me?" He paced back and forth. And as he did, he thought of the allotment. She had kept both the allotment and the phone a secret. He had doubts as to her dedication to him, and his pride was hurt.

She tried to explain. "I'm not hiding anything, Weber. It is for emergencies only. I promised Marshall… It's for an emergency, that's all."

"Marshall this and Marshall that. I'm getting tired of Marshall. What kind of emergency would you have that you would need to call someone in Florida instead of just calling me?" His voice rose.

"Weber, it's just that.." As a heavy, sharp, stinging force hit her cheek. A sensation she'd never felt before.

The unexpected slap made the side of her face feel like a wasp had attacked her. Having never been hit in her life, she felt devastated. The man she loved had hit her. She also knew this was not an acceptable action for any reason, least of all because of a stupid cell phone.

It hadn't knocked her down, but it might as well have. The impact was solid. She saw him raise his hand again, and she crouched down, raising one hand quickly to shelter her face from another blow.

Then suddenly he lowered his arm to his side and bowed his head.

"Weber?" She quietly whispered.

He immediately grabbed her, holding her firmly to his chest. "Oh, baby, I'm so sorry. I don't know what came over me. You are my life. I'm sorry, sorry, sorry. Do you forgive me?"

Stunned, she looked into his face so close to hers and saw the regret in his eyes. What should she do?

Again he pleaded, "I am just a fool, and I know you would never keep anything from me. It's just that I don't know what I'd do without you, and you talking to another man scared me a little. You're all I have, Glory."

To play it safe, not wanting any further confrontation, but wanting to speak in her own defense, she murmured, "I understand, Weber. I am sorry I upset you." That seemed to appease him.

He took her into the bedroom and begged forgiveness in his usual manner, suggesting they make
love, knowing that if he just showed her how much
he cared he would be forgiven.

He kissed her gently at first. The kisses lingering on the warmth of her cheek that had turned a
hue of deep pink. Then suddenly the kisses were
stronger. She gave in while still reeling from the
slap. But she was distracted. *When did his temper first
begin? Why did he detest Marshall so much? Was this
the start of more violence?* She found it impossible to
answer her own questions but knew this had better
be the last time.

She had lost track of the times he had repri-
manded her for silly little things, forgetting to take
the garbage out, not putting salt and pepper on
his hamburger, not making the bed, and other
things that were really not importance. He made
such a big deal out of nothing. Her determination
heightened as she considered trying even harder
to please him. After all, he was sorry.

But their lovemaking was quick and none too
satisfying for Glory. Her thoughts and the sting on
her cheek had made it hard to concentrate on giving her all.

CHAPTER 24

A DAY OF DREAMING

From time to time, Glory found time to sit on the front porch alone. She would read a book often setting it in her lap and gazing over the beauty of her garden. She had not done too bad a job of learning to pull weeds. Some days she pulled so many she felt her butt was in the air more that her head.

How she loved the smell of the roses and the bright, happy color of the marigolds in the mist of the lilacs and impatience. All the colors made her dream of beauty she missed. She would close her eyes and dream of Florida.

She missed the beaches, the palm trees, and the hustle and bustle of the city, but she dared not share that with Weber, knowing him to be a full-fledged country boy.

Sometimes she yearned to get a surfboard and run onto the soft sand then further onto the wet sand that would squish between her toes. She dreamed of hitting the water, paddling out past the breakers, and steadying her surfboard for the next wave. Sometimes she would just lie on her board, listening to the squawk of the seagulls as they surveyed the water in search of food.

She remembered the power of the sound the ocean made when the waves broke as they entered the shoreline and made a sound like a sigh as the water floated up the sand. It was like the beginning of a symphony to her.

And she remembered how the sea stopped at the top of the sand and reversed its course, swooshing like it was taking all the bad in the world and sweeping it back into a deep, black abyss so that only the music of the breakers stayed on top.

She remembered how it felt to sit on the warm sand, basking in the sun all day and waiting for the coolness of night and the golden orange sunset that rose up from the edges of the earth, glimmering across the water as if the heavens had opened up and were inviting her in.

The palm trees were her favorites, with their outstretched, leafy fingers swaying in the wind, dancing back and forth like a ballerina. Once in a while, a gust of wind would hit the tops of the trees, causing the fingers to gently bow.

The flowers and fragrances of her yard back in Florida filled her senses. The memory of the vast array of dark and light greens and bright, iridescent colors of the yucca blooms as well as the oranges, reds, and yellows of the ground cover transported her. The foliage in Florida made her feel alive, kept her revved up to do the next activity: hiking, surfing, water skiing, boating, or even just sunbathing. And then there was the scent of the freshly mowed grass as the gardener made his weekly rounds around the yard. Florida's forever shining sun turned her skin a golden brown. The warmth made her feel like she was never alone but wrapped in arms of comfort.

She was saddened when she thought of all the Florida plants that could never be planted in South Dakota. They would die from the cold. *Nothing is ever left unfrozen there.*

She indeed was happy in Florida. Of course she had her parents then. She could have lived anywhere, she thought. As long as her parents were with her, she would have been happy.

Some nights, as she dreamed, her eyes would fill with tears as she wondered if she would ever be able to even visit all that beauty again.

Her skin was as white as the snow now. She hated that; she didn't have time to lie out in the sun, and Weber wouldn't like it anyway. He'd say, as he had once or twice when she was gardening, "I don't know why you to spend so much time out here, and you need to quit flaunting yourself in those little tops."

She had to admit the snowfalls were beautiful in South Dakota, as long as she stayed indoors. She looked down at her stark, white arms, thinking it best never to get lost in the snow, because they would never be able to find her. It was too cold here—below zero many times in the winter, and when the wind blew you thought you could die in a frozen mass if you just crossed the street. She avoided going outside those days.

In the winter, the snow cover took on the appearance of a plush, white carpet, at least until a car or someone's footprints disrupted the fineness of it and turned it into an unappealing brown slush. When the sunlight hit the snow-topped trees, especially in the early morning hours, they would glisten and take on the guise of jewels, as if a jeweler had sprinkled his diamond stock on them and the gems were just waiting to be plucked off.

Then she remembered how stifling late summer in South Dakota was. The humidity had suffocated her to the point of losing lose her breath just from inhaling—and sweat, the sweat was continual. Cold showers after work always felt so good to her, but within minutes she'd be sweating again, unless she were lucky enough to be able to sit in an air-conditioned room. They had a small window air conditioner in the living room but every other room, though the house was small, was hot.

Her family had traveled a great deal. Glory liked the vacations, but after spending two weeks away from her home and friends, she was always ready to go home. Like her mother, she loved learning about different parts of the country. She loved the ocean as well as the mountains, and she thought she would live near both someday. But here she was.

Sometimes the daydreams would last an hour, sometimes ten minutes, but those were the times she had a smile on her face. She became aware of it when the daydream ended, and she went back to her sewing or reading or getting up to fix Weber something to eat. The side of her mouth would ache as she recognized she had been smiling the whole time.

Sometimes she would write to Marshall while on the porch, never failing to tell him how she missed the beach and the parks. She always told him her life was good, not wanting him to know her disappointment for perhaps making a wrong decision.

She never told him much about her day-to-day life other than about the café, the people there, and being a good housewife. She never wanted him to doubt her.

She wished she lived closer to Marshall so they could talk more often; 2,500 miles put a strain on the conversations. She felt him to be a kind of therapist to her. Always positive and upbeat, he helped keep her sanity intact, unbeknownst to him. Whenever a conversation concluded, she was cheerful and she was ready to keep trying to make her life better. Marshall always told her that everything would be all right and that someday all her dreams would come true.

The years had flown by faster than she cared to keep track of. So many things had happened in her life, good and bad. Now, years after what brought her here in the first place, more changes were in store.

She wondered if she should call Marshall and tell him her thoughts about the things she found strange. Should she tell him about Weber's behavior, the slap, expand further on her illness. Was it her imagination—she did daydream a lot. Was she dreaming up all this doubt too?

No, she thought, *I've probably just had a bad run of luck. Things just happen.*

Marshall spent a good deal of time daydreaming as well, a different kind of daydream though. In his, Glory was back in Florida, and he was keeping an eye on her. She was growing up now, becoming more beautiful with each passing year, and he had become more and more captivated by her.

But his hands were tied. He could never tell her or anyone about his true feelings. They would probably laugh at him and tell him he was perverted. Granted she was only sixteen when they met, but now she was a woman, a mature woman. No longer that little girl he first met when leading an investigation into her parents' deaths. She was now, he thought, more gorgeous than ever.

He couldn't have her; she belonged in the arms of another. His daydreaming continued, because he could not control it. He knew if he had her, she would be safe, she would be loved. And he knew at that moment he would never give up hoping.

With that Marshall decided to give it one last try to pursue the murderer of the McGuires. He asked the chief for a week's of vacation, which he granted.

Marshall waited until dark and went into the station to get all his files and documents. It took him twelve trips down the elevator to get everything on a wheeled cart and down to his car. He had only enough room to squeeze into the car himself. With no cart at his home, he knew it would take him thirty trips to get everything up to his second-floor apartment.

He moved the couch and the chair to one side of the room and piled the end table and coffee table onto them. Everything he brought up went onto the middle of the floor.

He went to the refrigerator, opened a beer, and gulped it like it was the last beer he would ever drink. Fatigue was setting in. His muscular legs ached from the steps he'd taken over and over to get the documents into his apartment.

He moved his desk out of the bedroom and into the living room then began to arrange the files in chronological order on the floor. He placed a tablet and pen on the desk, along with his computer. He decided to reference everything on the floor with the disk he had prepared from that same information. He thought he may have missed a clue, a hint of what happened.

He knew haste could have caused him to miss something. If you are in too big of a hurry, you scan documents that should be read thoroughly. He planned not to miss one word this time.

He began his work by pulling files and taking notes. After six hours, he got off the floor and sat in the chair near the desk. He laid his head down on the desk. Visions of Glory floated in his head, and that was the last thing he remembered. Had someone been there to take a picture, they would have seen a very tired man, asleep with a smile on his face.

CHAPTER 25

HIDDEN TREASURES

Washing greasy clothes was a daily chore that Glory did not look forward to. They smelled rancid, even when they were clean. Weber's work clothes had to be washed separately from anything else.

Keeping up with the laundry was one of the habits she had inherited from her mother. She folded the clothes properly: towels, washrags, T-shirts, carefully matching socks and even underwear. After all the loads were dried and folded, she took them into the rooms and put them away.

The kitchen drawers were for dish towels, the bathroom for towels and wash clothes, and the bedroom for clothing. She even placed everything in its place by color. She knew she was rather anal about her color coding but liked the idea of opening closets or drawers and seeing the arrangement.

She knew Weber could not have cared less what color was where, but it was important to her. She took her domestic skills seriously and was proud of her home. *When Weber opens his drawers, everything will be so easy to find and not wrinkled,* she thought. *But he won't even notice.*

One of Weber's habits the she found hard to tolerate was his sloppiness. If he chose a T-shirt out of his drawer and then changed his mind, he'd just wad it up and toss it back in the drawer.

Periodically she would straighten the drawers by taking everything out and refolding and replacing each one—even so much as matching T-shirt or sock or underwear colors.

It was late afternoon on a Friday, a day she devoted to giving the house a thorough cleaning; washing windows, cleaning out the refrigerator, and doing laundry. She went into their bedroom to place the folded laundry in the drawers.

Opening Weber's underwear drawer, the mess appalled her. In the first drawer there were usually five stacks of underwear, about thirty pair in all, some of them ragged. He didn't like to throw things away, and when she asked him about it, he said he would sort through them someday. But someday never came.

As she took each pair out of the drawer, she refolded it and set it by color on the floor. As she looked at the colored stacks, she was once reminded of the beautiful colors of her garden.

When she pulled out the last two pair of underwear from the drawer, something fell out and to the floor. She listened, thinking there would be a thump, but no sound came. Whatever it was had to be light-weight.

She looked down but saw nothing. She then crouched down on her hands and knees and put her cheek on the carpet so she could see under the dresser.

There lay a small, purple pouch. Golden strings gathered the top, and they were loosely tied. The pouch had floated down and under the edge of the dresser leg. She picked it up. Looking at it, she knew it was the kind of pouch you get from a jewelry store when buying a fine piece of jewelry.

Her mother would come home with little pouches like this, usually all purple with a gold string, and inside would be small pieces of fine jewelry she had purchased that day. Glory always enjoyed opening the pouches to see what her mother couldn't resist.

There was no company name on it, only the phrase "Fine Jewelry." She couldn't figure out why a pouch like this would be in Weber's drawer, with nothing in it, surrounded by underwear. She thought maybe it was from a bracelet Weber had gotten her some time ago. *Why wouldn't he have given me the pouch?* But as nice as the bracelet was, it couldn't be classified as "Fine Jewelry." She was confused but decided to put it back exactly as she had found it and finish refolding and replacing the underwear.

She decided to fold only a few pieces of under-wear to make it look like a new batch of clean underwear had just been put in the drawer. There were some folded and some just thrown in haphaz-ardly that she felt she should leave as they were so it looked like nothing had been disturbed in the drawer.

The next afternoon she had an urge to spend some time with Tanner. She got the car keys out and let Weber know about her stopping at the station, on the pretense something was wrong with the car. She felt that since he had to tow a car from halfway to Lambert that morning, she would take it in to Tanner.

Weber's response was, "Probably the spark plugs need to be replaced and if you'll just wait till I get back I can fix it."

Glory didn't want him to fix it; she just wanted to see Tanner. "Well, I haven't seen Tanner for a while, so I think I'll go ahead and take it to him."

Soon she was on her way, and as usual Tanner was all smiles when he saw her. Since she had married, they'd had less time together, and he wanted to have more. He nearly crushed her with a bear hug. "Hey, cuz, I've missed you. How are you doing?"

Glory hesitated, unsure where to begin the conversation she planned to have with him. They had become extremely close over the years, and she knew she could trust him. But to create any doubt in his mind about her relationship with Weber may be going too far. She just stood there as he waited. "I can tell something isn't right, Glory. What is it? Are you and Weber okay?"

She still hesitant, wondering if this conversation was needed at all. "Tanner, I need to talk to you about something, but have you keep it confidential. Can you do that for me?"

"Of course. You're my best friend. You can tell me anything."

"Am I really your best friend or is Weber your best friend?"

"You're both my best friends. Why, what's up? Now I'm getting worried about you"?

After he promised on his life to keep the conversation just between the two of them, he gave her a look indicating his trustworthiness and that he was all ears. "Okay, cuz, I promise."

She decided to be brazen with her questioning but careful not to sound like a crisis was occurring. She wanted no trouble between Tanner and Weber. She asked about Weber's past, especially his parents. She knew the facts from what Victoria had told her, but she felt Tanner knew Weber in a way Victoria didn't.

"Exactly what do you want to know?" he said.

"I know his parents died in a car wreck. What do you know about it?"

"Well, all I can tell you is that the cops said there were slide marks, but they were the kind made by steering one way and then another, like when someone is trying to get control of a car." Tanner went on. "Weber's folks were real strict, real church-going people. They were nice people; I thought they were great. Weber didn't like his folks forcing him to go to church either. That's about all I know. Is Weber treating you right, Glory? Is there a problem?"

"I understand you and Weber got in a lot of trouble when you were kids, right?" she asked, hoping she would get an honest answer and he would not ask her again about Weber and her relationship.

"Yes, a little."

"When Weber got in trouble I was there. It was never my fault. It was always Weber's idea for the mischief. Jeez, it was just kid stuff, Glory. Every kid gets into some kind of trouble. Weber was a little more daring than I was. If we did get caught, I was careful because if Lucen found out, I got a lickin'. I knew better than to try to fool Lucen, and I didn't want to be punished."

Then, he added, as if to defend himself, "But I've always been a good guy, Glory, just every day doing my thing. Sometimes Weber can be a butt, but I just ignore him—just got to, because otherwise he gets real pissy."

Glory thought, *A good guy he is, other than the fact he's like a Chatty Cathy.* Then she asked, "You mean Weber has a bad temper?"

"Glory, I don't know what this is about, and I don't want to talk bad about Weber—he's my friend—but you know if you're having any problems, you can count on me. We're pretty close for cousins, and I would go to the ends of the earth for you. You make my life better, and I expect to have my life keep getting better."

"What do you mean?" asked Glory.

"Oh nothing, it's just that because of you, I know life will get better. Just a feeling I have. You hang in there, and if there's any trouble, you come to me. About that temper, yeah, me and Weber are a lot alike. It takes a lot to tick us off, but watch out then. Guess we both been on our own too long. We like things our own way. Me and Weber butt heads on that once in a while."

At Glory's request, Tanner checked the car, and it took him about twenty minutes. "Purrs like a kitten," he said. With that he smiled, and she left.

She wondered why Tanner was so defensive when they talked about Weber, like Tanner was never part of the problem. She wanted to believe Tanner, but she also wanted to trust Weber. She thought, *Maybe it's just when the two of them get together trouble brews, but they have no trouble at the station and they are there most every day together.*

That night she again wondered if she had made too much out of her situation with Weber. He had been so good to her in the beginning of their relationship; maybe now he felt bored with marriage or else just tired. She would make sure she kept a positive attitude around him and smiled more; he always said he liked her smile.

When she stopped at the station a few days later, she noticed there was an area loose around the inside of the driver's door of the car. It was near the plastic strip down the inside cover of the driver's door. She asked Tanner if she could get a screw driver to tighten it. "Sure, back on the bench."

She went to the back of the station, where there was a workbench with tools, and she noticed five metal toolboxes on it, three red and two black. She looked around—no screwdriver in sight.

She opened the first metal box—nothing but screws, and bolts. She opened the second—a hammer, some vise grips, and other tools she did not recognize. In the next were several screwdrivers toward the bottom. She saw one with a red handle and liked it, so she pulled it out. It was tucked in pretty tight, so as she grabbed its handle, her finger caught onto a piece of cloth that pulled out a way then slipped out of her fingers.

Wondering what the cloth was doing it there, she put her hand back in and dug it out. It was wrapped securely around something hard, but not tied. She began unwrapping it, wanting to see what was inside. As the item dropped into the palm of her hand, she saw it was silver and shiny, very shiny. It was oblong, and there was a bump on one side of it.

As she removed the last side of the cloth wrapping, she could see what appeared to be a diamond on the top of the silver oblong object. It was a heavy piece of silver folded in half with a diamond centered on top. *It's a money clip,* she thought. It was beautiful. She remembered that her father used a money clip. She had only seen him use it a few times and never really paid much attention to it. He usually used credit cards.

What would this be doing here? she thought. *Maybe it's not real silver. Maybe it's a gift for someone. Does it belong to Tanner or Weber? How odd to find a money clip in a toolbox in a service station.*

She wondered if it had anything to do with the purple jewelry pouch she had found a few days before. She wrapped it back up and put it where she had found it.

Glory took the screwdriver and tightened the screw on the door cover then went back into the shop to replace the screw driver into the toolbox on top of the wrapped money clip. Before she left, she decided to ask Tanner about the boxes. "Tanner, whose metal toolboxes are those on the workbench?"

"They're mine and Weber's. Why?"

"So whose is red and whose is black?"

"Well, the tools were supposed to be separated, but in time our tools got mixed up, so they really belong to both of us. We put stuff in the wrong box all the time; it's a big joke with us. If we ever split the partnership, we're screwed." He chuckled then asked again, "Why?"

"Oh, you just had so many, I was curious." She doubted the idea of Tanner being deceitful regarding ownership of the boxes.

As she got into her car, she thought of the money clip belonging to her father. Was it one of the personal items she had taken from the house to keep with her? If so, what had she done with it? She had brought her mother's hairbrush, hair pins, and a few other things. She had a tie of her dad's that she had given him on his last birthday. But she could not remember if she took his money clip.

That dreadful month after her parents were killed was still foggy, and there were too many things about it she wanted to forget. Maybe she forgot this too. She hadn't looked at the items since the day she moved into Lucen's. She kicked herself for having doubts.

That night Glory tried to avoid Weber because she knew if she wasn't careful, she would ask him about the toolboxes. When she got obsessed about something, she couldn't seem to control the "want to know" side of her. She thought about calling Marshall and asking his advice.

Surely she brought it with her, and maybe Weber saw it and wanted to keep it for himself, not realizing how important it was to her. Maybe he just put it in his drawer. But that would still be stealing from her. Her imagination was running wild.

She decided not to call Marshall, not yet anyway. Not quite yet.

A few days later, Glory remembered the money clip again, and curiosity started annoying her like a mosquito bite that won't quit itching. She decided to call Marshall.

She told him about the items she had brought with her from her Orlando home and thought she might have brought a money clip belonging to her father, but she could not find it. She asked Marshall to check with Mr. Sanders and see if a money clip was listed in the inventory. He said he would get back to her.

She didn't like telling him a lie, but what if the money clip had nothing to do with her at all. She knew Weber and Marshall would never be the best of buddies, and there was no sense starting trouble without a reason. She knew that Weber would defend himself to the end and that Marshall wouldn't hesitate to pounce on Weber the first chance he got.

Marshall contacted Sanders that very afternoon and inquired about the inventory. Sanders said he was off to court and couldn't get specific information to him right then. He said he would have Jill fax him a complete list of the inventory items for him to go through in his spare time. He made it sound as if Marshall had nothing better to do, which irritate him.

"Yeah, go on to court. I'll check it out when I get the fax." Marshall waited. Within the hour, the faxed copy came through. It took another forty-five minutes to review it between phone calls. No money clip.

Marshall decided to go to the bank and speak with David's associates. He first asked Mr. Johnston, the vice president, if he knew anything about a money clip belonging to David McGuire. Johnston said yes, David did have a money clip. Most of the bankers did, but he was not able to give a description of it.

He then went in to see Louise, David's assistant. Quickly she responded, "Oh yeah, Janice gave him one on a wedding anniversary. I only know because I went with Janice when she picked it out. David had a plain gold one previous to that, and Janice had said, 'Gold is out, silver is in.' She picked out a beautiful piece. It was sterling silver one with a pretty good-sized diamond right in the center, a real showpiece for sure. Why?" Marshall told Louise he was just verifying items listed on the McGuires' inventory.

She interjected. "You know, David never left that clip anywhere. He always carried it with him. It meant a great deal to him."

Marshall decided it best not to call Glory right away. If she lost it or it was stolen, she would feel terrible. And if she failed to take it, and it was missing from the inventory, she would be heartbroken. More importantly, if it was David's, what was it doing in Spalding if Glory hadn't taken it?

He went right back to his apartment and scattered items around, trying to find everything that pertained to the items from the residence. Between the document of inventory and what Glory told him, he had a hunch that Lucen, Tanner, or Weber knew more than they were telling. But what did they know, and how would he prove any of it?

CHAPTER 26

A PETAL FALLS

Eight months from her twenty-first birthday, Glory arose early. It was a cold December day. The air was brisk but no new snow had fallen since the day before.

Olivia had asked her to come in earlier that morning and help her with the breakfast crowd. Typically there was never a breakfast crowd at the café, usually just coffee drinkers, but there had been a wedding in the family that lived a little further in the hills the night before, and Olivia had been told most of the wedding party would be in for breakfast.

Glory was ready to leave by 4:30, went out to her car to head to the café, and backed out of the driveway into the street, as she normally did. But when she pressed the brake pedal to stop before moving the car forward, the pedal almost hit the floor. She pumped the brakes lightly, and with each pump they tightened a little more, so she continued on her way.

It would be busy that morning in the café. Glory was pleased Olivia asked her to come in; she could not have handled that bunch alone. Nothing worse than a bunch of hungry people, who celebrated all night showing up at 6:00 for a meal to wake them back up to a new day. Glory knew it would be slow by 2:00 o'clock in the afternoon and if so Olivia had assured her if it was slow Glory could leave a little early.

Since Glory had some time to spare before her 6:00 o'clock a.m. shift she decided to drive up to Lucen's to have coffee with Victoria first. Victoria was an early riser, and Glory wanted her advice on baking some bread for Weber's supper that night; he loved homemade bread.

She enjoyed the beauty of the leisurely drive to Victoria's. She loved how the trees sparkled this time of year with a light dusting of snow. Though they weren't palms, they were tall and green and swayed in the wind just like palms, and she loved them.

When less than a quarter-mile from Lucen's, still daydreaming about Florida and what her life would be like had she not stayed in Spalding, she realized her daydreaming had caused her to push the gas pedal a little too far and she was going too fast for the coming curve. She surprised with herself for not paying more attention and knew she had to brake quickly to get around the curve.

Taking a quick look down at the speedometer, she realized she was going forty-five miles an hour, and sign before the curve said "25."

As she lifted her right foot to press the brake pedal, it hit the floor. No resistance at all. Remembering what happened that morning, she immediately started pumping the brakes, but they didn't grab like they had at the house earlier. Nothing happened.

The rear end started to slide as she got about halfway around the curve. When she brought the steering wheel back around, it swung back the other way and started rocking as if in an earthquake. She held the steering wheel so tight her fingers began to turn white, and she moved her hands left and right with the wheel, trying to regain control.

There was a large drop off on the driver's side of the road. Anyone soaring over it and down the raven would have surely been killed. There was a deep ditch on the passenger's side, then a fence, then some trees, then a field that was rippled with small rises. Obviously heading for the ditch, she continued to pump the brakes. Still no response. She concluded this was her doom. She started screaming, yet she knew no one could hear her.

She hit the ditch at an angle and the back of the car started to tip, then the front, and then she felt the surge of her body as it rose several inches off the seat for an instant. Suddenly she realized the car was flipping end over end. She briefly saw the ditch, then was aware of hitting a fence, narrowly escaping ramming a tree full force. The car seemed to angle a little and went between two more enormous pines, and she heard a screeching sound as the side of the car brushed against the tree trunk as it flew by.

When the car got to the field, it gained momentum and went down the hill. It slowed going up, but then flew over two small rises, and on the second rise it lifted, twisted, and rolled twice. Snow and dirt were stirred up in chunks soaring high then landing as they speckled the window. The view became less and less clear.

She had screamed as she went through the trees but once she hit the field, she couldn't scream anymore. Fright had taken her over, and she knew nothing else but frozen fear. She wondered if she had died already.

The car twirled and spun until it finally ran out of momentum and rested its side, the passenger door to the ground, so Glory was hanging toward the passenger window by her seat belt and she was justifiably shaken. She had suffered several whacks to the head as the car had flipped.

She had gripped the wheel when she started to flip then moved her hands up to the roof of the car to keep her in her seat. Her left hand had broken somewhere along the way, she could tell; it was just hanging on the end of her arm.

Suddenly blood began racing down her forehead, and she felt the wetness of it in her eye. She lost vision in that eye as it filled with the blood. She tried desperately to keep it closed; it wasn't of much use to her.

When she fully came to terms with the accident, she discovered she was suspended, bleeding, and broken. Again she began screaming. "Help me, somebody help me."

Within a few minutes, she was over the initial shock of the catastrophe and another type of terror set in. *What if the car goes up in flames, like in the movies? I need to get out of here!*

She smelled the gas, confirming that maybe the movies were more real than fiction. She knew that with all the jolting, gas probably poured out all over the car. Unsure about the extent of it on the car and convinced she didn't want to end up in ashes if it was located near the hot engine, she knew she had to get out.

Being able to use only one hand would be difficult, to say the least. *First things first,* she thought. *I've got to unbuckle the seat belt.* She had no doubt she would most likely fall to the passenger side of the car and then have to crawl back upward to get out of the window. But when she hit the button on the seat belt, nothing happened. She tried again and again, to no avail.

She prayed there would be something in the glove compartment that would jimmy the belt lock so she could open it. She leaned over and opened the glove compartment, but the pain was horrendous; she cried out. The only thing she could locate was a ball point pen. She began wedging the end of it into the latch. Nothing happened.

Then she saw a lighter. *I can burn the strap off me.* she thought. *Oh sure, and set myself on fire.* But she was positive that no one would see her back behind the trees and over the rises, and if she didn't get out pretty soon and to the road, she could die. The sun would start to set, it would get dark, and she'd be there all night.

The belt strap was nylon, and she knew it would be dangerous and tough to burn through, but she grabbed the lighter and took off her outer shirt. With her broken hand, this accomplishment took ten minutes.

She began to pray as she gripped the lighter with her good hand and flicked the side cylinder. The first spark ignited the belt, and it started to melt. If the flame only lasted a few seconds, she would have to relight the lighter. The nylon belt would melt much like candle wax when she held the lighter to it.

She had placed her shirt under the belt area, next to her skin, so the hot nylon would not land on her, and it worked. She used her broken hand as best she could to hold the safety belt as her good hand continued its objective: keeping the flame going. When the flame would go out she would rest for a minute then try it again.

After struggling with five or six small burnings, there was just a single, strong nylon thread holding her in place. She knew once that was burnt off, she would fall, but she had no choice.

When she set the lighter to it, the strap quickly melted. And suddenly her head, shoulders and upper body were in the passenger seat and her feet were hung up on the steering wheel. She wiggled until her feet were free, noting that her leg or foot or both were broken.

Exhaustion was consuming her. Her chest hurt and she thought she remembered it forcefully hitting the steering wheel during the wreck.

She stood up on her one good leg and thrust her head up and out the driver's side window, which was absent of glass. She was in the middle of the field, about four hundred yards or more from the road with the car's front end facing toward it. She wondered how she would ever be found.

She began a one-handed climb out of the window, again smelling the strong odor of gas. She prayed, "God please don't let me blow up." She credited him for keeping her safe thus far.

It was a struggle inching her way out. She finally had to use both feet—even the broken one, pain or no pain—to climb over the seat and middle glove compartment, pulling her full weight to the top window.

Once she had gathered enough strength and courage to hurl herself over and down to the ground, she landing with a thud as a sharp pain tore through her chest. When her left leg hit the ground, there was a horrid sound of more bone cracking, and she knew in an instant that was the sound of another break. And then—only darkness.

Glory came to, woozy and shaken and unclear as to where she was - until the pains began to grow to an almost unbearable height which awakened her senses.

She knew walking was out of the question. She would have to crawl if she expected to be found. She began, one arm in front of the other, and went about fifty yards as the pain throbbed in every limb. She knew she couldn't stop or she would die out there, bleeding to death or freezing to death.

She continued at the snail's pace, and once again everything went black.

She woke up in the Lambert Community Hospital. There were tubes in her arms and a tube down her throat. Her hand was covered in a white cast, and her leg had a cast on it from thigh to toe. There was gauze above one eye and a bandage that wrapped around her head.

She turned her head slightly and saw Weber, Victoria, Lucen, and Tanner sitting only a few feet from her bed. She moaned, trying to construct words, but to no avail. Weber saw the movement, took two steps, and was beside her, taking her good hand. "Oh, baby, you're all right. Thank God, you're all right." Did she see tears in his eyes, or were they her own?

Victoria rushed to the other side of the bed, bent down, and kissed Glory's forehead. "Glory, Glory, honey, it's Aunt Victoria. Can you hear me?"

Glory blinked her eyes; she couldn't speak.

She turned her head just a little and saw Lucen sitting in a chair; his arms crossed, staring right at her. He looked upset, but there seemed to be a glaring anger in his eyes—or was she wrong and his eyes were wet too? Probably not, she guessed. It may have just been the light in the room, and her focus was not the best.

Weber headed out of the room to get the nurse, and she came in, checked Glory over, and went back out. She came back in and removed the tube. It hurt Glory badly.

Then she felt a great deal of pain and her chest hurt. "My chest, my head." She was nearly unintelligible.

The nurse tried to comfort her. "Honey, you are going to hurt for quite a few weeks. You really banged yourself up. You broke your left hand, your left leg, and you have severe lacerations on your head. You also punctured a lung, so we have to watch you very close. No sudden movements, honey, no excitement. Breathe in and out slowly."

Weber was back by her side after the nurse left. Glory looked into his eyes and was happy to see the concern washing over his face. "You've been out for two days, baby. I was a mess worrying about you. Everything will be okay now."

Victoria approached her again. "Honey, do you know what happened? Did you hit a deer?" Glory could only whisper and that was labored: "Brakes, no brakes." It was not decipherable to those in the room. They figured when she was better, she could tell them what happened.

Weber was holding Glory's hand tightly. "Thank God someone was driving by and saw skid marks and a trail of broken debris, and broken and scraped trees, and pulled over. They followed the rubble and found you."

Victoria said, "Let's let Glory rest and go get coffee. We'll be back in a little while, honey."

Glory looked at Tanner, and there was a strange look on his face. He said, "I'm going to stay with Glory till you all get back, then I'll go." Glory looked at Tanner and said, "Purs, purs."

"What is it, Glory?"

She found it hard to say her words clearly, but she tried again. "Purs, purse."

"You want your purse?"

Glory blinked.

"Let me look for it." He found her purse in the cupboard along with her clothing and brought it over to the bed.

She struggled to form words with her lips. "Cell, cell fon, fon."

He looked in her purse. "Glory, there is no cell phone here."

Tears welled up in her eyes, and she said, "Help, Marshall."

"You mean the detective, Marshall?"

She blinked twice.

"Why do you want Detective Marshall? You'll be okay. This was just an accident, Glory. Why do you want him?"

She pleaded as best she could. "Pleeees, Marshall."

"I don't know what good it'll do, but I'll try to reach him."

She rasped, "Tell no one," and hoped he understood her.

He went to the pay phone to contact Marshall. He knew he was with the Orlando sheriff's department, so he called information for the number and then went to the cashier for a fist full of change. He hesitated a few minutes, not sure he wanted to make the call at all.

He dialed the number and asked for Detective Marshall. Marshall was not in, but he left a message on his voice mail: "Marshall, Glory's in the hospital, had a car accident, lost her cell phone. She'll be all right; you don't need to come here. She wanted you want to know. Oh, this is Tanner McGuire."

CHAPTER 27

THE WILTING HEART

When Detective Marshall entered his office that evening, after just spending the day at a family reunion, he was jubilant. The fellowship and day's activities had left him spent, but he still had his shift to do. The brothers and cousins had played touch football and then gone to the beach for a dip in the ocean.

That was the first day he'd relaxed since becoming the lead detective for the division. There had been an abundance of food at the reunion, and he had paced his intake so as not to be too tired for his shift. If he ate too much, he knew he would start a snoring match he couldn't win with the others on the night shift. The day's laughter had refreshed him, and he wished life could always be that simple. He wished he had his own immediate family to share such times with.

He sat at his desk, leaned back in his chair, put his arms behind his head, and smiled, remembering his brothers and the fun they'd had. He looked at his desk and was wondering where to start when he saw his phone blinking. *Oh crap,* he thought. *Who can that be?* As he picked up the phone he heard Tanner's message.

And he suddenly lost all his jubilance. "Oh my God, Glory." He sat upright in his chair. A chill drifted over him, and the jubilation he had felt moments before turned into adrenaline.

He tried to call her on her cell phone, but there was no answer. *Lost her cell phone, Tanner said. How did that happen?* Something bad has happened; he knew that. He had told her to keep that cell phone close, no matter what. And why would Tanner tell him he didn't need to come. Why wouldn't he go there if she was hurt?

Good God, something's going on, and she won't confide in me about it—the fall off the ladder, being so sick, rushed to the hospital, and now this. This is too coincidental. I don't like this a damn bit. And why did they wait two days to call me?

He looked up the number of the Lambert Hospital on the internet and immediately dialed it. When he firmly declaring his status as a detective from Orlando, Florida checking on the condition of Glory McGuire, the nurse told him the condition of her hand, leg, head, and lung. His heart sank as she spoke.

She said all she really knew was that there was a car accident and the girl was lucky to be alive. Panic seized Marshall. Sweat began to form on his brow. He asked to speak to someone in the room, and the nurse connected him to room 422. The phone rang three times before it was picked up.

Everyone had gone home for the evening. Glory was alone. It was impossible for her to reach the phone, try as she may. A nurse passing by heard it ringing, picked it up, and hand it to Glory. "You need to stay still, very still," the nurse said in a firm voice.

Glory held the phone to her ear. "Yes?"

"Glory, it's Marshall. Are you okay?"

Glory responded as best she could. "Marshall, help me. I'm scared."

He said he would catch the next flight out and get a car in Lambert, and be there as fast as he could.

She started to cry and dropped the phone. The nurse retrieved the phone and placed it back on the stand.

Marshall immediately called the local police and told them of his concern for Glory's safety and asked to have an officer posted outside her room.

The officer began to laugh but caught himself after the second chuckle. "Man, we have only one cop in this town, and that's me. I can't go protecting one person 'cause of a simple car accident. There's no proof anything happened that she needs protection from. What if something else happens in this town. Who's going to respond to it if I'm at the hospital?"

"I don't care if it's just you. Either you do it or get an officer from Lambert, but by the time I get there, I'd better see an officer posted outside that room, or you can look for another job first and a plastic surgeon second. Do I make myself clear?"

The officer simply acknowledged he would do his best.

Detective Marshall booked a flight and told his superiors what had happened. The chief said, "Marshall, this is a cold case. I think you're wasting your time. Didn't they say it was a car accident? Those things happen. You can't keep pursuing this murder case and everything that goes on with that girl when she is 2,500 miles away."

Marshall didn't appreciate that comment, but then the chief hadn't known there was more to Marshall's involvement than just the investigation. "I think I'm close to being able to put this puzzle together. Do I have permission to go?" Marshall knew full well he would go whether the chief approved or not.

"You can go, but if you don't come up with anything more than you have today, nothing more than you've put together over the last few years, this ends this case, understand?"

"Yeah, I understand."

Marshall began to go over things and placing them in his mental notebook once again:

- Lucen and Victoria are in line for fifty thousand dollars as soon as Glory turned twenty-one. That would benefit Lucen, Victoria, and possibly Tanner.
- The ladder accident may not have been an accident.
- Glory was sick and in the hospital with the flu, or maybe it wasn't the flu at all.
- If anything happened to Glory, Weber would be in line for her inheritance.

- The only people that should be aware of the inheritance were himself and the attorney, Garrett Sanders, supposedly. Lucen and Victoria are aware of the twenty thousand a year for her care, and he had told Victoria when Glory turned twenty-one a substantial sum would come to them as well.

So Lucen, Victoria, Tanner, and Weber all had motives for harming Glory. The motive was money, but who knew about the inheritance?

He headed for the airport and booked a flight to Lambert, but could only find one with a stopover in Sioux Falls. This gave him plenty of time to construct some plausible scenarios.

When Marshall finally arrived at the hospital, he asked the entrance nurse what room Glory McGuire was in. "Room 422," she said, "but you won't get in. There is an officer posted outside the door." A smile crossed Marshall's face as he realized his threat to the officer had been taken seriously. It was a relief to him knowing Glory was under police protection, even if she didn't require it.

He didn't wait for the elevator to descend to the lobby floor. Instead he rushed up the stairs, taking them two at a time, to the fourth floor. Located just off the elevator was a nurse's station with three long halls jutting from it.

He quickly showed his badge to the on-duty nurse. "Glory McGuire's room. Where is 422?" He barely gave the nurse a chance to answer. "Where is it?" The nurse pointed toward the left hallway, and off he ran. Coming down the hall, he observed a uniformed officer blocking one door. He assumed that was Glory's room.

He introduced himself to the officer, showed his badge, and entered the room. No one else was there.

Shock hit him full in the face when he saw Glory. She looked as though she had gone through a meat grinder. He saw the cast on her arm and leg, saw the bandages around her head, bruises and swelling on her face as well as distinct bruising on nearly every exposed part of her body, especially noticeable on her arms. He could only imagine what the rest of her must look like.

"Hello, beautiful," he said, while he thought, *Oh my God, that beautiful face.*

He casually walked up to her and took her hand carefully in his. He was afraid at this point, in her condition, he may hurt her. She began to cry. As her tears began to run down her black-and-blue face hitting her swollen lips, he cupped his arms as gently as possible under her neck and shoulder, holding her close to him. With her less-injured arm raised, she wrapped it up and around his shoulder. They remained like that for several minutes. It was all Marshall could do to reject his desire to pick her up and carry her off.

He gently released her and backed up with his eyes fixed on her. He reached for a chair moving it very close to her bed. "Glory, what happened?"

She was able to talk by this time, the third day since the accident, but didn't need to say anything. Marshall could read the fear in her eyes. She explained the brakes were not working right when she left for work, and they went out completely on her way to Victoria's house.

She said Tanner had just gone over the car and assured her it was running perfectly. "But maybe he didn't check the brakes," she said.

Marshall immediately asked where the car was now, and she said Weber towed it to the station. He left the room and, seeing the officer had a Lambert Sheriff's Office insignia on his uniform, instructed him to leave his post at the door and do whatever he had to do to get the car towed to the sheriff's office for inspection. He was not to tell anyone before actually seizing the car. Marshall requested a full search of the vehicle, instructing the officer it was to be gone over with a fine-toothed comb—the brakes especially.

The officer hesitated. Taking orders from someone out of his jurisdiction was not a custom he was used to. When he saw the look of authority on Marshall's face and heard the determination in his voice, he felt he'd better do as told. However, hesitancy showed on his face.

Marshall said, "If anyone has a problem with it they can call me for authorization. I'm still in charge of a murder investigation related to this young woman. I don't expect anyone to question my orders or inquiries, understand?" The officer took his cue and left the premises.

Marshall went back into the room. The fear on Glory's face was obvious even through the bandages, swelling, and discoloration. She had lost the youthful, happy glow Marshall always looked forward to seeing.

Marshall came close, his face just inches away from hers. "Glory, I don't want to scare you, but I think someone is trying to hurt you. I hope I am wrong, but I will be close by for a while. I can only stay a few days and have to return to Orlando but I will see to it that you are protected and that may not please some people." A smile inched its way up one side of her lips. "If *anything* isn't right—no matter what, no matter who it comes from, someone you love, a friend, a family member—if it doesn't feel right, if it doesn't sound right, then it's probably not. You absolutely must let me know if you are uncomfortable about anything."

It was then that Glory released her feelings about her marriage to Weber. "He wasn't like this in the beginning, Marshall, and I haven't told this to a soul until now. He gets angry at me. I think it's because he was alone for so long. Sometimes he just gets mad and stomps around; I don't know why. Most of the time he is really good to me and we are happy enough." Marshall thought that "happy enough" was just not good enough.

"His parents died and that hurt him a lot. I think he may be afraid of losing me. I just thought things would be different. I'm sorry, I don't mean to whine."

It may have been whining to her, but it was music to Marshall's ears. He must not hope for too much, but he always felt Weber was not the man for Glory. Even more disturbing was that Glory was not happy, and she was in danger, but not necessarily from Weber.

"I'll stay around for a while," he said. "I'd like you to go to Victoria's house when you get released."

She simply said, "No, Weber wouldn't understand."

Marshall conjured up the ability not to say what was on his mind. As far as he was concerned, it didn't matter to him if Weber did or did not understand.

A few minutes later, Weber came in. Upon seeing Marshall, he said defensively, "What the hell are you doing here?"

Marshall instantly and abruptly stood tall, causing Weber to take a step backward. Marshall walked right up close to Weber. He began to reach his hand out, and Weber stood for an instant not wanting to respond. Weber reluctantly put his hand into Marshall's outstretched palm. They shook. "Weber, you must have been worried sick about Glory."

Weber's glare said it all, but it didn't answer the question Marshall had asked. "Yeah, sure. What are you doing here?"

Marshall thought, "*And jealously rears its ugly head once more.*" His response was the good-guy cop response. "I heard about the accident and wanted to come see for myself that Glory was all right. I knew you'd take good care of her, as you have been, but felt I should come anyway."

"She's doing better, so you don't need to stick around. How did you find out about it?"

"Sorry, pal, privileged information, and I do plan to stick around, so get used to it." You could almost see the hair on the back of Weber's neck stand up as he scowled at Marshall even more. Weber knew better than to question this detective's motives.

"Do whatever." Weber walked over to Glory. "How you doing, baby? You feeling better? I was so worried about you. Doc says you are doing real good. Thank God you're okay."

"Yes, I'm much better Weber."

Tanner walked in. "Hey there, Marshall," he said with surprise in his voice, not wanting to tip his hat to Weber that he had called Marshall. He sat on a chair opposite Glory and Weber.

The next few days flew by quickly. Weber, Tanner or Marshall took turns like going through revolving doors in passing to ensure someone was always in the room with Glory. Marshall had his doubts as to whether to leave her at all but he had work to and could not stay with her all the time. He made it a point to contact the head nurse and request one of the nurses check on Glory every half hour. The head nurse said she couldn't have a nurse committed to checking on Glory saying they were short staffed. Marshall had to explain he felt uncomfortable about some of the family members staying with Glory and he would make it worth her while if she could assign a nurse on each shift to keep checks on Glory. The head nurse hesitate then assured him she would see the task assigned. Marshall thanked her by grabbing her hand and placing two bills in her palm.

She immediately put her hand in her pocket and not until she left her shift had she dared to look. There were two one hundred dollar bills there. When she arrived home she called the hospital requesting to speak to the nurse on duty on her floor. She reiterated her request for the nurse to check on Glory every half hour and to write down her checks so the times could be reviewed the next day. She wasn't about to see the two hundred dollars she received be returned for lack of service.

After a day it was like they were competing to see who the best knight in shining armor might be, each trying to outdo the other in caring for her. No one won; Glory slept most of the time and was not conscious of the day or time.

A few days later, Marshall needed to head home. He had a few things to wrap up in Lambert and Spalding, but that he would call her at home after her release. It had been decided Glory would go home and Victoria would check on her periodically to make sure she was getting along all right.

Before he left, he caught Tanner alone in the hall and asked for a conversation with him. They went to the cafeteria, and both order black coffee. They chose a table away from any other visitors, and Marshall began, "God, this was an awful accident, wasn't it, Tanner?"

"I was scared to pieces for Glory."

"Tanner, I understand the car had been in your shop a few days earlier and you had looked it over. Did you check the brakes?"

"Oh, sure. Glory came in with the car, said she didn't think anything was wrong with it; she just wanted it looked over. It had been in the shop once before, when Lucen bought it, but I checked it anyway. Everything worked great—weren't any problems with it at all."

"But Glory said the brakes went out on the car. How would you explain that?"

"Well, speeding was the main factor, and the corner she was rounding is a bad one. There have been a lot of near misses there. Maybe when she tried to slow down she got the brakes screwed up from pushing so hard or maybe they got wet. I don't know."

"Sorry, Tanner, that scenario doesn't fit. She had to be going pretty fast and I'm not convinced that's what happened. I am convinced those brakes were bad, and I'm having the vehicle checked over thoroughly by the sheriff's department in Lambert. Any objections."

"Are you accusing me of something? I don't have anything to hide. The car was working fine when I checked it, so if something went wrong, it was after I was done with it."

Marshall thanked Tanner for his time and went back to his room in Lambert. He called Glory from his room. "I'm going to have you checked on a regular basis until I return by someone from the Lambert sheriff's office. They'll stop by, and you let them know if you are okay or not. And don't lie; tell them the truth."

"Why would I lie?"

"Glory, I know you too well. You have always been protective of everyone around you. You want no one to worry about you. Yes, you're a big girl, but I don't think I could stand it if anyone were to scare you. I don't think I could stand it if you were hurt again. If you're in trouble, call me or tell the officer checking up on you. Promise?"

"Yes, I promise." At that moment she knew it wasn't just the investigation of her parents' deaths but that Marshall had another motive for watching out for her all these years. He really cared.

CHAPTER 28

A PERPLEXING PUZZLE

Marshall had all the documents related to the case still in his apartment in Orlando. He rushed there after returning from Spalding and pulled everything related to the case out of cold storage.

He again reviewed each and every detail, reviewed his computer analysis as to what did or did not match. From his initial call from Richards, the search of the residence, the interviews, the forensic report, the coroner's report, he was starting to see someone had a plan, a long-range plan. Someone surely knew about the money.

Marshall knew that two plus two didn't equal four in this case. He left his apartment and headed straight for the station. As soon as he went into his office, the chief all but ran out of his office to Marshall's desk.

"We've got to talk, and I mean now." Marshall rose to follow the chief to his office and noticed the other officers in the station staring at him, following every step as he trailed behind. His first thought was that a pink slip may be waiting for him.

Along the walk, which was from one end of the open offices to the other, Marshall kept his concentration on the case.

Lucen is mysterious. Maybe he couldn't wait to get his hands on all that money, if he knew of it. And if he were to get both Glory and Weber out of the way, he would be the remaining beneficiary. He would inherit the rest of— or at least most of—David's estate.

Tanner is a nice kid but somewhat evasive, sometimes sarcastic. Does he know more than he is letting on? Had Tanner ever heard a conversation between Lucen and Victoria about the money? Had he ever seen the paperwork, the will? Were the bills he showed me from the day of the murders legitimate repairs; he could have doctored the receipts, showing he was at the station. Did he really check that car over, and if so, did he check the brakes or just say he did to save face as a mechanic? Why did he not like me asking questions when you'd think he'd want to protect Glory?

And Weber, a jealous and possessive man. Is he more in love with Glory or more in love with the yearly allotment they could get if Glory would allow it. Does he even know about the allotment? Is he mad at Glory for not taking the money every year but instead making him and her both work full time? Does he even know anything about the final inheritance.

And sweet Victoria—is she as sweet as she appeared or does she have a greedy itch that just can't be scratched by Lucen. And wouldn't Lucen be less annoying if she had an abundance of money to spend?

Did Lucen, Victoria, Tanner, or Weber hire someone to murder the McGuires? Would any of them put their necks on the line for a "kill for hire"? How would they have found out about the money?

Were Glory's accidents related to the murders of her parents or were the two incidents totally unrelated?

Now, if Lucen did not do this, maybe he hired Weber or Tanner to carry it out for him. If it was Weber, maybe he hired Tanner. If it was Tanner, maybe he hired Weber. And then maybe any of the three of them hired someone else, an out-of-towner. There seem to be a lot of anger issues here, and all three are short on cash.

He knew now that Glory's life was in jeopardy, but he didn't know from whom and he didn't know what "accident" might happen next. His gut once again told him to concentrate on Spalding, not on a local burglar.

As they sat down across from each other in the chief's office, the chief asked, "Okay, what did you find in Spalding?"

Marshall, unable to tell him that what he had were only hunches, said, "It seems like there are some connections here, and I need to follow them up." He thought that was it and stood up to leave the room.

"Sit," the chief said in no uncertain terms.

"What's up, Chief?" Marshall tried to sound as casual as possible, hoping he wasn't going to be raked over the coals for not letting the McGuire case rest.

"An odd sort of fellow came into the department yesterday, announced he had a report to make. I asked him, you know, 'What kind of report?' He said about some murders, a long time ago. The McGuire murders." The chief paused and studied Marshall to see his reaction; thinking he may lose his temper. His prediction was extremely close to that.

Marshall sat straight up. "What the hell?"

The chief continued, "Yeah I know what you're thinking Marshall. Four years later some jerk shows up. Well, he said he picked up a fare at the airport and drove him somewhere on Sycamore Street. All the officers in the room froze and stared at this man, this grubby little man. I think the guys knew that when you heard this, you'd blow a gasket."

"Enough about my gaskets. What the hell did he say?"

"I demanded to know his identity and what information he had about the murders. I was none too happy at this point. The man had on a grubby cap that said, "Geno's Cabs." His name was Nick Garcias, a cabbie, usually works the airport. Best money there, he said."

"Crap, Chief, get on with it. What did he know?"

"That day he had a fare, like I said, dropped him off at Sycamore, and he heard the next day there were murders on that street. He remembered the fare from the day before. He looked like a sales-man, and the cabbie just forgot about it until now."

"*Then* what, for God's sake, Chief?"

"The guy said it was in the morning, maybe eight or thereabouts. He said the guy was about twenty-five, could have been as much as forty, hard to tell he said, probably about five eleven. He wore a blue suit and looked like anybody. He said he wasn't sure but he thought the guy wore dark glasses. He had brown, or maybe black, hair, kind of greased down and shiny." Marshall knew that was a big enough spread in age and description that it could have been just about any man in the country.

The chief went on. "I asked if there was anything distinctive about the man that he could remember. He said, "'Maybe the case. It was an odd one, all black but it had a big old chain on it. It ran from the handle down to the side of the case. Heck, I thought he might have been a diamond dealer like in the movies.'"

"Why was he telling you this now? It's been years," Marshall asked.

"Well, seems this cabbie went and got himself arrested for theft, evidently after one of his fares got out and left a bag in the taxi. He took it home and kept the stuff in it. The fare reported it, and the cops found it in his apartment. It had clothes, jewelry, and lots of cash, and it was still in the bag when the cops found it. The cabbie is up on a felony rap. He got scared and decided maybe he could work out a deal. Not all that dumb, was he?"

Marshall was sitting back in his chair, and the color had drained from his face.

"I then asked again if he could identify the guy," the chief said. "The cabbie repeated the same exact description he had before with no variations. He begged for me to talk to the D.A. to tell him he cooperated."

"So, do you think he can actually help with this case?" Marshall asked.

"Nah, I think he just wanted a break, probably can't ID the guy after all this time. Anyway, he said he was scared the guy might remember him and come back to shut him up, if it was the same guy.

"At that point I got so pissed off, I slammed my hand down on the desk right in front of the guy and muttered a few words—unintelligible but sharp enough to know they weren't nice—and nearly scared the cabbie to death. He shook like a little baby."

The chief and Marshall knew that this case could have progressed and maybe even the killer could have been found if this idiot had only opened his mouth four years earlier. "At that point," the chief said, "I wanted to walk over and hit the guy in the mouth and lock him up for a couple of years and see how he liked being in the dark as much as we have been."

Marshall hesitated and then said, "Tell that guy he doesn't need to worry about his passenger coming back to hurt him but that when I see him, I may kill him myself."

The chief was quick to respond. "Calm down. I know this isn't much to go on here, but it is *something*."

Marshall immediately went back to his desk and called the Lambert sheriff's office asking about the report of Glory's car from the accident. After being transferred twice, his blood pressure was to its limits.

A rep from the sheriff's office mechanic came on the line. "Detective Marshall, the brakes were cut. Not completely, but severed so at some point they would have broken off cleanly."

"Are you saying it was deliberate?"

"Well, I can't officially say it was deliberate, but I know this much: this is not normal wear and tear. I think you've got a problem. I also had the guys from the lab dust, but there were no prints around the brakes or mechanisms."

Marshall's mind began to spin. Lucen bought the car; he took it to Tanner's station to have it checked out; Tanner and Weber were both there. Could Lucen have taken it somewhere else first?"

He felt he was inches away from an answer but confused as to why it wasn't coming together now. There were too many people with a motive; too many who may have known about the money. Yet, there was still a remote chance this was random, this was a burglary gone wrong. The brakes were another matter altogether.

Marshall knew the killer had not left a trace at the house. There was no murder weapon, no ransom, and no threat to Glory. No threat until she arrived in Spalding and settled down, at least. Until the brakes there wasn't a clear threat, just bad luck. Could be, but he thought not.

He knew Lucen hated his brother, though he was pretty sure he had not gotten the whole story. Lucen would have a motive—hatred for his brother—he did have access to a copy of the will, and could have known about the money; if he had opened it. He and Glory were the only living relatives, so he knew if she dies, all the money would come to him. He could have easily planned the whole thing.

Marshall knew that Tanner was a good suspect: not a decent dime to his name and didn't get along well with his father—well, who did? Maybe he was out for revenge against his father for being so strict or for being mad that he didn't like the farm, or maybe he knew about the money and that there would be something in it for him. Tanner could have planned this whole thing.

Victoria was another possible suspect. She lived with Lucen and could have seen the will at any time. Did she want the money, especially after Marshall had told her about the lump sum? Did she discover the fact that Glory would have to stay with them, giving her access to Glory's day-to-day living. She could have planned the whole thing.

The only evidence connecting anyone in Spalding to the murders was the money clip, a clip Glory herself wasn't sure if she had taken with her. Or did someone else take it; the diamond in it was worth a great deal of money. It may not have been David's at all, but it may have been.

Any one of them could have planned it, or planned it together. Lucen or Tanner could have easily gotten to Orlando without anyone knowing they were gone. Tanner could have been gone on repairs all day or even overnight.

The cabbie said the guy's age was between twenty-five and forty. Either of the boys could look any age, and Lucen could have disguised himself to look younger. Would Lucen have the strength to carry it out alone, it would have had to have been well thought out.

Any one of them ... Any one of them. Could any one of them expected to stay in the clear? Would no one talk?

Marshall knew it was only a matter of time before Glory was dead and someone would be very rich.

CHAPTER 29

IT'S NOW OR NEVER

"Not so easy anymore." At this stage in his plan, he was getting more than a little nervous. Maybe he should slow down, not take so many chances.

If he kept on schedule, soon he could get out of this hell hole and start a real life. He would take one of those jumbo planes like he had four years before. He would go to a big city, enjoy himself, maybe even travel to a far off island with sexy native girls.

He would never return to Spalding, never set foot on this god-forsaken part of the country again. No one will ever know who was responsible or where he was. They will just think him so distraught with this loss that he had to get away. Soon people would forget about him. He had made a small mistake this time, the accident hadn't killed her. It was a mistake he could rectify. Next time he would have to be more careful.

If he could just stay in control for a few more days or weeks, he would be home free. He didn't plan the flight to Orlando four years ago and do all this just to have things fall apart. He wasn't going to allow that to happen.

He had always been held at bay by that old coot Lucen, so when an opportunity presented itself, he took advantage of it. He remembered four years earlier, when he had gone over to the house to talk to Victoria.

It was a Sunday, and no one was home. She had mentioned they might go to Lambert for the day. He walked up to the front door. He knew no one would see him, out there surrounded by trees, but he looked around anyway—guilt perhaps. He knew the front door was never locked, so he walked in. He came to the house frequently, so it would be no surprise if anyone should they see him there.

Victoria always impressed him as a good-natured woman, kind, generous, a good cook, a good gardener, a woman who cared about everyone. He felt good around her, unlike his feelings around Lucen. Victoria saw the positive side to everything. She believed in everybody, which had helped him a lot throughout the years.

The kitchen was neat as a pin. There was a small nook area, with a desk, where he knew Victoria worked on her recipes. He looked through the papers on the desk and then went on to the living room. Nothing out of the ordinary there.

He headed for Lucen and Victoria's bedroom. They would be furious if they knew he was mulling around in their personal belongings. He carefully began going through the jewelry box, the closet, and the drawers making sure he put everything back just the way he'd found it.

In the bottom drawer of the large mahogany dresser were farm magazines, hunting magazines, and envelopes with receipts for utilities and the like in them, just papers in general. He thought this an odd place for Lucen to keep his magazines. He thought maybe there was a girlie magazine in the group, which would explain the other magazines.

He fanned through two magazines. Found nothing. As he fanned through the third one down, out dropped an envelope. It was old and had yellowed a bit. On the front was written. "Lucen McGuire, Dear Brother." He knew it was a legal document of some kind.

He took his small pocket knife out of his jeans pocket and carefully worked it under the seal, but the seal was so brittle the envelope broke open. Pulling the document out of the envelope, he opened it fully.

Not being a legal scholar, he had a hard time deciphering what each paragraph meant, but he wasn't too stupid either. He was able to decipher out the important points, such as Lucen and Victoria being Glory's godparents. The next sentence explained that if anything were to happen to David and Janice, Lucen and Victoria would have full custody of Glory until she was of age.

The part he liked best had to do with money, enough money to care for Glory, a twenty-thousand per year allotment and then a fifty-thousand lump sum to Lucen and Victoria when Glory turned twenty-one. The bulk of David McGuire's estate was to go to Glory, in all its "glory."

His body shook with disbelief as he read on. He started on the first page again, deciding to read each and every word. He read slowly, missing nothing. As he came to the final page, his plan began to take formation.

He knew it would take time to put together, but he had time. He knew Glory was about sixteen years old, so he had to calculate a timetable.

The second reading gave him a vision of opportunity, maybe the only opportunity he would ever have to make it big. It was right in front of him. He decided to take advantage of it, for his own greedy success.

And now, having reminisced about how this whole thing started and that Glory would soon be twenty-one, it was time to make his final move. Her final accident could have no errors. This time he had to be precise. He didn't want her mishap to look like anything other than an accident. He had to get an alibi, he had to decide on the method, and he would have to grieve.

CHAPTER 30

LET THE IMPOSTER EMERGE

Though Lucen felt he did not have enough information for what he felt may be the inevitable, he knew there was a sticky situation brewing. The predicaments Glory had endured over the last few years were just not normal.

Most people had one or two crises, but it seemed Glory was always in one. Who has so many accidents and illnesses? He saw her as a strong, young, healthy girl and yet not the sweet, energetic girl she had been when she came to Spalding.

Sure, she had grown into a woman but the laughter, the smiles, and the bounciness he so enjoyed had subsided since her marriage, so he knew she had troubles. He had heard Victoria and Glory discussing some of Weber's antics, and he thought it wasn't right. He felt Weber was taking advantage of Glory.

Now he thought he should get up and make a move.

First he would check the will; his curiosity got the best of him. If it was still intact, he may very well be wrong and all these things that happened would just be unfortunate luck. Lucen hadn't touched the will for twenty years, and he had never opened it. He entered the room and shut the door behind him. The magazines he needed were in the bottom drawer of his small dresser. The only one he needed was exactly where he had left it, third one down.

He fanned through it until it reached a page where it stayed open because of the large envelope tucked inside. There was the will. It had yellowed but seemed intact. He turned it over in his hand and noticed that the seal was broken. Could it have just cracked from heat, humidity, or cold—or had it been broken? Had Victoria or Tanner found it?

This document was not to be opened until Glory reached twenty-one; the attorney had told him that. That had been twenty years ago, yet he heard the attorney's voice, saying those words, as if it were yesterday. The attorney had reiterated those very words when he contacted him that his brother died. Lucen had not checked on the will then. *Maybe I should have,* he thought.

As he retrieved the document from inside the envelope, his hands were shaking. He began to read. His first reaction was shock; he had no idea his brother was so wealthy. He read on. Glory would inherit it all, or if something happened to Glory, her family and/or spouse would get it all. As the usual scowl on his face became deeper, he knew he had been right: Glory was in danger.

Lucen tried to organize his thoughts. He did not want to think Tanner had read this and tried to do what he could to ensure his family would receive the money. "Damn that boy." Lucen thought back to the ladder accident. When he looked at the leg of the ladder that day, he had been confused at the way the ladder leg had broken. An accidental clean break on an aluminum ladder leg is next to impossible.

He also remembered when Glory was so sick she had to go to the hospital. The doctor found nothing; could it have been poison? She had been sick like that more than once, but once she had been near death's door. Then the car accident.

The next two hours went by slowly as Lucen tried to make up his mind what to do next. He sat in his recliner, contemplating his decision. If he was wrong, Glory would hate him—probably Tanner and Victoria too.

But if right, he might just save Glory's life. He decided to bite the bullet and go talk to Glory.

He waited until the next day after spending the night experiencing cold sweats. He worried about Glory, but he also was not sure he was making the right decision.

The next morning at about ten, he finally decided to call Marshall. He dialed the number on Marshall's card, which he'd found in a desk drawer. He assumed Glory had left it, and was thankful she had.

Marshall answered, "Detective Marshall, how can I help you?"

With no formality, as usual, Lucen said, "You better get up here right away. He found the will. I think Glory is in danger." Lucen's nerves got the best of him, and he hung up the phone, put his head in his hands, and began to cry.

"Hello, hello." No response. Marshall knew he had no way of contacting her except through Lucen, and Lucen had just called him. He tried to redial the last number, but the phone rang with no answer.

Marshall immediately called the chief, gave him a life-or-death scenario, and asked permission to use the police charter. He then booked the flight for Lambert. Since it was a police charter, he could leave as soon as the plane was fueled. He knew there was no time to waste.

Lucen sat for two hours, knowing Marshall would be coming but not when he would arrive. He made a point of not talking to Victoria; he didn't want to worry her. Finally he got up and took care of the essential chores. He tarried around the yard until after three, when he decided not to wait any longer. He decided to go to Glory's and bring her home with him, at least until Marshall arrived.

Lucen was well aware Weber had been a bad influence on Tanner over the years. He used to tell Tanner, "If you hang out with that kid, you better see you get your butt home before you get in trouble." And "I don't want him hanging around here." So Tanner and Weber did not spend much time at either parents' houses when they were together.

Tanner knew better than to rile Lucen. Lucen was not someone anyone wants to face in a confrontation. Tanner faced little, because Lucen's stare was enough to make him stop cold, no matter what he was doing at the time. Whether he was feeding the cats or watering the chickens, he always felt that, if Lucen came around, he'd better pray for forgiveness, even if he didn't know what he'd done.

When Weber's parents died, Lucen had been uncomfortable with Weber's reaction. Sure, he cried, but he seemed to get through the upset very quickly: he was back to his usual self the day after the funeral and went right back to work part time for an independent mechanic. Though Weber was seventeen at the time, the courts decided to emancipate him.

Weber presumed he would inherit a great deal of money from his parents' deaths. He presumed wrong. The property, house, and cropland, were sold by the estate. Weber discovered his parents owed money on the house, at the local stores, at an auto garage, and of course at the attorney's office.

When the debts were paid, Weber had been disappointed to find only a small balance remained. Lucen expected Weber to squander his inheritance, spending every cent on himself, and he did.

Weber found a small, two-room apartment—actually a remodeled gardening shed. Weber spent money on his friends. Playing the big shot, he paid for everything: going to Lambert, eating out, and drinking beer. Soon the money dwindled down to nothing except for the small amount used to go into business with Tanner.

At that time, Tanner couldn't wait to get out of the house; he didn't want to farm. He wanted a better life, but did that mean the money from the will? Lucen realized money was a motive, but was not sure if Tanner or Weber was the one full of evil and greed.

Before Marshall left the office, he called the Spalding Police Department. Of course there was no answer, so he left a message when the recording came on: "This is Detective Marshall, from Orlando. Please check on Glory. I think there may be trouble. I'm on my way to the airport. I'll be there in a few hours."

Lucen finally headed for his truck.

Marshall was still airborne but within minutes of landing in Lambert.

CHAPTER 31

THE BEGINNING OF THE END

That afternoon Weber came home early from work, parked his truck in the back of the house, went inside, and waited. He had told Tanner he had a repair call to make between Spalding and Lambert and would be back soon.

He got a beer, even though it was only two in the afternoon, and sat in his chair contemplating his next move. He decided Glory would have her final accident today. Yes, it would be her *final* accident.

After spending the morning settling on his modem operandi, he chose the garden as her final resting place. She spent so much time there, he knew an accident there wouldn't be questioned. The hoe, the shovel, or any of the tools she used to spruce it up could cause a fatal injury if her head were to fall on it. It was simple; instead of her Garden of Eden it would become her Garden of Death. He opened another beer, and then another.

Glory arrived home at about 4:15 and was surprised to see Weber sitting on the couch with a beer in his hand. She thought it strange for him to be home so early. The beer caused her alarm; there was usually trouble when he started drinking early.

She said, "Hi, honey. Are you okay? Do you want something to eat?"

"No, sit down. I want to talk to you." He seemed agitated.

Glory became very nervous. Whenever he wanted to talk, it ended in an argument. She really didn't want to have to go through that today. She said she would put the few grocery's she had away and be right in to speak to him.

She took her time, wanting to avoid a confrontation, hoping he would fall asleep before she returned to the room. She heard Weber go to the refrigerator and then heard the pop of a beer can tab.

She came back into the living room and sat on a chair across from the couch. "What is it, Weber?"

Weber suddenly became brazen. "You know Glory, over the few years we've been together I've really come to love you."

All of a sudden Glory "got it". "Glory suddenly realized that in the three and a half years they had been together, Weber had never once said, "Glory, I love you," not even on their wedding day. He said things like "You are the most important person in my life" or "I can't live without you" but never

"I love you." She had accepted any words he said because she really did want her marriage to work; she had hoped he felt the same way. Her heart began to sink.

She responded with what she hoped he wanted to hear. "Well, I love you too." But an eerie feeling came over her in that instant. It was the same chill she had felt walking home from school many years ago, turning the corner block to go to her house, and finding her parents dead. She wondered why on earth she would have that feeling now.

Weber continued, "But Glory, we can't be together any longer."

Glory was shocked. What was he talking about? Her face showed surprise. She had never expected to hear those words.

A smile, a grimacing smile, appeared on Weber's face.

She had no idea there was that big of a problem in their marriage; she had always been faithful, taken good care of him, kept a nice house, and never asked for much. "Weber, what on earth is the matter, what have I done wrong?"

That's about the time Marshall's chartered plane was landing in Lambert. He ran through the airport, not even stopping to retrieve the one small piece of luggage he had packed. He knew he had to get to Spalding before it was too late.

Lucen, too, was on the road, heading to Glory's house. He had to tell her what he suspected. He had to protect her; he didn't want her to come to harm. Though he had never been very friendly or loving with her, in secret, he loved her like a daughter.

"As cute as you are, and you are cute, our relationship is over. I have to move on with my life now."

"I don't understand, Weber. What are you talking about? What's wrong?"

"Well, you see, I have another girl."

Glory struggled for a breath. She felt betrayed. *Another girl?* "Who, Weber? What other girl and when did you have time to see her? Why would you have another girl?"

"Well, baby, it's like this. She's been my girl for five years. You are a sweetie, but you are not who I want. I want a better life; I want to have some fun. I'm sick of working on cars for peanuts."

"Who is she, Weber?"

"She's a peach; stuck with me for five years now. And Glory…do you know how much money you are worth?"

Glory wondered where that comment came from. Why he was being so despicable, so vile, so unemotional? "Weber, I don't understand. Why would you have another girl and marry me? What are you talking about 'what I'm worth'?"

He glared at her with a fierceness she had never seen before. His face was distorted, transforming as it had been on the day he slapped her. Weber was no longer in front of her; a madman had taken his place, someone she didn't know. She began to question herself, *"Why have I not seen this side of him before, or have I?"*

"To be honest, baby, I love *her*, that's why. Oh, and I like money, that's why too. So I'll be packing my bags soon to leave Spalding, with her."

She suddenly remembered the only person who ever called her baby was her father. He always referred to her as baby rather than Glory, and all this time Weber had called her baby. Since they'd first met that had been his nickname for her—one that endeared him to her. It was comforting and reminded her of home. It reminded her of her father.

She said, "I don't have much, but whatever I have is ours together. Don't you know that? I thought everything was fine between us."

"Yet you wouldn't share your twenty thousand a year with me, your allowance. But I guess I'm not good enough to share it with, right? And I know that on your twenty-first birthday you'll be worth millions more, baby."

"The twenty thousand is ours whenever we needed it, but I thought we were doing fine. If it's the money that has you upset, we can get it any time. I can call Mr. Sanders right now, if you want."

"You wouldn't even tell me about it. I had to hear about it from someone else. That wasn't a nice thing to do; you should have shared it when we got married. You're greedier than I am." And he laughed.

"Weber, are you crazy."

Weber practically leaped like a lion out of his chair, landing directly in from of her. He threw his beer can at the wall then set his hand on the arm of her chair while the other went around the front of her neck just under her chin. "Wrong, baby cakes. Crazy, no, not me, I am the smart one here; I saw the will. When you turn twenty-one, you're getting every dime your precious daddy ever made. Did you know that?"

"Of course not. How would I know that? How do *you* know?" She was too afraid to ask more.

Weber chuckled a little in a sinister manner. His breath was putrid and stale, smelling of beer and hatred combined.

His face and body contorted into an almost ogre-like figure. "You get all the money, all of it. Your daddy left you a fortune. If you're not here, your family gets it. If you are married, well, guess who gets it? Little old me." His grip tightened a little. Her hands went up to her throat, and she tried to pull his away but his grip was too strong; his hand wouldn't budge.

She gasped for air, terrified for her life.

A light went on inside her head. "Do you have my father's money clip?" He let go of her throat, stood upright, and placed his hands on his hips. "How did you know about that?"

"I found it in a toolbox at the station. Was that my dad's?"

In a heartless and yet arrogant tone, he bent his head down so they were face-to-face. "Yeah, guess I didn't hide it good enough, did I? I got it, quite a piece of work, diamond and all, probably worth some bucks." Glory was both despondent and terrified.

He said, "Sorry, baby, but I plan to be the one with the dough in my pocket. You understand, don't you? You'll forgive me, won't you?" His hand once again gripped her throat.

Her mind was swimming. *He is crazy. He's deranged. He's going to kill me.*

She could only whisper with his hand so tight, almost cutting her air supply. "No, I don't. What are you going to do?"

"I'm not going to do anything, but you, sweet pea, are going to have a little accident."

She now felt the full horror of his words. "What accident?"

He seemed to truly enjoy tormenting her. "The one you are going to have today, in just a few minutes, actually. So don't go making any plans for tomorrow." His voice became deep and raspy. "I think your garden is beautiful, you know. You worked so hard making all the little flowers pop out in pretty colors. That will soon be a new bed for you. You can lie down with your pretty little flowers."

A chilling cackle rose up and echoed through the room. "It'll be kind of like the ones you had before, just another fall. People think you are acci-dent-prone, you know? And it's so close to your twenty-first birthday—how sad is that? You won't even get to have a birthday party. I'm sorry, dar-ling, but I've spent the last four years working to get here."

Glory's will to live intensified as she finally accepted that he intended to kill her. "You, Weber. It was you that tried to hurt me."

Weber's laughter then came grumbling from the very depths of his soul. He sounded like a ranting lunatic, babbling his sentences out. "Who did you think, or did you think it was just accidents? 'Course it was me. Who else would it be?"

"Anybody but you."

"Now, that's funny. And all the better for me, I guess. What a great pigeon Tanner will make, if a suspect is needed. Hopefully, it will look like you just took a fall and, oops, must have hit your head. But if there is a problem, I'm sure I could get people to believe Tanner had something to do with it. He worked on your car more than I did. Tanner can take the heat; it would look like he wanted the money for his family and his crappie little repair business."

Glory was surprise and a shudder went through her body. She tried to relax, tried to hold her own in the situation and her voice shook when she spoke, "But Tanner is your partner, your friend. I had the money saved for us if we needed it. I wasn't trying to hide it."

He scowled. "I've never counted on anyone in my life. Whatever I've done, I've done on my own. I used Tanner when I needed to get close to you. Yeah, I guess you can say he's my friend." With that he let out a laugh that made her shudder. "If they do think it's more than an accident, Tanner is the man. Everyone knows I love you, that I'd never hurt you."

Now she wished she had shared the awful moments with Weber with at least Victoria or Gloria. She knew she would soon die, and everyone would think it was an accident—or worse, Tanner would be blamed for it.

"I did all I could for you," Weber continued. "But you never shared, you never shared a dime. Now I get it all. See what happens when you are so greedy? They might even link Tanner to the death of your parents too, and that actually is perfect."

Sweat began to run off Glory's forehead as she thought of her parents. There was a raving maniac in her face and she knew she was minutes from death. She knew she had to hold onto every shred of sanity she could muster. "My parents? What has this to do with my parents' deaths?"

Weber smiled, shrugged a little, and then presented a grin that the Cheshire cat would be proud of. "It's because of your parents that you are here today. Baby, we should thank your daddy for working so hard. He made big bucks there in the bank."

She screamed at him. "Oh God, Weber, did you kill my parents?"

He sighed like he couldn't believe she waited until now to ask.

"Ah yes, it was me. It had to be done. I did it for us at first, for you and me. Well, no, I didn't actually do it for you. I planned for us only to be together for a short while. You were a little stronger than I anticipated and didn't let any of your accidents stop you. It is not working exactly quite how I planned."

He seemed to mellow and made an unexpected confession. "I came to care about you, but that torment between caring for you and caring about my future was tearing me apart. I didn't plan to like you. I didn't plan that you would be a beautiful girl with a good heart. That just got in the way, screwed with my head a little."

Then he reverted back to the madman raging about the next accident. "But now I'm back on track and your misfortune today will set me up for life. Sorry, baby. It's just that there is so much more than Spalding, South Dakota, and I intend to find it all. I never did like the thought of being married. It's just like having parents, someone telling me I can or can't have something, can or can't do something. That's what my parents did – and they paid, too."

"Weber, what are you saying?" At that moment she had clarity. She saw how dire her situation was. Her only access to staying alive now was to keep him talking.

She was also suddenly conscious that she had never loved Weber but instead had accepted him for his kindness, for being there when she needed someone to love her, someone to care, like her parents did.

She knew there were things wrong in their married life but she had pushed the doubts aside so she wouldn't lose another person in her life who she cared about. She clung to his words for so long, before his words had turned to just unmeaning words with no feeling, no thought.

She could see that now it had been a mistake all along. Even if it had not come to this, she would have eventually seen it was a mistake and would have left. She thought about her father and how disappointed in her he would be.

Thank God she did not have children. Oh *God, what would have become of them?* She was strangely thankful that some things were not meant to be. She now knew Weber killed his parents, her parents, and was willing to kill anyone who got in his way. He was after money. All this time, he was after the money.

Marshall rented a car and sped to Spalding. It was only a forty-mile drive, and he hoped there were no officers on the road to stop him.

At the same time, Lucen was heading to Tanner's station. When he arrived, no one was there. The door was locked. Both Weber and Tanner were out. Fear gripped Lucen; his chest tightened. He headed for the café.

Olivia informed him that Glory had left at 4:15 because it had been a slow day. "Oh my God," he said as he got back in his truck and headed for Glory's. Usually Lucen drove like a turtle in a race, but today his foot was to the metal. It was a race against time. With only a few blocks to Glory's, he knew even one minute could make a difference.

Olivia saw something she had never seen before in Lucen. Was it compassion? Was it fear?

His worst fears were coming to fruition. Either Weber or Tanner was to blame for those accidents. One of them was after Glory. His protective senses took hold, rising to the surface of his being like oil on water. He pushed the accelerator as hard as he could as he prayed, "Let my girl be okay."

CHAPTER 32

THE DARK OF KNIGHT

As Weber tightened his grip on Glory's throat she knew she would have to take action or be killed. At the same time, she lifted her knee so it would meet head-on with the most tender area of his body, hoping to drop him to give her enough time to run.

A split second later, Weber heard a crashing explosion behind his ear as something made contact with the side of his head. There was a deafening silence in his ears, then just as quickly his head seemed to split open.

His grip on Glory loosened as he collapsed to the floor, one hand grabbing his head while the other grabbed his crotch. Pain shot through his entire body, and he wasn't sure where it hurt the worst.

Lucen reached out his hand for Glory. "Oh my sweet, are you okay?" She began to cry and stretched her hand out to him, their fingers just touching.

Weber moaned and turned over, grabbed Lucen by the calf of his leg and pulling him down. Lucen let out a yell as he let go of Glory's hand and toppled to the floor, falling with a thud.

The two men grappled with each other, both intending to kill the other. It could have only been minutes, but Glory felt it would never end. Lucen's strength amazed her - Lucen the old, skinny, wrinkled man who shuffled about and was never in a hurry. Lucen was much older than Weber, but he was certainly a formidable opponent; his adrenaline had peaked.

Lucen's voice rang out. "You bastard, I'll kill you!"

Weber tried his hardest to get his arm around Lucen's neck. "You'll not spoil this for me, you old coot. You're dead." Weber loosened his grip and Lucen attempted to pull himself up off the floor.

As his head rose Weber pulled his arm back and swung it forward, hitting Lucen in the jaw with a straight-on, calculated blow, causing him to stumble backwards. The hardwood floor seemed to come up to meet Lucen as the side of his face slammed hard into it. He was out cold.

Weber reached out for Glory, knowing he had very little time to complete his plan and make this look like an accident. He had to get her outside. He would come back in and take care of Lucen once and for all. *Now,* he thought, *Lucen could be the fall guy. I'll make it look like he killed Glory then fell himself. It will look like he was responsible for hurting Glory cause he knew about the money. Jesus God why did*

Lucen have to show up?" He choices were few but he thought he could make that scenario work.

Weber reached for Glory, who had been stunned by the fight and never moved. He gripped her arm so hard, pain shot around and up into her shoulder. She screamed, "Weber, no. No, please, no!" He had turned his head and was looking directly at her when suddenly, out of nowhere, came another blow to the back of his head. Again he loosened his grip on Glory as he rose a few inches off the floor then fell.

He had closed his eyes when he went down, but as he began to open them, there came a crushing weight pressing on his chest.

Marshall with his foot directly on the middle of Weber's chest. Weber started to form words with his lips, until he saw the nose of a .44 pistol positioned within inches of his forehead.

"I would like to invite you to get up as soon as I release my foot," said Marshall. "You may want to attack me or Lucen or go for Glory again, and when you do, I will have an excuse to blow your selfish, perverted little brains out."

Marshall removed his foot from Weber's chest. Weber did not move, not an inch. To some degree, Marshall was hoping Weber wouldn't listen to him. Marshall even considered begging him to get up; satisfaction for Marshall was only moments away, but Weber did not move. Marshall could see the fear in his eyes, but even more so he saw hatred. Weber's plan had failed, and he knew it.

Marshall handed Glory his cell phone and told her to call the local police and to wait for him in the dining room. She obeyed. A few minutes later, Lucen groggily began to stir and slowly rose. Seeing Marshall there, holding the gun in Weber's face, Lucen extended his hand and said, "He opened the will. Give me the gun, Marshall. I'm going to blow this damn kid to smithereens."

Marshall told him to calm down. "Nobody's getting killed today, Lucen. Go check on Glory. She's in the other room calling for backup." Lucen's body jerked; exhibiting he still more adrenalin flowing through him than perhaps at any other time in his life. He wobbled into the dining room.

Marshall heard the sirens and knew his backup was coming. He wondered why the Lambert sheriff's office hadn't responded immediately when he had called them earlier that morning. They should have been there before Marshall. Now he was really hot under the collar.

At the same time Tanner came in the front door.

"What the hell is going on here?"

Lucen was standing near the door and put his arm around Tanner's shoulder. "I'll explain it shortly son. Come with me."

Tanner was dumbfounded because in many years this was the first time Lucen had touched him, extended a welcome of sort from father to son.

Lucen and Tanner entered the next room and saw Glory standing by a window. She turned and saw them. She was looking directly at a man standing there with no scowl on his face, no frown on his brow, and with big green eyes full of love.

She was seeing something she had never seen before - something Victoria had known all along. This was a good man. And in that she saw the compassion breaking through that solid surface of a stony-man, and she then saw tears.

She walked over to Lucen, knowing he was still rattled from the collision of his face to the floor. He reached out for her. His arm encompassed her and held tight. She, in turn, wrapped her arms around him.

"Thank God you came, Lucen. If it weren't for you, I'd be dead." Lucen took a long time to release his hold on Glory; the fear of losing her still gripped him, yet he said nothing. She knew at that instant that Lucen was not only her savior but her family. She knew he loved her.

The local police and the sheriff's officers arrived at the same time. Marshall knew he would be putting in a complaint. *Talk about lackadaisically doing your job,* he thought. *Both these officers should have been here hours ago.*

A few minutes later the phone rang. Thinking it was Victoria Glory started to pick it up, but Marshall intervened. "No, I'll answer it." Weber was now securely handcuffed to a radiator grate with a pounding headache. Marshall entered the dining room to pick up the phone on the second ring. He held it to his ear and said nothing.

"Hello, hello, is Glory there?"

"Who is this?" he asked.

"Liz, a friend of Glory's. Is everything all right? Who is this?"

Marshall told her to hold the line. He turned to Glory. "You know somebody named Liz?"

Glory's face went white. Liz, her friend, all these years. It had been Weber and Lizzy. No wonder Liz asked so many questions about Weber and Tanner and tried to tell her over and over Tanner was stalking her. They were setting Tanner up while also keeping their cover.

She looked sadly at Marshall. "I know Liz. She was my friend, or so I thought. Weber mentioned he had a girlfriend. He called her Lizzy. I hope not, but it may be her. If so she knows about Weber's plans today."

Marshall returned to the call. "Liz, Glory's been hurt. She said you were her good friend and asked if you would come and help her. She needs you."

Liz immediately responded, "Is Weber all right?" Marshall noted that question: not "is Glory okay," but "is Weber okay?"

"Sure, he's fine. Can you get to Glory's house as soon as possible? He's worried about her and she needs you." Liz said she would check out at work and drive right over. It would take her about thirty minutes.

Lucen had taken a few minutes to brief Tanner in on what had been taking place before his arrival just before the phone rang. Once hearing it was Liz Tanner looked at Lucen. "Good God dad, is Liz involved in this crap too?"

"It appears so son." That is the second time in less than twenty minutes Lucen called Tanner "son" and Tanner had definitely made a note of it in his mind.

Thirty-five minutes later, Liz was at the door. Marshall opened it as she approached. She had seen the police cars and was apprehensive about going any further but she knew she had keep going. Marshall said Glory needed her and she believed it. Her main concern was really Weber. At the door she said, "Where's Glory and Weber?"

"Right this way." Marshall let her into the living room, where she saw Weber handcuffed to the radiator, mumbling incoherently about never having a dime to his name.

All the color drained out of her face when he saw her. She made a hasty turn and found that she was looking directly into the face of Marshall. Before she had time to say anything, he grabbed both her arms, put her hands behind her back and placed the handcuffs on her as tightly as he legally could. He then sat her down on a chair in the dining room.

Glory walked up to her.

She began to cry. "I'm sorry, oh Glory, I'm so sorry."

"Why, Liz? Why?"

Weber chimed in. "Don't say nothing, you little tramp."

Her response was expected but unwelcome. "The money. Weber wanted the money so we could go away, so we could have some fun. You see, Glory, he is my Prince Charming. I'm so sorry, Glory; he really is my Prince Charming."

Now Glory knew it had been Weber in the apartment with Liz that day. The time Liz insisted on talking outside the door. Weber was her mystery lover.

Marshall interjected. "Your prince won't look so hot in an orange jumpsuit, Liz, and neither will you."

Glory glared at Liz and took a deep breath before speaking. "You're sorry. So sorry that you were willing to see me killed? Sure you're sorry. You're a poor excuse for a human being, Liz."

Lucen was in the corner with Marshall telling him about checking the will. It had been opened. He said he didn't know how long it had been opened; he hadn't seen it for twenty years. "I'm sorry Marshall. I see now that you were only trying to protect Glory. I got in the way and I am sorry."

He said he read the will for himself and learned about the money, then started to put two and two together. Even then he wasn't sure if it was Weber or Tanner who knew the information contained in the will. He said when he found out about the inheritance to Glory, he knew she could be in serious trouble sometime before she turned twenty-one.

Now the pieces finally came together for Marshall and he understood the full impact of Weber's plan. He explained to Lucen and Glory what happened: "Weber had found the will at Lucen's. He did further research and found out as much as he could about David and Janice McGuire. He knew David was successful and probably worth many thousands of dollars. I wasn't sure Weber was smart enough to find out David was worth millions, but to Weber Arturo, thousands would have been enough to kill for. The money was his motive, so he started hatching his plan.

"Weber obviously had been seeing Liz and was hooked on her. So when he started his plan, the only way to keep her quiet, so they could continue seeing each other, was to tell her about it."

"He saw that Lucen and Victoria were the god-parents of Glory and that if she was under-age, they would have to take care of her. If that came to fruition, she would have to move to Spalding. From that point on, all he had to do was woo her and get her to trust him completely. His plan had to be perfect."

Marshall told them about the cabbie finally coming forward and that he had been stumped until he started rechecking plane flight lists the same morning that Lucen called him. He had checked them once before with everyone's proper name listed but had found nothing. The killer had been picked up at the airport, so he had to have flown in.

Marshall shook his head, "I should have done a double check on the flight lists a long time ago. There was one flight from Lambert the day of the murders. I looked at the boarding manifest again, and I saw what had happened. The manifest read Arturo Weber while his ID read Weber Arturo."

As Marshall Lucen, Tanner and Glory sat at the dining room table, with Liz and Weber hand-cuffed and uncomfortable at the opposite ends of the living room, Marshall explained how he came to be there from Lucen's call, saying he had already made plans to take off for Spalding because he had finally put the pieces together.

"If it had not been for you Lucen, I would have waited another three hours to board that plane. If it hadn't been for you, Glory would probably be dead, we are grateful."

Lucen took a quick glance at Glory and then at Marshall. "I was worried. I didn't want nothing to happen to her. I love her." Glory got up and wrapped her arms around him. She knew this would be the start of a wonderful new relationship.

Marshall said, "I started putting two and two together when the cabbie came forward and Glory mentioned the money clip. I knew then the money clip was David's, and I knew you hadn't taken it. David's assistant at the bank knew about the clip, Janice showed it to her; it was a present from Janice. It was not on the inventory list from Garrett Sanders. The indications were that someone in Spalding had been to Orlando."

"I think Weber contrived this plan from the time he found the McGuires' will in Lucen's drawer, perhaps as much as four years ago.

"He would have been about nineteen then. He knew he had to move quickly to assure you were underage and for it to be mandatory that you come live with Lucen and Victoria. He thought up the plan and was very careful in his implementation of it. He wanted no suspicion to come back on him, and he did a good job of it all these years."

"As far as anyone knew only the attorney and your parents knew what was in the will. Lucen was not to open the sealed envelope until you were twenty-one. Today I found out it had been opened and he didn't open it. Neither you nor Lucen knew that Lucen and Victoria were to receive fifty thousand dollars when you were twenty-one.

"Sanders is to tell you this but, well, I'm going out on a limb here. When you turn twenty-one, you inherit your parent's estate and, Glory, you will indeed be worth millions. Only someone opening the will and reading every detail would have known this." He watched her face as she absorbed the news from him.

"When you arrived in Spalding, Weber was going to do everything in his power to win your heart, which he did. He wanted you in his clutches, and then before your twenty-first birthday he would kill you so he would inherit all the estate. I think he tried to kill you with the ladder accident and the car accident. I also have a hunch he tried on a number of occasions to poison you. If it weren't for Lucen, his plan would have worked."

It was almost too much for Glory to take in. She had been betrayed, and she would never forget that. She had not one ounce of caring or concern left for Weber, and she thought about how devastated Marie would be to find out her only daughter had been involved in this.

The officers from the Lambert sheriff's office arrived and were in the living room trying to get a word from Weber, but he had completely lost it, and just mumbled nonsense.

Shortly after talking to Lucen and Glory, Marshall finally allowed himself to lose his temper. "Good God, man, I flew in from Orlando and, I rented a car in Lambert, and I still got here before you guys. Did you have too many donuts to eat before you left the office?" The officer turned beet red and simply said, "Sorry."

"You could have gotten this girl killed. Are you guys nuts?"

Within a few minutes he did calm down long enough to explain the circumstances and said Weber was to be charged with the murder of his parents, the murder of Glory's parents, and the attempted murder of Glory. Liz was to be charged with accomplice to murder, four counts, and this one for Glory. They were taken away.

Glory, Lucen, Tanner and Marshall were now alone. They sat at the dining room table and Lucen was the first to speak. "Glory needs to come home with me." Short and sweet as always.

"Thank you Lucen, but I am fine now. Weber's gone and I'm not afraid, really."

Marshall felt Lucen's idea held merit but then he also knew he was not leaving right away and could watch out for Glory. "I'll be around a while yet and can check in with Glory until she feels comfortable. Glory, if you want to go to Lucen's it's not a bad idea either. What do you want to do?"

"I will be fine here. I'm tired and just want to sleep. Thank you Lucen, you are a good, kind man."

Lucen turned to Tanner. "I'm sorry for doubting you son. You are a good man and I am proud of you. Let's go home." Now Tanner felt something he had not felt in years. He had a father.

With that Lucen and Tanner said their goodbyes as Lucen once again hugged Glory, and headed for home in his dusty, dirty old truck, Tanner in his truck. Marshall stayed for "just one more cup" of coffee. He hesitated and drank slowly as he didn't want to leave Glory.

"He was going to kill me in my garden, my beautiful garden. What a hateful man. Just an ugly, awful, hateful man." Tears were streaming down her cheeks.

She asked. "Would you mind sleeping on the couch here tonight? I'd feel better if I were not alone." Marshall gladly agreed.

As Glory lay on her bed, assessing the events of the last four years, she knew she had wanted to be loved so badly after losing her parents that she grasped at the first chance at a happy life offered to her; Weber. She thought of the wedding, the bungalow, how hard she had worked to be a good wife.

And what about the garden? She knew that her garden would become overrun with weeds. There would be no more flowers, no more dirty hands. The bungalow was no longer her home, the garden no longer her haven. She would let the responsibility of her garden die just as her parents and her marriage had died.

CHAPTER 33

REVELATIONS

The next morning Glory received a phone call from Victoria. "Are you alone? I've got to talk to you, Glory, Lucen told me what happened and I've got to talk to you now." Glory was surprised at her insistence and still trying to wake up from a troubled sleep.

"What's this about, Victoria?"

"I can't say on the phone. I've got to see you in person. I've got to see you right now." Because of her insistence and the urgency in her voice, Glory told Victoria to come over.

With that, Marshall awoke on the couch. She told him about Victoria's call, and he asked if she wanted him to stay; he would if she was afraid. She said she had no fear of Victoria and preferred he leave so they could talk in private.

He said he would go to the café for breakfast and return in a couple of hours, but to call him if she was scared at any time.

Within half an hour Victoria drove up to the bungalow, got out of her car and actually ran to the front door. Glory was watching for her and opened the door just as Victoria reached out her hand and grabbed the knob. As Glory swung the door in, Victoria's hold on the knob caused her to be pulled in, quickly putting them face-to-face and foot-to-foot.

Within an instant their arms encircled the other as they hugged like there was no tomorrow. Victoria started crying so Glory directed her to the dining room table.

As Victoria's crying simmered down to a whimper Glory spoke. "Marie, Liz's mother is going to be facing a pretty hard time for awhile. She's all alone. Would you stop by and see her sometime?"

Victoria looked up and realized what a good heart this young girl had. *At a time like this, her near murder, she is thinking of others.* Then she said, "You're such a thoughtful girl. Of course I will, but Glory, I have something very important to tell you."

So much had transpired that Glory was a little unnerved about what Victoria had to say, but she let her continue. "You must never repeat what I tell you. Can you promise me that?"

Glory assured her that whatever was said would go no further than that room.

"You know, Glory; there was a time, many years ago, that your father and I were an item."

Glory nodded and responded. "I know that, but it was a very long time ago. It doesn't create any problems, truly it doesn't. I love you, Victoria".

"Wait, there's more. I was very much in love with your father, practically obsessed with him. I know how much your mother loved him, too. When he let me go, broke up with me for your mother, I was devastated, to say the least." She paused to wipe a tear.

"I tried very hard to forget him and tried to go on with my life, but my heart ached, I missed him and Glory, I loved him dearly. One weekend shortly after David and Janice met, I went to David and begged him to see if there was something we could do to rekindle our relationship. I wanted to be with him. He said no. He had just started dating your mother and hadn't made any commitments to her yet. That I knew of anyway."

"I began to cry, and I cried so hard my body shook. He was a compassionate man, a good man. I think that's one of the reasoned I loved him. There weren't many like him. I think when he saw me so heartbroken, he felt bad, took me in his arms and I clung to him, I clung like I would die if he let me go. I reached up and kissed him and begged him to love me just once more.

"He hesitated, but we did make love. Well, I made love to him, and he just let me." Again her emotions got the best of her, tears flowed.

"After it was over he cried and begged my forgiveness. He said he would never, and I must not either, mention to anyone that we had been together, because he truly was in love with your mother and planned to marry her. I hadn't known their relationship was to that stage already, and I felt bad. I agreed never to tell."

"Victoria, why are you telling me all this? You don't need to. I understand."

Victoria lowered her head slowly and began to cry. "I loved him, Glory, more than he would ever know. I loved him with my entire being, I was crushed that he didn't love me back."

"Go on." said Glory.

"That's when Lucen stepped in. He always had a crush on me, even in elementary school. He would watch me swing and play with the other girls, and when he tried to talk to me, I would run away. In high school we dated once. There was a little brunette girl I think he dated once, too. She didn't care for him much; she liked athletic guys. We both know Lucen didn't fit that bill.

"Lucen was David's brother, but they were polar opposites. Lucen tried to talk to open up to me more. He didn't have a lot to say, but he tried. At games we'd sit together and watch David on the field. I knew Lucen liked me, but I loved your father."

"When your father broke up with me, I was drawn to Lucen. He gave me comfort; he loved me, you know. Then very soon after I started feeling strange and knew the worst. To cover my tracks, I started coming on to Lucen more, and soon we made love."

Lowering her head and taking in a deep breath and raising her head so her eyes would meet Glory's, she said. "I was pregnant, Glory; I was pregnant with David's baby."

Glory quickly grasped the information. "What?"

"I never told Lucen, I told him I was pregnant with his baby. He thought it was his and we married. When the baby was born, I told Lucen it had been an early baby. It wasn't though, the baby was full term. You see, Glory, Tanner is that baby. I never told Tanner or Lucen, and I don't want either of them to ever know."

"I grew over the years to love Lucen, mostly because he loved me so much and was good to me. He is a quiet man, but he has a large and loving heart. Don't let his appearance fool you; he loves you very much, too. I'm sorry, Glory, but Tanner is your brother."

Glory reached for Victoria embracing her like a mother and daughter would embrace. She knew her father was a special man and now she knew two women had loved him deeply.

Glory sat in awe remembering the love story her mother had told her years earlier. She adored Victoria and wanted her to be assured the secret would go no further than the two of them. "Victoria, I will never tell, I promise. Lucen and Tanner will never find out from me." At that instant, they smiled at each other, their hands entwined as if their commitment to secrecy was being made official. Victoria wiped her face and patted Glory on the shoulder. "Thank you, sweet Glory. Thank you." Victoria opened the door.

Now Glory faced a new dilemma. There is a fortune that was to be hers when she turned twenty-one, now she found out Tanner is her brother. She knew he deserved part of the estate. But how would she get it to him without telling him the truth? She couldn't let Lucen know; it would destroy him if he ever found out that Tanner is David's son. Could it be an anonymous gift? No, it would be too much money to just give someone anonymously. This is something she will have to give a great deal of thought to.

An hour and a half passed before Marshall returned from breakfast. He asked what Victoria wanted, and she hated to lie but told him. "She just wanted to make sure I was all right."

Marshall knew Glory had been through a lot, but now that Weber was out of the picture and they were alone, he knew he would not be able to contain himself any longer.

She poured them both coffee and they sat at the table, across from each other, both looking up at the same time directly into each other's eyes. Marshall let it out. "I know this isn't the best time but, Glory, I have to tell you I think I've loved you from the first moment I saw you in Orlando. You were so beautiful and vulnerable, sitting on the couch in your parents' home."

"When I spoke to you that day, you had the voice of an angel, and at that point my heart became yours. It was there and then I vowed to protect you, no matter what. I was heartbroken when you married Weber, but I cared about your happiness and said nothing. When things started going awry and you started getting hurt, I knew I had to be there for you."

"I prayed someday you would be able to see the love I had for you, you'd be able to see your money was not important to me. You and you alone were the reason I existed. I love you, Glory. I've always loved you." Now she understood why he had given her the heart bracelet and the lifetime pass to Disney World in Orlando. He was suddenly irresistible. She got up and fell into his arms.

E.J. OBERMEYER

The author was born and raised in the Monterey Bay area of California and brought up in Santa Cruz, California, loving both the mountains and the ocean. She moved to Nebraska in 1969.

She writes poetry, paints, quilts and loves to travel and read and spend time with her grandchildren and great grand child. Her lifelong dream, her ultimate goal as an avid reader all her life, was to write a series of books spanning the life of Glory McGuire.

Her career carried her through law and the legal system, then into banking. As an active member of community organizations and state organizations, and having held offices in woman's organizations as well as her career positions, she knows the hard work it takes to make life great.

"It's all about God, family, having a positive attitude, never saying 'never,' and being committed to fulfilling your dreams."

This year she fulfilled her lifelong dream with the writing of *"Garden of Death,"* the first in a series. The soon to be completed sequel, *"Garden of Iniquity,"* and the third book *"Garden of the Sinister"* will continue the life and mysteries of Glory McGuire.